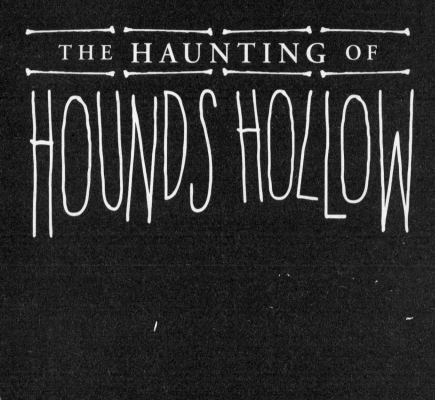

THE HAUNTING OF
HOUNDS HOLLOW

THE HAUNTING OF HOUNDS HOLLOW

JEFFREY SALANE

Scholastic Press / New York

Library of Congress Cataloging-in-Publication Data available

ISBN 978-1-338-10549-0

10 9 8 7 6 5 4 3 2 1   18 19 20 21 22

Printed in the U.S.A.   23
First edition, October 2018

Book design by Nina Goffi

For Wren and Dez,
who wanted a scary story . . . and a dog.
—JS

"A [kid], before [they] really grow up, is pretty much like a wild animal. [They] can get the wits scared clear out of [them] today and by tomorrow have forgotten all about it."

—Fred Gibson, *Old Yeller*

"Darkness cannot drive out darkness; only light can do that. Hate cannot drive out hate; only love can do that."

—Martin Luther King Jr.

Breathe in, breathe out.

The boy with tousled brown hair huddled low behind a tree, trying hard to steady his rapid breathing. He leaned into the shadows as the bright moon cast a glow like a searchlight overhead. Forest sounds shuddered to life, and the leaves whispered a warning on their branches. This world was out to get him. The warm wind blew down his neck like a breath in the darkness as smaller animals scurried past in sudden bursts. He wasn't alone anymore.

The boy stayed put and kept still with his fingers pushed into the soft, damp earth, like a sprinter waiting for the start signal in a race for his life.

Breathe in, breathe out.

The silence was deafening. There was no other noise than his own thin breath. Still, he clenched his jaw and waited, preparing for what came next.

And then, the signal. A lone howl cracked through the empty forest, scaring everything away, even the wind. The horrible sound was like a monster breathing through a dead animal's bones. When the boy heard it, his insides froze. He had no idea what made that terrifying sound. He hoped he never would.

Breathe in, breathe out.

As the cry went silent, the boy sprinted. He ran violently. He didn't care about what was in his way. Trees, rocks, cliffs, snakes, he darted past everything to keep away from the howl at his back. His knees hurt from running over the uneven ground, but the boy kept moving forward. It was the only way he might be safe.

The forest behind him erupted. The beast had found his scent. Steady, unsettling gasps chugged like a hungry train chasing him. The boy's breath sped up to match the beast's wild rhythm.

Breathe in, breathe out.

Breathe in, breathe out.

Breathe in breathe out breathe in breathe out breathe in breathe out breathe in breathe out breathe in breathe out breathe breathe breathe breathe breathe breathe breathe.

A sharp pain tore across his shoulders, shoving the boy face-first to the ground. Dirt flew into his eyes as a heavy weight stepped onto his back and legs.

"Please, please," the boy pleaded as he spit earth from his mouth. "What do you want?! What are you?!"

But there was no answer. There was only the wet smack of a tongue licking its chops followed by a low growl that resonated through the boy. The race was over.

Even though he was filled with fear, the boy opened his eyes. The forest was illuminated by a light cast from behind him. He could see the trees and bushes, but they seemed to look away somehow, as if nature itself did not want to witness what was about to happen. But the light . . . maybe someone had come to stop this from happening again?

"Anyone? Please! Someone! HELP!" he screamed.

That's when the beast took its first bite.

CHAPTER 1

Lucas Trainer woke up in his bed for the last time.

It was dark, but the city streetlights gave his room a twilight glow through the closed venetian blinds. He hated those blinds. They always let in too much light. But after Lucky, the family cat, shredded the curtains Lucas had picked out, he was left with the blinds that had been installed when they first moved into their New York City apartment. And now they were moving out.

But the streetlight wasn't what woke him. It was the dream again. A strange nightmare for a kid who lived in the city, but when were nightmares ever supposed to make sense?

Outside, a sound rang out—most likely an animal scrounging the trash for food. Lucas had learned to tune out most of the neighborhood sounds in the city. People on their phones loved to stop in front of his window to have their deepest, most personal conversations. Dog walkers, kids singing at the top of their lungs, skateboarders, police sirens, fire engines . . . they were basically white noise to him. There was even a guy who collected cans from the building's recycling bin under his window. He always whistled a creepy tune while he foraged through the clinking glass bottles and crinkling soda cans. Lucas had asked his mom one time why the guy whistled.

"Probably to announce himself," she had told him. "That way we know he's not a stranger or a thief."

But he *was* a stranger, thought Lucas. And he could be a thief, right? He was stealing their recycling, wasn't he? Of course, Lucas never said that to his mother. She would have gone off on how society forgets people on its march into the future, and how it's our responsibility to remember and help all those left behind. She was a social worker, after all. With an emphasis on the *was*. But it wouldn't matter in the morning: Everything in their lives was about to change. This was his last night at home.

The sound in his dreams, though . . . *that* was a different story. It was a mixture between a howl and demented laughter—a guttural and haunting sound that tugged him out of a deep sleep like a claw reaching into his dreams.

Wiping the sweat off his brow, Lucas sat up. He removed the face mask that covered his nose and mouth, the hiss of air from the oxygen tank filling the room. Rubbing the bridge of his nose and around his chin, Lucas tugged on his necklace, which was suddenly tight. He still wasn't used to it. The small key attached to the necklace flipped out from his collar. He traced it, then reached over and shut off the machine. The hiss stopped. Lucas took a breath of the night air for the first time and shifted to the lip of his loft bed.

His father built the bed into the wall seven years ago.

"Are you sure it will hold me and all my stuff?" Lucas had asked.

"Oh, definitely," Dad told him. "This bed is a monument. It won't break even if your room is invaded by an enemy army. Heck, I don't think I could get it down again if I tried! If we ever move from here, we'll have to leave this bed behind."

Lucas stared down at the floor as his feet dangled over the edge. The bed had seemed so much taller when he was five years old. Now it felt like a little kid's bed. His feet almost touched the ground, for crying out loud! He was kind of happy never to sleep in it again.

He jumped and landed with a thud. The entire room shook under his weight. He winced at the sharp pain in his knees. His parents had warned him about jumping down from bed in his condition. Not that anyone really knew what his condition was. But still, he had a long list of things that doctors said he couldn't do. Lucas interpreted that as things he *shouldn't* do. So every now and then he broke the rules.

Lucas made his way to the window through the shadows of packed moving boxes. He flicked the shade open with two fingers to search the street. No one was there.

"Just a dream," he mumbled to himself. "What'd you expect? A werewolf? Come on. With your luck, maybe you'd spot a vampire rat. *Maybe.*"

Whatever Lucas had heard before was gone. His alarm clock was perched on boxes filled with his books; 5:30 a.m. glowed green and stared back at him. He'd meant to wake up early before the move, but not this early. Usually a room looked bigger when it was cleaned and packed up, but his room looked tiny now. The bookshelves were empty and so was his dresser, but they all jutted out from the wall and cluttered the space.

It also didn't help that his life was crammed into ten boxes in the middle of the floor. Ten boxes. That's literally everything he owned. Books, clothes, video games, baseball mitt, and collectible Star Wars Legos. Those Star Wars Legos were never going to make the trip south without breaking, who was he fooling? Still, he packed them like his parents asked. They told him to pack everything, so he did. Well, not his alarm clock. Or his iPad. Or his headphones. Or the *Haunted History* book his parents gave him during his last hospital visit. Or his CPAP mask. Or the clothes he was going to wear tomorrow, which he was technically sleeping in—or not sleeping in—at that moment.

Another rumble came from outside. Lucas tugged on the chord to the blinds and they zizzed up quickly. A newer, fancier building had gone up across the street from their house last year. The entire exterior was made of glass like one giant, building-sized window that reflected everything like a mirror. Lucas studied his building's trash cans in the reflection. They seemed undisturbed.

Then he saw a set of eyes flash in the darkness.

"What the crow?" he said aloud.

The sudden glare pulled him forward as he tried to look directly down into the front of his building, but he couldn't quite see it from his sixth-floor window. Whatever had been there was tucked away and hidden, but the sounds always reached him.

When his family moved into the apartment, they were thrilled to be on the sixth floor.

"Lucas, you can have the front bedroom. The air will be better up here," Mom had said. "Plus, I guarantee you'll never hear anything this high up."

But he heard everything. The sounds from the street rose and converged like hot air, collecting in his room every night. Sometimes he wondered if the noise actually clouded the breathable oxygen, too, because he still coughed and wheezed in his room at the top of their six-story building. So Dad built the bed to make getting his weirdo CPAP mask cooler, Lucas supposed. It didn't change the fact that he still had to walk up and down six flights of stairs each time he wanted to leave the building or come back home. Dad thought it would be good for his stamina. Mom thought the distance from the road would cure him.

Lucas just wondered why groups of stairs were called *flights* if he had to walk up and down them all the time. But all that was going to change in a few hours.

Lucas surveyed the well-lit street again. No one was out there. The eyes he'd seen were probably from a stray animal anyway, if that. He could be imagining things again.

"You win, mysterious noise," Lucas said to himself. "If I'm up, I'm up."

The trip to the kitchen was a maze of more stacked boxes and furniture that also had boxes sitting on top of them. It was less of a home now and more like a museum for boxes. Tall boxes, small boxes, fragile boxes . . . there was a box for everything in their life.

Lucas stepped on a loose floorboard that creaked, a reminder that even their rugs were rolled up and ready to go. From somewhere in the boxed darkness, a sharp and frantic scattering of claws scraped across the wood floor at his sudden intrusion.

"Sorry, Lucky, it's just me," he whispered, as if their family cat could understand him. But, in a deep-down way, he wasn't sorry. He actually felt silly. Who apologizes to their cat for walking through their own apartment? Lucas was glad no one else was around to see him.

Past the den, there was a skinny hallway that led to the kitchen. Lucky stood at the end of the hallway, tucked deep into the shadows. Lucas waved and knelt down, holding out his hand. Lucky was still spooked, though, and retreated toward the back of the apartment.

In the kitchen, the refrigerator was completely bare. Dad had made good on his promise to measure out exactly what food they needed until the day of the big move.

Still, Lucas instinctually reached inside. It wasn't even cold anymore. He shut the door and saw the pulled plug curled up on the counter. Dad had thought of everything. He'd even started to thaw out the fridge.

There were three cups on the kitchen table, which was the only bare surface in the apartment. Lucas grabbed one, filled it with water from the tap, and drank it down. The cold water tasted crisp. He held the last gulp in his cheeks and swizzled the water around as he walked to their tiny bathroom. Then he spit the water out in the sink.

And that was the end of the apartment tour. Almost. He peeked into his parents' bedroom at the back of the building. They were both asleep in bed. Part of Lucas wanted them to wake up, too, as if they were supposed to have a sixth sense that warned them when he was feeling what his mom called "the feels" and just wanted another person around.

The other part of him wanted them to oversleep, because maybe if they slept late, the movers wouldn't be able to make it upstairs and then he simply wouldn't have to leave this life behind. Then he'd wake his parents up and tell them that he'd overslept, too. And those movers, well, you know, they have a lot of other people to move and a schedule to keep, so you snooze, you lose.

But neither of those things were going to happen. His parents were deep sleepers at night, but prompt waker-uppers in the morning. It was like a superpower . . . the lamest superpower ever, but it impressed him nevertheless. Lucas always had trouble sleeping at night *and* had trouble waking up in the morning. He was like their exact opposite, which maybe explained his condition, too.

Lucas did have his own superpower, though he didn't tell anyone about it. He had a great sense of timing. Like right now, he knew that the app set to track his CPAP machine was about five minutes away from sending its alarm to his mom's phone announcing that the machine had been switched off. It was designed to give him just enough time to go the bathroom.

Lucas was about to go back to his room when something furry brushed against his leg.

Mmrrow.

Lucky wound between his feet like a fluffy snake. Lucas knelt down and petted the cat on his head. The poor thing was blind in one eye and had a snaggletooth that stuck out all wonky, but the cat didn't seem to care. Lucky nudged his head harder against Lucas's palm and started to purr.

"You're right, I can't just sleep through this," whispered Lucas.

Lucky stared at him and then, like all cats, flicked his tail without warning and scrambled away into the den for no good reason at all.

Back in his room, Lucas flipped the machine back on and plopped onto the oversized beanbag underneath his loft bed. Turning on the reading lamp, he let the mask dangle down with the oxygen hissing gently.

Lucas held up the small key that he wore around his neck. He'd stared at it every night since his parents had received the special delivery. There'd been two envelopes in the package. The first was addressed to his mom—the deed to a house that belonged to some uncle no one had ever heard of in some tiny town called Hounds Hollow. The second envelope was for Lucas, which contained a tiny key on a ball-chain necklace. It was so small that he had no idea what it could possibly open. There'd been no letter, no explanation, not anything except the lightweight necklace sliding around in the sealed envelope. Lucas studied it again, as he did every night since the package arrived. Tomorrow the tiny key mystery would finally be solved.

Lucky trotted over to the window and pawed at the glass.

"I heard it, too, but nothing's out there," Lucas told the cat.

Lucky ignored him. The cat was scanning the street below and the trees outside. Lucas listened for the familiar clicking sound that Lucky made whenever he spotted a bird. His mom had told him that cats made that sound because deep in their

DNA coding, they have an instinct to be ruthless hunters. Even the cutest little kittens know in their cute little kitten bones that if they were ever to pounce on a bird, the first step in the hunt would be to grind their kitten teeth together in a saw motion, which makes that clicking noise. Then the kitten would bite into the back of the bird's neck to sever the spinal chord. This way the bird couldn't fly away or hurt the cat with its wings. Lucas had almost thrown up when his mom was done with that particular biology lesson. He definitely never looked at Lucky the same way after that.

But Lucky didn't click tonight. He hissed.

Lucas meant to get up and check out whatever was bothering Lucky, but his beanbag was suddenly too comfortable. He picked up the *Haunted History* book and flipped through the pages, but his eyes became heavy again, and before long, he fell back asleep.

CHAPTER 2

It was true, and Lucas had definitive proof. Moving sucked.

He hadn't expected the day to be easy, but he didn't think that it would hurt as much as it did. His eyes burned and his throat was still sore from trying to hold back that weird lump feeling when he was saying goodbye to his home. Even his forehead hurt from leaning against the window as his parents drove away. And that was just during the first five minutes.

Lucas spent the rest of the eight-hour trip playing on his iPad in the crowded back seat while his parents listened to their audiobooks or talk radio. Lucas wasn't sure which because he was wearing headphones and trying to exist only in the digital world. Minecraft, Five Nights at Freddy's, YouTube, those worlds lived online and streamed everywhere at once. He wished he could move to one of those worlds instead of Hounds Hollow, but real life didn't work that way.

The car drove past cities, mountains, factories, and farms, but Lucas kept his head down, eyes glued to the screen. The only time he resurfaced was when they stopped for gas, a bathroom break, or to eat. His parents planned their trip carefully with him in mind, because they stopped at nine Dunkin' Donuts on the way down. Normally they never let him have Dunkin' Donuts, but there seemed to be one at every stop. By the fifth time, Lucas noticed that they didn't even need gas, but his father still topped off the car while his mother ran into the store to buy him another chocolate glazed donut. By the ninth stop, he barely wanted another one. Barely.

"I get it," he told his parents when they were back in the car. His mom and dad were sipping on what seemed like their hundredth coffee of the day.

"Ah! Did you hear something?" Dad joked. "The creature from the back seat speaks! He's alive! ALIVE!"

"Calm down, Kyle. I think you've had enough coffee," Mom said as she took his cup and poured it out the window. She turned back to Lucas and asked, "What do you get, honey?"

"Your plan," Lucas replied. "You want me in some sort of chocolate glazed donut sugar coma so I don't mind the drive."

"Pfft, no way. What are you talking about?" Mom said. "This amount of sugar should put you in a happy coma for at least the first month at Hounds Hollow. *That* was our plan."

Lucas should have known his parents would aim straight for his Achilles' heel—his sweet tooth. He looked at Lucky sleeping soundly in the carrier next to him. "You guys are treating me like the cat, you know."

"Not true," Dad said matter-of-factly. "We didn't give Lucky any donuts. He just likes to ride in cars."

"So you're treating me *worse* than the cat?" Lucas flicked the side of Lucky's carrier, and the cat gently lifted its head and glared at him. Then Lucky inched over and rubbed against Lucas's hand.

"Well, you're not in a cage," said Mom. "Yet."

Outside the window, trees crowded the side of the road. His family had pulled off the interstate almost an hour ago and were traveling down a two-lane street that spent more time winding than going straight. The effect of each curve made Lucas feel like they were driving through a curtain of forest. And it didn't help that they were the only car on the road, too. Even at that last gas station/Dunkin' Donuts combo outpost, the workers had been really surprised to see them.

Of course, their packed-to-the-brim car *was* an odd sight. The bumpers were dinged and paint chipped from years of parking in the city, and the engine was loud with a squeaky noise that sounded like a banshee singing through the woods. Plus, with most of their suitcases strapped to the roof and folded blankets blocking out the back window, the Trainers must have looked like they lived out of their car.

His mother tapped him on the knee. "Aren't you going to ask us the age-old child-on-a-road-trip question, 'Are we there yet'?"

Lucas shook his head. "Honestly, I don't want to know when we'll get there . . . because I don't want to *be* there. I want to know when we'll go back home."

His parents exchanged a quick glance before his mom worked her way around in the seat to face Lucas. "I know this is tough. I do. You left your entire life back there in the city. We left ours, too."

Lucas peered out the window as she spoke. He was afraid that if he looked at her, he might start to choke up again, just when his throat had finally stopped hurting.

Lucas's mother pressed on. "Honey, between your father getting his new job and Uncle Silas leaving me the house in his will, it was like the stars aligned and the universe made the decision for us. Plus, the doctors say—"

"I don't care what the doctors say about me." Lucas tried to turn his back dramatically to his mom, but the back seat was so crammed, all he could do was squirm.

His mom put her hand on his knee. "I know you don't. You're not supposed to, Lucas. That's for us to worry about. We know you're upset, and probably mad at us, too. Still, like it or not, we're on this new adventure together. You, me, Dad, Lucky . . . and the Dark Cloud."

The Dark Cloud was what Lucas's parents called his condition. There was no other name for it, because no one knew what it was. Doctors from all over had tried to diagnose the dark clouds that marked Lucas's X-rays ever since he first started having trouble breathing. Test after test came back inconclusive, which was hospital-speak for *We have no idea what's going on.* The clouds grew with him, an expanding atmosphere inside his body that started in his lungs and spread outward. At this point,

Lucas's X-rays looked like a weather tracker with a storm swirling over his bones. He didn't like to think about it, because on the outside, he looked absolutely fine. But his insides stung with a dull ache he'd learned to live with.

He squirmed away from his mother's hand and began to cough.

"Do you need your CPAP? I have it back here." His mother quickly unlatched her seat belt and pulled at the pile of things beside him. Lucky gave her an angry meow as she shifted his carrier.

"I'm fine, Mom," Lucas snapped. "Not every cough is the end of the world."

There was a silence before his dad spoke up. "You're right, Lucas. And not every move is the end of the world, either. Think of it as a new kind of life. You've lived in the big city, and now you get to live in the great outdoors. Fresh air, grass under your feet instead of concrete, space to explore. I mean, our new house is so much bigger compared to our tiny two-bedroom apartment, you could get lost in it."

But Lucas didn't want the great outdoors. He didn't want nature or cavernous space to get lost in. He wanted his normal life back, but that life was already hundreds of miles away. It wasn't the apartment he missed, necessarily. It was the hustle and bustle, even the random sounds in the middle of the night—the liveliness of the city that you just couldn't get out in the quiet country. Lucas straightened up and said, "Do you realize that we might never hear another ice-cream truck song ever again?"

His mom laughed and snorted at the same time, like his joke had surprised her. He loved making his mom laugh like that. "Oh, you and that song. You had the sharpest ears, like a guard dog. That truck could be nine blocks away and you'd be at my side asking for ice cream."

Now it was Lucas's turn to laugh, but he felt that lump stick in his throat again. How could some stupid, twinkly song make him feel so rotten now, when it used to make him so happy?

"Are you okay, sweetie?" Mom asked.

Lucas nodded back to his mother. He hadn't been paying any attention to his parents during the drive, but now he saw all the telltale signs. Her eyes were puffy and red, she held a tissue in her hand, and her nose was running. She didn't want to leave the city, either.

After a moment, Lucas caved and asked, "Are we there yet?"

"Oh, we're close now!" said his dad as he pointed to a wooden sign up ahead.

The weather-beaten sign with cracks at the edges read WELCOME TO HOUNDS HOLLOW. There were two mountains on the sign, behind the words, and as the car sped by, Lucas could have sworn the two mountains looked more like a creature howling, though whether this was intentional, Lucas wasn't sure. It was less than welcoming. In fact, it looked kind of evil.

"Well, isn't that . . . cute," Mom said.

She thought everything was cute. The scary movies Lucas watched were cute. His demon costume for Halloween was cute. Even after Lucas's operation, she told him his scar was cute. He'd lived with his mom for a long time now. When she said cute, she didn't mean cute. It was her code word. It meant she didn't know what else to say.

Lucas tipped back his head and closed his eyes. When he opened them again, he stared at the car's tan roof. Some of the upholstery had become unglued and created a little pocket of air. He reached up and poked it, then turned his head toward the window to watch the treetops streak by. What in the world had he gotten himself into?

After what felt like twenty minutes, Lucas asked the prizewinning question again. "Are we there yet?"

The radio cut in and out as his mother searched for any station signal. Nothing stuck. "I don't know. Kyle, are we close?"

"I think so." His father slowed down at every possible path that veered off from the main road, looking left and right. "I mean, there's not really a sign for the place."

"But I thought you'd been here before?" asked Lucas.

"Sure, but only with the estate lawyer," said Dad. "I think I remember that tree." He pointed to a tree that looked like every other tree in the forest.

"A tree, Dad?" said Lucas. "Great. Admit it: We're lost."

"We're not lost, we're . . . momentarily displaced," said Dad. "And that's not the tree. So we press on."

Dusk had settled in and the roadway was beginning to get dark. The car lights automatically flicked on as his parents swiveled their heads to either side of the road.

"It's gotta be around here somewhere." His father stared down at a map absentmindedly as the car went around another turn.

Suddenly Lucas saw a shadow dart into the road. In the fading light, the figure was hard to make out, but it crouched as the car approached. Time seemed to slow down. First, Lucas noticed the shadow's shaggy black hair. Then he saw it rise up, standing on two legs. It held something round in its arms that could be either a head or a wizard's fireball. Lucas really hoped that it was neither. Finally he realized that the car was heading right for a kid, and she was very, very real.

CHAPTER 3

"DAD, STOP!" screamed Lucas from the back seat.

Lucas's dad looked up from the map and slammed on the brakes just in time. The abrupt stop sent Lucas lunging forward into his seat belt; the strap tightened against his chest and threw him into a coughing fit, as though the Dark Cloud were trying to escape his lungs. Piles of blankets flipped over and buried Lucas, but he caught Lucky's carrier just before it tipped sideways and fell off the seat. The screech from the tires echoed in the evening as Lucas frantically tried to dig himself out to see what was going on.

The girl stood in the headlights, but she didn't look scared or surprised. She looked to be around Lucas's age, but while Lucas was pale as a ghost, this girl was sun-crisp tanned. Lucas could now see that the thing in her hands was a basketball. The girl calmly bounced it as she walked around to his side of the car.

Lucas's dad rolled down the window. "I'm so sorry—are you okay? What are you doing in the middle of the road?" He was breathing heavily. "I could have—you could have—"

"No one drives up this way 'less they live here," the girl said flatly. "And no one lives here anymore. So are you lost?"

"Yes—no . . . maybe," Dad managed to say.

"Well, sir, which is it?" asked the girl as she bounced the basketball again.

"We're looking for the Silas Sweetwater residence," Lucas's mom said. "Do you know where it is?"

The girl nodded. "I can get you there, but I'm afraid I have some bad news about Silas. He passed away some weeks back."

"We're not looking for him," Mom said. "We're looking for his house—I mean, *our* house. Silas Sweetwater was my great-great-uncle." She picked the map up from the floor and passed it over to Lucas's dad, who held it out of the car to the girl.

"You won't find it on a map," she said without even looking at the paper. "But I can take you there if you have room in your car."

Lucas's parents exchanged a look. Even he knew that letting a stranger into the car was high up on the list of horrible mistakes to make when driving down backwoods roads at night.

"No, that's okay," said Dad. "We can find it on our own, I'm sure."

"Doubt it." The girl bounced the ball again. Lucas could hear it crush against the small dirt pebbles in the road and he saw the cloud of dust lift up from where it hit. "Silas built that place out past where anyone ever goes."

"In that case, what are you doing out here, sweetie?" Mom asked.

"I'm the closest neighbor." The girl nodded to the other side of their car. Lucas followed her motion and was surprised to see a house sitting inside the woods. The lights must have just turned on because it was impossible to miss, now that he saw it.

"Bessie Ann Armstrong, what are you doing out in that road!" The call came from the driveway leading to the house as an older woman made her way over.

Lucas's mom rolled down her window. "Sorry, Mrs., um, Armstrong. I'm Holly Trainer, your new neighbor."

"That's right. Y'all must be the ones taking over the Sweetwater place," Mrs. Armstrong said. As she came out of the shadows, Lucas could see that her hair was tied back under a bandana and she was wearing short-shorts under a long polo shirt. "Welcome to the neighborhood! I'm Mae, and goodness, clearly I wasn't expecting company tonight. Look at me, I'm a fright."

"No, no, it's our fault," said Mom. "We basically stopped by unannounced. Not very neighborly of us."

"Awe, please, darling. Y'all are welcome to drop by any-time." Mae leaned into the car and gave Lucas's mom an awkward hug as if they'd been friends for years.

When Lucas turned back around, Bessie was right by his window, peering inside. He flinched back in his seat and the blankets tumbled on top of him all over again.

"You're a jumpy one, huh?" she said. "Mom, they need directions to their new home. Okay if I show them the way?"

"Of course, Bessie. First time to the place, is it?" Mae Armstrong reached over across Lucas's mom to shake hands with his dad. "Howdy, I'm Mae."

"I'm Kyle," said Dad. "I suppose we could use a navigator, if that's okay. We can drive your daughter back, too."

"Oh, no need, Kyle," said Mae. "Bessie can just walk back through the woods. See, by the roads, our houses are far apart, but by the woods, well, we can practically spot each other from our kitchen windows! Funny how that is."

"Sounds like a plan," said Mom. "Lucas, scoot over and let Bessie inside."

Lucas widened his eyes at his mom, sending a telepathic message begging for her to not let this girl into their car, but his mother sent a telepathic message back to him letting him know that if he didn't scoot over that instant, she was going to make him get out and wait with Mae Armstrong. The whole magical communication lasted probably five seconds, before Lucas gave in and opened the car door.

The girl handed him the basketball, and then she climbed inside. Lucas was crushed next to her, stuck between Lucky, blanket piles, his backpack, her basketball, and this odd girl whose legs were now touching his. Yuck.

"Head straight," she said as she clicked her seat belt into place. "Then 'bout three miles down, you'll turn right."

"Okeydokey," his dad said as they pulled away, leaving Mae waving behind them.

Lucas leaned his head against the basketball out of embarrassment before realizing that the basketball was covered in dirt. He jerked back and tried to wipe off his forehead, but his hands were now covered in dirt, too.

"Jumm-pee." Bessie drew out the word so that it became two long syllables.

"Bessie, this is our son, Lucas," his mom said.

"You can call me Bess," the girl said. "Only my mom calls me Bessie, and that's usually when I'm in trouble."

Even though Lucas's mother had already introduced him, Bess made no friendly moves. She didn't shake his hand, or smile, or even give him a nod. She just kept her eyes on the road.

The car was eerily quiet as the next three miles crept by. Lucas stared at the floor and leaned forward, wishing he were anywhere but in that back seat right now.

Suddenly Bess leaned down next to him and softly said, "You aren't gonna hurl, are ya?"

"What? No, no way." Lucas was shocked as he sat back.

"Good. Cause if you hurl, I'll hurl." Bess cleared her throat, and Lucas could hear the phlegm slug its way up and back down. "And I don't want to ruin all your blankets back here."

"So, we're gonna be neighbors," said Lucas.

"Take this right," Bess called out.

Dad listened and turned, but he was going so fast that Lucas slid over into the strange girl. His face went straight into her wild, black hair. It smelled like the trees and sunshine. Bess was expecting the turn, however, and caught Lucas as he leaned into her. Then she steadied him and went on as if nothing out of the ordinary had just happened.

"Are you sure this is a road, Bess?" Mom asked from the front seat. Lucas could hear the tires rumbling over the dirt path.

"It's not a road, it's your driveway." Bess peered over the driver's-side headrest. "Is this all-wheel drive? If not, you might want to invest in a new car. Driveways get muddy around here in the winter."

The drive narrowed as they went along and then Lucas's father stopped the car. There was an old covered bridge ahead. "I don't remember there being a bridge when I came here."

"You must have come from the south side, then," said Bess.

"South side?" asked Lucas's mom. "How many driveways does this house have?"

"Four," Bess said matter-of-factly, holding up four fingers, as if that was going to drive the point home even more for the Trainers. "North, south, east, and west." She paused a second before adding, "That I know of."

"Sounds . . . busy," said Mom. She shrugged her shoulders as his father drove onto the bridge.

The car bounced on the old wooden floor like a boat on the

water. Boards outside creaked and cracked as Lucas felt the back of the car dip lower than the front. He gripped Bess's basketball tighter and wondered if it could also be used as a flotation device in case of an emergency water landing.

"I'm gonna need that back, you know," said Bess.

"I know," said Lucas. "But I'm holding it for now."

"I can see that," said Bess as the car eased off the bridge and back onto the road. "The bats must be out searching for food. They're usually sleeping in there."

"Bats?" asked Lucas, making sure he'd heard her correctly.

She ignored his comment and changed the subject. "*Haunted History*? You like ghost stories?"

Lucas saw his book peeking out from the pocket on the back of the driver's seat. "Huh? Oh, yeah, sort of. What about you?"

Bess smiled, then pointed dead ahead. "There's the house."

The forest cleared and was replaced with what Lucas could only describe as a ramshackle mansion. It was somehow majestic and decrepit at the same time. The front porch stretched fourteen windows across and two stories high. Above the windows were several of those towerlike things that stick up from the top of castles. Lucas couldn't remember the name for them, but he'd seen things like them before in video games and YouTube videos about haunted houses. At the center of the porch, there was a giant front door with an intricately carved pattern of a tree with branches spiraling in every direction. The middle of the tree, though, parted to make way for a stained-glass window. There was a light on inside the house that made the window in the door glow, and Lucas could swear it looked like a wolf glaring at whoever dared enter. Whatever this massive house was, it was definitely not home sweet home.

What had his parents gotten him into?

Without warning, Bess opened the door and stepped outside, pulling Lucas and the basketball with her. The night was completely silent except for the sound of the car's engine and the sound of Bess's footsteps kicking up dirt as she walked.

"I'll let you move in now," said Bess as she started back toward the forest. She stopped by Lucas first but didn't say anything.

"What is it?" asked Lucas.

"You doing anything tomorrow?"

"Um." He paused, trying to find any reason to be busy. "Maybe, with the moving in and apparently making a map of my new house."

"I'll come by, then," Bess said, not taking the hint. Then she motioned to his chest and added, "You've got a scar."

Lucas's hand went up to the scar that peeked out of his shirt by his throat. "I know" was all he could think to say.

"I've got one, too." She twisted her leg around to show a similar scar on her calf. Four white stripes stood out against her dark skin.

"Oh," said Lucas.

"Maybe I'll tell you more about it tomorrow," Bess said. "And you can tell me about yours. Not often you meet a kid with a scar like that."

Then she bolted into the darkening woods, leaving Lucas behind with his family, his scar, a giant, creepy house, and oddly enough, her basketball, which sat in the dirt at his feet. He really was a long way from home.

CHAPTER 4

Lucas started a list when he first became sick. His parents took him from doctor to doctor, searching for the answer to what was wrong with him. He called it the Last Thing list. It wasn't like a bucket list; it was more of an anti-bucket list. By now, there were so many "last things" that Lucas didn't want to do, but he was always ready to add more to the list:

The last thing I want to do is get back in the car.

The last thing I want to do is find our new house.

The last thing I want to do is unpack my stuff because then it means I actually live here.

The last thing I want to do is hear my parents arguing about the new house.

The last thing I want to do is find a room in this giant place.

The last thing I want to do is hang out with that weirdo Bess tomorrow, or the day after that, or the day after that, times infinity.

He held his breath, and the night seemed to hold its breath, too. Facing the house, time felt like it had stopped, and the silence made him feel like he had walked into a creepy painting. To break the spell, he exhaled, and the night seemed to breathe again, too. Sounds of nature erupted around him. The hot wind rustled through the trees, and a burst of clicking noises hissed like a million rattlesnakes hidden in the dark forest. The clicks swelled in waves, pitching up, then down, and made Lucas's skin crawl as sweat trickled down the back of his neck.

Add that noise to the Last Thing list, too, he thought. That noise wasn't the sound of the city. He was in a new world here, but he was still the same old Lucas. He'd survived lots of things on the Last Thing list, because things on the list needed to be done. Even if he didn't want to do them.

~~The last thing I want to do is get another CAT scan.~~

~~The last thing I want to do is give another blood sample.~~

~~The last thing I want to do is see how the nurses look at me during my checkups.~~

~~The last thing I want to do is move.~~

His dad helped him make up his mind on which new Last Thing to scratch off the list first. "Get in the car, Lucas. This isn't our house. The home I visited was much smaller. I think our little navigator might have been confused. This place looks like no one has lived here for a long time."

"Yes, sir." Lucas picked up the basketball and got in the back seat again. The night buzzed around him. "What's that crazy clicking sound outside?"

"Cicadas," said Mom. "They're a type of insect."

Slowly, Lucas realized that this place was nothing like the city. The buildings he was used to were replaced by giant trees. The crowds of people were replaced by giant trees. And the sound of traffic was replaced by the now deafening sound of bugs whirring deep within the forest of giant trees. Even inside the car, it was like they were drilling into his mind, the noise was so loud and persistent.

His dad drove around the mysterious house, and as the tires scrunched against the dirt, lights started to come on both inside and outside.

"Are you sure no one lives here?" Lucas asked before his mom shushed him.

"That's odd. The lights are linked to motion sensors," Dad said, pointing to the eaves of the house. Tucked under the roof were small but noticeable cameras. "Whatever this place is, someone was really protective. Those are top-of-the-line, infra-red laser–based cameras along the roof. They work by trimming the beam thin and wide to—"

"I don't care how they work, Kyle," Mom interrupted. "Why in the world would anyone need them?"

"Bears, maybe?" he suggested. "Do they have bears out here?"

His mom sighed and pushed playfully against his dad's shoulder. "All right, you. Let's just get to the house so we can finally sleep."

Lucas was tired, but he hadn't thought about sleep until his mother mentioned it. He closed his eyes and felt himself relax. When he opened his eyes again, there was still more of the mysterious house. It jutted into—and out of—the yard. Lucas thought it actually looked like twelve completely different homes connected to each other. Like patchwork, or like Frankenstein's monster. And the house wasn't the only larger-than-life part of the property: They drove past an honest-to-goodness hedge maze! Lucas made a mental note to walk back that way in the morning to test it out. Maybe he could lose Bess in there forever.

Finally, after another few minutes of driving, they found a house next door. As they drove toward it, the lights from the larger house turned off. Lucas peered through the rear window. It was as if the mansion behind them had disappeared.

The neighboring house was small, like a cottage. Seeing the air conditioners sticking out of the two top windows made Lucas smile. He'd had an air conditioner in his old room and loved falling asleep to its hum. The cottage was made of wooden slats and, other than the air conditioners, looked like it was one huff-and-puff away from falling over. The roof sagged like it was hunching its old shoulders. In the moonlight, Lucas could make a face out of the house—the two top windows were its eyes and the faded red door was its mouth.

"So *this* is the place?" Lucas asked.

"This is the place," his dad said proudly, noticing the look of horror on his wife's face. "It's a fixer-upper! Actually, it looks much better on the inside. A fresh coat of paint, some elbow grease, and we'll get this house in tip-top shape."

"But not tonight, right?" asked Lucas.

Lucas's mom tried to smile, but there was no heart behind it. "No, honey, not tonight."

Lucas nodded. "Good, I'm zonked." Sure, the mansion and the cottage shack were creepy, but he wasn't about to sleep in the car after a long drive.

"It's settled, then, the Trainers have arrived!" His dad parked the car outside the house and popped the trunk. "Help me with the bags, Lucas."

Lucas joined his dad to carry the luggage into the house. The car was packed full with suitcases and a few boxes that his mother wouldn't trust the movers with. Inside were old photo albums, jewelry, and what his mom called the good silver, but just looked like regular knives, spoons, and forks to him.

A walkway made of tiny pebbles led through some small bushes up to the front door. Lucas listened to the sound of his dad's crunching footsteps and the rolling suitcase behind him, though it wasn't easy to drown out the clicking hum of the cicadas. They really *were* everywhere. But at that moment, as if someone flicked an off switch, the noises around them stopped.

"Kyle, pick it up," said Mom. Her voice sounded extra loud in the new silence. "You're ruining the landscaping and scaring away the cicadas."

"Don't worry about the rocks, I'm sure they'll be fine," Dad said. "I'll sweep them back in place tomorrow. Just be happy those cicadas turned in for the night. I didn't think those bugs would ever shut up."

Lucas moved forward in the darkness, following the path between a row of shadowy bushes. Below the bushes, the walkway was impossible to see, so he stepped carefully and wondered if there were snakes in Hounds Hollow. If there were, they might live in the bushes and come out at night. Maybe he should add stepping on snakes to the Last Thing list.

The clouds were merciful and let just enough moonlight through to show the cottage and the forest around them. Past the trees, though, there was still a curtain of darkness. The city had never been this dark. Lucas could even see stars in the sky. Stars! Suddenly Lucas's imagination got the best of him.

Peering deeper into the woods, he saw something move. Maybe there really *were* bears in the woods here. Lucas had only pictured bears living in zoos, but that seemed silly now. Of course bears lived in the wild. Without fences or barrier pits. And that was more than a little terrifying.

A rustle of branches sounded out behind them and the whole family jumped. His father was the first to laugh. "Well, we are definitely *not* in the city anymore."

Lucas realized just how quiet things were in the great outdoors. There weren't any cars or taxis. There weren't any people talking on cell phones. There certainly wasn't a whistling guy who collected cans here, either. In that moment, Lucas realized how much he missed his home. He craved the great *in*doors. Even the droning noise of the cicadas would be better than the quiet that sat around them right now, because with the noise gone, Lucas couldn't help but think that something else was out there.

Lucas turned to his father, who was trying to find the right key, lifting each one on the key chain close to his face and squinting. "Dad," he whispered. "I . . . I need to go, like, now."

"Hold on," his father said, more to himself than to Lucas. "It's got to be one of these."

"Dad, for real," Lucas urged.

"Go in the bushes, Luke. There's no one around—"

"No," Lucas interrupted. "Just hurry—*please*."

"Aha!" His dad waved his hand in the air in success, but fumbled finding the keyhole. There was a series of clicking taps, followed by the key entering and the lock unbolting with a loud thwack that made Lucas flinch.

The chipped red paint on the front door flaked off when it was opened. Lucas's dad reached his arm inside and patted the wall, searching for the front light. When it finally clicked on, a dirty bulb over the front door flickered on to a murky brown color. It wasn't bright, but the dull glow startled something in the forest. The branches on a tree close to them were shaking slightly, as if a creature had just skittered away. Then a muffled howl erupted in the mysterious distance. It was long and lonesome, wailing up, then slowly down until the animal was finished.

A shiver ran up Lucas's spine with the howl, then trickled back down like melting ice. He'd heard that howl before—in his nightmares. Lucas held his breath and closed his eyes. It couldn't be his nightmare; he was with his parents. He was safe with his parents, right? Time seemed to stand still, until the cicada song rattled back to life and started again.

"Bathroom!" Lucas squeaked as he darted past his dad into the house.

Lucas took only four steps before he slammed into something soft and leathery. He thrashed quickly, trying to stand.

back up, but something held on to his leg. The harder he pulled, the tighter the grip bit into his leg. It was all he could do to not scream for help. His parents were right behind him anyway. Then the lights came on and Lucas froze.

"You're not going to pee on the sofa, are you?" asked Dad.

Lucas opened his eyes. He'd knocked himself head over heels on the back of the sofa and tangled his foot in a blanket. His chest began to tighten, too, as he wheezed, "No jokes, okay?"

"No jokes, bud. We promise." His dad pointed to the left. "Bathroom's over there. But watch out for the closet. I hear it's hungry."

"Stop it," Mom scolded.

Lucas untwisted the blanket and quickly walked to the bathroom. The house was bigger than his old apartment, but not by much. The kitchen, living room, and dining room were all in one open space, and included a fireplace that had seen better days. He heard the wind wheeze through the chimney stack, and for a moment, Lucas felt like the house was breathing around him.

"Keep it together, Lucas," he whispered to himself as he stepped into the bathroom. In the darkness, he felt around for a switch on the walls before he ran into a thread dangling in the middle of the small room. Lucas swatted at it like he'd walked into a spiderweb, and then he realized that the string was attached to the light. He turned the light on with a click and saw his reflection in the mirror. Startled, Lucas jumped back and slammed the door shut accidentally.

"Sorry," he apologized to no one. Then he pulled out his inhaler and took a deep breath. He felt his lungs fill again and began to relax.

Leaning closer to the mirror, Lucas tried to give himself a pep talk. "Stop it, right now. You're a city kid; you're tougher than the country. There are no crazy bears out there—just a weird neighbor, and you've known a lot of weird neighbors. And that sound in the woods, it's just a stray or something. It's not your nightmare . . . it's not your stupid nightmare."

The collar on his shirt was stretched out, revealing the scar on his chest. No wonder Bess had noticed it. That scar was the star of the freak show known as Lucas Trainer. Even after living with the scar all these years, it still shocked Lucas every time he looked in the mirror.

As he went to touch the scar, a tiny flash of light blinked from his chest. It was the key he wore on his necklace. It must have fallen out of his shirt when he tripped over the couch. Lucas tucked it back in, then turned on the faucet to splash water on his face. It felt so cold and wonderful that he rubbed some on the back of his neck to break the heat. Refreshed, he summoned the courage to go back out there and get on with the rest of his life.

Lucas turned off the water and opened the door. In the hall-way, a shadow slipped out of the darkness. It was an old woman in a white nightgown, with frost-gray hair that fell around her head like a wild, glowing haze. Her face was wrinkled with dark freckles and her eyes were a cold shade of green. As he stood face-to-face with this stranger, Lucas thought he might be imagining things again. Had his daydreams followed him all the way to Hounds Hollow?

Slowly, the old lady pointed her finger toward him and cleared her throat. "You!"

CHAPTER 5

Lucas stumbled backward, surprised that the old lady was actually real and not just a figment of his imagination. He caught himself against the sink and screamed, "DAD! MOM!"

His parents ran over and screamed, too. The woman whipped her head at them like a cat hissing, but kept pointing at Lucas. "Is this your son?"

"Y-yes," Mom said with a slight nod.

"Well, he forgot to flush. I don't like no-flushers. Don't like 'em one bit."

"Who . . . ?" Dad struggled to find the right words. "Who are you, and what are you doing in our house?"

The old woman sneered. "*Your* house? This here is *my* house."

"Impossible," Mom said, though she seemed unsure. "Unless . . . this *isn't* Silas Sweetwater's house?"

Suddenly it seemed entirely possible to Lucas that his parents had broken in to someone else's house.

"Oh." The old woman frowned. "So you're the fancy-schmancy new owners from the city. I should've known from your no-flusher son." She glared at Lucas like he was a rotting piece of meat. "I don't care how they use the bathroom where you're from. In Hounds Hollow, we flush."

"Yeah, I get it," Lucas said. "But I didn't even use the toilet."

She eyed him suspiciously. "That's what they all say."

"What? That doesn't even make any sense," Lucas said.

"Eartha Dobbs." The woman walked into the kitchen, grabbed a fresh pot of coffee, and poured two cups.

"Excuse me?" Dad asked.

"My name," Eartha said as she set the coffee mugs on the counter. "You wanted to know who I am. I'm Eartha Dobbs. I work for Silas—well, *worked*—for Silas. Near thirty years now."

"That still doesn't explain what you're doing in our house." Dad pulled out his cell phone and held it up like a police badge announcing the seriousness of his presence.

"First, you're not gonna get any reception out here," Eartha explained. "That phone is worthless. Second, I told you, this is *my* house."

"No, this is the house that the estate lawyer showed me," Dad argued.

"You think a fool lawyer's gonna mistake a groundskeeper's cottage with a mansion?" Eartha waddled over to the refrigerator. "Well, maybe. Maybe they would make that mistake. Never did like lawyers. You like cream in your coffee?"

"Do I . . . like cream?" Dad asked, confused.

The old woman moved around the kitchen effortlessly. She slid open the drawers and pulled out spoons, then closed the refrigerator door with a ballet-style kick. Then she put every-thing on a tray and carried the drinks to the dining room. Like it or not, Lucas could see Eartha Dobbs was telling the truth. She belonged here.

Dad realized it, too. "Yes. Yes, we do take cream, thank you . . . wait, did you say *mansion*?"

"Well, sit, why don't ya?" The old woman smiled. "Looks like we need to talk."

Lucas joined his parents and Eartha at the table. His father and mother sipped their coffee, but he didn't touch the water she'd poured for him. He didn't want to go to the bathroom again that night. Not with the old lady watching him.

After his parents introduced themselves, Eartha led the con-versation. Apparently, she was going to stay on as the groundskeeper of the Sweetwater estate and continue living in the cottage.

"And you don't have anywhere else to go?" Mom was trying, kindly, to give Eartha a hint. "Any family you want to visit? I just don't think we need a groundskeeper. Frankly, I'm not sure we could afford it."

"I don't need your money," Eartha said proudly. "Only pay-ment I need is the roof over my head. Only family I had was Silas, so that makes you my family now."

Lucas could see his parents deflate. It looked like the Trainers were stuck with Eartha Dobbs. She came with the house.

"But you can't move in tonight," Eartha snapped. "Wasn't expecting you. Didn't know when or even *if* you'd show up. I'll need to turn the electricity back on, make sure the water heater is boiling again, and get the air conditioner up and running."

"Move in to where?" Lucas asked. "I'm confused. If you live here, then where are we supposed to live?"

Eartha let out a cackle that rattled in her chest, then slapped her hand on her knee. "Ha! From the mouths of babes. Where are we supposed to live? Ha!"

Then the old lady saw the puzzled looks on his mom and dad's faces. "Oh mercy, y'all really got no idea, do you? Bless your hearts. Okay, stay here tonight. Morning makes everything clearer—wait. What is that?"

Eartha pointed at Lucky's carrier, which his mom had placed by the front door.

"It's our cat," said Lucas.

"Cat?" Eartha said the word like it was a hairball stuck in her throat. "You don't let it outside, do you?"

"No," assured his father. "Lucky's an indoor cat."

"Hrumph." Eartha glared at the carrier before turning to Lucas. She put her pruney hand on top of his hand. "Keep him in, boy. Always keep him in. Those woods are full of things that might like a cat snack."

Lucas nodded and tried to pull back his hand from under hers without recoiling as fast as he wanted to.

His parents took long sips of their coffee that passed like a secret conversation between them. Lucas had no idea what they were saying, but he'd seen this kind of secret code happen before whenever he wanted to have a friend spend the night or rent a movie that they thought was too scary for him. Or when doctors gave them options about his treatment.

But Eartha was not going to wait for them to finish their silent code. "It's settled, then. Y'all will stay here tonight. There's a guest room upstairs. Leave your things in the car. No one's gonna bother it way out here."

"No, we couldn't," Mom said. "I'm sure there's a motel nearby."

Eartha shook her head with a husky giggle. "No hotels or motels near Hounds Hollow. Ain't no reason to stay! Now, please, I insist. You're just steps from your new home."

"If it's no trouble, then thank you," Dad said, relenting. Lucas could see Mom's eyes nearly pop out of her head. "We'll take the upstairs room and Lucas can sleep down here on the couch. You already know where it is, right, son?"

"No," Eartha blurted out. Then she caught herself. "I'm sorry, but I, er . . . I'm up so early, I'm afraid I'd wake poor Lucas. And a growing boy needs his sleep! There's a pullout upstairs; he can use that."

This time Lucas deflated like a balloon. There was no escape from Eartha or his parents tonight.

"You said our new house is steps away," Lucas said. "Were you talking about that mansion?"

"Well, I wasn't talking about the forest outside," Eartha said with a yellow-toothed smile. "Y'all must have seen it on the drive in. Darn near impossible to miss. You're moving into Sweetwater Manor."

CHAPTER 6

A haunted house. In the middle of nowhere. His parents had moved him to a haunted house in the middle of nowhere. It had to be haunted; there was no other explanation. Either it was haunted or this Silas Sweetwater was one seriously weird dude. Lucas gulped and the gulp echoed in the kitchen.

"Honey," Mom began, "it's been a long day. Why don't you head up? We'll be right behind you."

Lucas nodded because he knew that this was parent code for *We need to talk privately when you're not in the room.* He was used to hearing that, but this time he was pretty sure that they weren't going to be talking about him or his health.

Lucas carried his portable CPAP machine and Lucky's crate upstairs into the small room that barely fit the bed. In the closet he found the rollaway cot where Eartha told him it would be. When Lucas unhooked the latch, the moss-green mattress flopped open like a dead fish and fit in the room like the last piece of a puzzle.

Lucky hissed angrily from inside his carrier and reached a paw through the front grate. After such a long trip, who could blame the cat for wanting to escape? Lucas opened the carrier and the cat bolted out and bounded around the small room, under the bed, and even climbed the wall at one point before he froze and snarled. Then Lucky charged forward, nearly crashing through the window. The cat scratched furiously against the glass, then stopped and peered outside. Lucas was spooked by Lucky's frantic trip. Silently and carefully, he joined the cat, trying to spot whatever he was staring at. From deep in the shadows of the trees below, Lucas saw something move. It was hard to make out, but it looked like an animal with white, glowing fur. It moved carefully between the trees, almost like it was sneaking closer to the house. With every soundless step, Lucas felt his heart beat faster. He exhaled sharply, fogging up the edge of the window. Lucas couldn't decide if he was really seeing the animal, but Lucky seemed to see something, too. The cat pinned its ears back and crouched down low on the mattress.

Outside, the animal's movements were . . . glitchy. That's the only way Lucas could describe it. The animal's body was unnaturally blurred—like it was an image still loading on a computer. It seemed to be almost tearing through the night as it walked.

Suddenly a tiny flash popped in the woods, followed by a high-pitched whine that filled the quiet world outside. Lucas searched to find the animal again, but it was gone.

As he moved back from the window, a second flash

popped farther from the house. Then a low shudder erupted from the other side of the room, causing Lucky to skitter over Lucas, claws digging into him frantically as the cat ran to hide for dear life. Lucas flinched, but it was only the air conditioner whirring to life. A drift of cold, crisp air crept into the room.

"Okay, so we're both scaredy-cats," Lucas said as he reached down for Lucky. The cat poked its head out from under the mattress and playfully pawed at Lucas's hand. "And we probably both need sleep."

He made a mental note to look through his *Haunted History* book tomorrow. Maybe there was a section on people imagining things in the forest, the same way people saw mirages in the desert. With a yawn, Lucas grabbed the blanket that was neatly folded at the end of the guest bed and tugged it around him. Eased by his owner, Lucky laid down on the cot, and Lucas felt the familiar weight at the foot of his blanket just as the air conditioner sputtered on. Without even changing clothes, he slipped his mask over his nose and sighed with relief. He was more tired than he thought. And animal or no animal outside, Lucas had no problem falling asleep that night.

Hiss. Hiss. HISS.

Lucas woke groggily, but he knew that sound. It was Lucky. He reached to pet the cat and felt claws dig into his hand.

"Ow!" Lucas cried.

This wasn't a playful swipe. This wasn't a cat looking for food or for Lucas to wake up and give him attention. Lucky was scared. Lucas flipped his CPAP mask off and jerked back his hand to study the scratch in the gray, early morning light. The cut was deep, long, and red.

"What was that for, you crazy cat?" Lucas whispered. He blew on the cut, shook the pain away, and looked at his hand again as if he were expecting the scratch to have disappeared.

The room had turned stiflingly hot even with the AC running at full blast. Lucas leaned forward and touched the vent where the cold air should have been. He could feel a rush of air blowing out, but it burned hotter than a hair dryer. He jerked his hand back for the second time and peeled back his covers. The entire bed and his clothes were wet. He'd fallen asleep in an icebox and woken up in a sauna. Lucas switched the temperature all the way down to COLD, but the hot air stayed on.

Lucky crouched at the foot of the rollaway cot with his ears pinned back and his tiny teeth showing. The cat hissed at the door and bristled with a nervous energy that made the hair on the back of Lucas's neck stand up, too. In a flash, Lucky streaked across the cot and hid under the bed where his parents were still sleeping soundly.

Lucas carefully crawled to the bedroom door and put his ear against it. From downstairs he heard other scratching noises, like more animals scampering away, nails clicking and sliding against the hardwood floors. And then silence.

Instantly the heat left the room and was replaced by a frigid cold again. Lucas's teeth chattered as his wet clothes clung to his back. Suddenly he was freezing.

Lucas opened the bedroom door and a wave of heat rushed over him. It felt warm and safe and it pulled him forward. He didn't know why, but he started walking downstairs. It was as if he was being led there.

An old clock chimed seven times as he stepped into the den. Eartha was already up and in the kitchen. She was putting away two stacks of large plastic bowls under the sink.

"Aah!" Eartha said, flinching as soon as she saw him. "Boy! Hasn't anyone ever told you not to sneak up on an old lady!" She clutched her heart. "Mercy."

"S-s-sorry," Lucas chattered. The downstairs felt cold and drafty. Lucas realized that his sweat-drenched clothes weren't helping, either.

"Oh, now you must have set that AC on frostbite," said Eartha. She left the room and came back with a blanket for Lucas. "Wrap yourself up before you catch cold."

He pulled the blanket around him like a cloak and sat down at the table. "Thank you."

"So you're an early morning type, huh?" Eartha asked.

"Not usually, but . . ." He paused. "Lucky woke me up. Something spooked him."

"The cat?" Eartha looked past Lucas, searching the room for signs of Lucky.

"Don't worry. He's hiding upstairs."

A smile broke over Eartha's face. "Oh, I wasn't worried. I'm just not a cat person, is all. They are too lonesome for my taste."

Lucas nodded; he kind of understood what she meant. "I'd never been a cat person, either. I always wanted a dog, but we weren't allowed to have one in our old apartment."

"Still doesn't seem like a good reason to get a cat," said Eartha.

Lucas didn't know what to say, so he changed the subject. "Do you have dogs?"

"Dogs?" Eartha asked, wiping down the already spotless counter. "What's it to you?"

"You were putting away dog bowls," said Lucas.

"Dog bowls?"

"Yeah, under the sink," said Lucas. "At least, they looked like dog bowls."

Eartha waved her hands, motioning around the empty room. "You see any dogs round here? I think that cold's froze your brain, hon."

"So there's nothing under the sink?" asked Lucas.

"Just sink stuff," said Eartha. She walked over to the cabinet, opened it, and pulled out a plastic bowl with a dog bone border. "Is this what you're talking about?"

"Yeah. Doesn't that look like a dog bowl?" said Lucas.

"I s'pose," said Eartha. "Except you won't find any dogs in here. I moved the bowls to get my cleaning supplies. Not sure where they came from. They've been here since I showed up."

Lucas felt his nose start to drip. He tried to wipe it without Eartha noticing, but that forced him into a sneeze.

"Bless you," she said, handing him a box of tissues. "I know what might help that cold. A cup of orange juice with a splash of something special."

"Something special?" asked Lucas, when he felt a slap on his back.

"Morning, champ," said Dad. He was wearing the same clothes he had on the day before. "I'm surprised to see you up this early after that long drive."

"Yeah, I guess," Lucas agreed as Eartha put a cup in front of him. The orange juice was still swirling from whatever she'd added to it.

"What do you say, Lucas?" Dad prompted.

"Thank you," he mumbled and picked up the juice. He sniffed it, but there was no weird smell, just the brightness of pure orange citrus. Lucas took a sip and it was surprisingly delicious. "Wow . . ."

"Mmm-hmm." Eartha nodded. "That'll clear you right up in no time."

As he drank, Lucas looked out the front window. The entire outdoors was newly colored by the morning light. The murky shadows from last night had been cast away and replaced by bright greens, deep browns, rich yellows, and a blue sky so perfect that he wanted to name a color after it.

But just as the world outside had become more vibrant, so had the noise of the cicadas. They were blasting now, far louder than they had been the night before. Lucas was taking it all in—the beauty and otherness of his new world—when a man walked out of the forest. He was followed closely by a fleet of other men and women dressed in jeans and flannel shirts. Lucas stared at them through the window as they made their way past the cottage and over to the mansion that was about to be his new home.

More people arrived, wearing tool belts and hard hats. Some carried sheets of lumber and piping, as if they'd just been pulled off a truck. But every worker looked like they were doing the most normal, mundane task in the world, like it was business as usual. None of them bothered to give a single glance to the weird, sweaty kid wrapped in a blanket and drinking possibly poisoned orange juice.

"Um, Dad?" Lucas called, pointing outside.

Dad shook his head. "Don't look at me. I didn't order any home improvements. Until last night, I didn't even know which house was mine."

A knock on the back kitchen door broke the silence. Framed by the yellow curtains around the door window, a man in a green hard hat stood waiting. His stare fell on Lucas, and a shiver crawled up Lucas's spine again. The worker's eyes looked right through him as if he weren't there. Lucas waved, but the man only hovered in the doorway, staring.

"Hold on, hold on," Eartha called out. "I'm getting the keys. Hold on."

Lucas looked at his dad, who only shrugged.

Eartha shuffled over to a closet and pulled out a gigantic ring of keys. Each key had a brightly colored rubber cover with writing on it. She slid key after key around until she landed on the one with a lime-green cover and unhitched it from the ring.

"Number 108," Eartha said, opening the door and handing the man the key. "Now, you know the rules for your team."

The man nodded stiffly as he took the key and left without saying a word.

Lucas saw Eartha give the man a royal side-eye glance as she added, "And you best be gone by five. All that hammering makes a racket and I need peace and quiet to calm my nerves."

The man stopped without turning around to look at Eartha and, in a strangely hollow voice, said, "You'll hardly notice we're here."

"Oh, you always say that, and I always notice," complained Eartha as she shut the door.

"What is this all about?" asked Dad.

"It's just the builders, hon," said Eartha. "You'll get used to it."

"Get used to what?" Lucas asked. "What are they building? What are all those keys for?"

Eartha held up the giant ring. Lucas had never seen someone with so many keys in his life. The groundskeeper for the White House maybe had a collection like that . . . *maybe*. Or the warden at a prison. There must have been well over a hundred keys dangling on a ring that could have fit around his neck.

"These are the keys to your house," said Eartha. She tossed them on the table with a clunk. "The same house those people outside are still building."

"*Still* building?" Dad repeated.

"How much do you know about Silas Sweetwater's home?" Eartha reached into the jumble of keys, found one in a red cover, and pointed it toward Lucas. "There's lots of rules to living in Sweetwater Manor, but three are most important."

Lucas looked at Eartha, wide-eyed, both fascinated and frightened by how much she reminded him of a drill sergeant in that moment.

"Rule number one: Don't move anything. Silas put everything in there for a reason. Rule number two: Always keep building. And rule number three . . ."

"Wait, hold on," Dad interrupted. "There are rules?"

Eartha shook her head in disbelief. "Oh, yes, there are rules. Why do you think I live over here, instead of in there? Listen, hon, maybe y'all should take a look at the house yourself. It's hardly my place to ruin the surprise."

Lucas's dad let out a frustrated sigh and ran upstairs to wake up his wife. Lucas was left wrapped in a blanket with what he now realized was the most delicious glass of orange juice he'd ever had in his life.

"What's the third rule?" he asked.

"For you? Always flush. Now put that glass in the sink when you're done," Eartha instructed. Then she winked and left the kitchen.

Lucas nudged the keys as if they might be alive. He felt the cold metal and weight against his knuckle. They were all different shapes and sizes, like an evolution time line of keys. There were old wide-toothed brass keys, short silver keys, even the credit card type of keys that hotels use for their rooms. A scent of grease and chimney fires loomed in the air over the keys, which made Lucas feel oddly relaxed and at home. The spell was quickly broken when he heard shredding buzz saws come to life outside. Shaking his head, Lucas downed the rest of his juice and brought his empty glass to the sink.

Out of the window, Sweetwater Manor towered over the trees. The house was yellow with green shutters . . . or at least *this* side of the house was yellow with green shutters. It was the first time he'd seen the mansion in the daylight, and it was gorgeous.

He washed the glass in the sink. Knowing how crazy Eartha was about no-flushers, he didn't want to find out how she felt about dirty-dish-in-the-sink-leavers, too. He reached for a towel to dry the glass, when he heard a loud bang. The noise came from the base of the kitchen door, where a small metal flap was swinging open back and forth.

"Is that a dog door?" Lucas got on his hands and knees to study it. As he pushed it open, the heat of the outdoors tumbled inside as if the morning was breathing on him.

The forest was close to Eartha's house. Lucas reached his hand outside and could almost touch the trees. He'd never in his life lived this close to nature. He stared at it like he was studying a statue in a museum. The wilderness was a mysterious work of art to him in the same way a statue was once a hunk of rock and then something new had blossomed from it. Just then, a shadow moved in the trees—or at least Lucas thought he saw a shadow.

"Stop freaking yourself out," he whispered. He heard a scuffling sound outside, and the bushes next to the back door bounced as if they were alive.

"Hello?" asked Lucas, as if anyone was going to answer him. For a moment, the morning remained quiet.

Until he felt something sharp dig into his leg.

CHAPTER 7

If Lucas's parents had heard the gasp that erupted from him, they would have called an ambulance right away. It sounded like all the air had been sucked out of his lungs.

He whipped around to find Lucky kneading away at the blanket around Lucas. The cat's claws plucked carelessly at his legs.

"Get off!" Lucas said, then he flapped the blanket and sent Lucky skirting across the floor and back upstairs with a hiss.

"It's not nice to scare the cat," said Mom from the bottom of the stairs.

"He scared me first," Lucas argued.

"That's still no reason to scare the cat. What in the world are you doing?" She was putting on her shoes and wore a very determined look on her face.

"Uh, exploring?" He went to stand up but slipped on the blanket and fell back to the floor with a smack. "Uh, exploring . . . gracefully?"

"Congratulations, Einstein, you found a dog door," said Mom. "Now if you really want to explore, let's go see our new house. Your father seems to think it's haunted. Wanna find out?"

Lucas didn't. But when Mom had her determined look on, it was best to follow her into battle. This was the face that launched a thousand bake sales for his school and single-handedly took over the PTA. Plus, Lucas wasn't sure if he could handle another night at Eartha's. It was time to confront his weird future home. "Yeah, I'd love to. Just let me get dressed."

As they headed to the giant home, the first thing Lucas noticed was how the house shone in the sunlight. It was almost too bright to look at.

A small group of trees separated the two homes, but walking through it, he realized that every tree, plant, and bush had been cultivated to build an artistic barrier from the cottage. What seemed like a wild forest last night was actually an intricate garden that ushered visitors toward the house. As the wind blew, Lucas felt himself being pulled forward.

A porch stretched across the entire front of the mansion. It was tucked under an extended roof that gave the open space plenty of shade. Arches jutted up and down along the porch to give the house a ski lodge look.

"It's a craftsman," Mom said.

"A what?" asked Lucas, wincing in the bright sun.

"A craftsman is a building style," his mom answered. "Craftsman houses are known for their beauty and hand-built design. You see the arches over the deep porch, the stained-glass windows, the detailed woodwork that covers this house from top to bottom? Those were all created by hand. Probably by builders that were more artists than contractors."

Lucas could see exactly what his mother meant. The place looked like a living dollhouse, but not a plastic one. More like those weird, old, collectible dollhouses that people on TV showed to experts who guessed how much their dollhouses were worth. And they were usually worth a lot.

The house didn't seem like it belonged here, in the middle of the forest, hidden like a diamond. It was the kind of home that was made for a movie set or the cover of a magazine, the kind of house that's supposed to make the rest of the world envious. Lucas counted three stories to the house. At least that's the way it looked from the outside. The front of the house weaved in and out of the lawn and then disappeared behind a row of trees.

Who knows, thought Lucas. *It could be one hundred times bigger than it looks from the front.* Then he remembered their long drive the night before just to get around the enormous building. Lucas had a feeling they were only seeing the tip of the iceberg.

Mom held up the red key and walked toward the front door. "Let's take this puppy for a drive, shall we?"

Lucas followed, tiptoeing up the wide wooden stairs that had grown smooth but rickety over time. He could feel the house ease under him, creaking and sinking with every step. The front door was a deep brown slab of wood with a full stained-glass window set in the middle of it. The placement of the stained glass was eerie under the porch, where the bright sun almost disappeared. Lucas felt a cold breeze in the strange shade that made him shudder. The pattern on the stained-glass looked like a hooded figure lurking in the doorway—a shadow waiting for them just on the other side. In the folds of the figure's cloak, Lucas thought he saw the shadow holding a whip trapped forever in a lashing motion.

"Oh, that's a shame," said Mom. "Why would someone put a stained-glass window in a place where it would never see sunlight?"

Then, as if by magic, a light came on from inside the house and the window was transformed. What looked hidden and dangerous to Lucas one second became beautiful the next. The design wasn't a creepy demon holding a whip; with the light shining through the stained-glass, Lucas could see a sun with beams breaking through the clouds. It was heavenly and inviting. He felt himself drawn closer to the house again.

As his mom set the key in the lock, the light pulsed brighter. *It's angry* was Lucas's gut reaction. *The house is angry and it doesn't want us here.*

Suddenly, the light flared into an explosive flash and the sound of shattering echoed from above them. Lucas's mom practically tackled him out of the way as shards of glass rained down on where they had been standing.

Then the worst possible thing happened: Lucas lost his breath.

"No, no, no," Mom said in a quiet but serious tone. "Not here, not now. It's okay, just focus, relax, and breathe." She rubbed his shoulders and took deep breaths with him. The low, haunting drone of white noise brought him back to the moment.

"I'm okay," Lucas wheezed.

Her hands moved from his shoulders to trace over his face and scalp, looking for any cuts from the glass. Lucas looked past her and up to the ceiling, where a black mark charred the paint. It floated above them like a disturbed spirit.

"Voilà!"

Lucas and his mother jumped at the sound of a voice behind them.

"We have electricity!" Dad said, appearing out of nowhere.

"KYLE!" Mom snapped, clutching her chest. "You blew up a light bulb and the light fixture exploded right above us! You could have given Lucas another serious attack!"

"Sorry, didn't mean to," Dad said with a shrug. "It looks like everyone's okay, just a little spooked."

Mom shot him a glare. "No. Jokes. Kyle."

"What? I promise," he continued. "It wasn't a joke, it's an

old house. I had the electric company turn the power back on. Are you okay, champ?"

Lucas's mom stood up and slid the broken glass over with her shoe so that no one would step on it. Then she unlocked the door and turned the oblong, brass knob until it clicked. As the heavy door swung open, an unexpected odor drifted from the inside.

"Is that . . . ," Dad began with a sniff, "roses?"

Lucas nodded. The house smelled like the cleanest, safest place he could imagine, like the Garden of Eden from the Bible, or his kindergarten classroom. He inhaled the scent deeply and the high-pitched whistle from his wheezing disappeared.

"See?" Dad whispered to Mom. "Lucas is better already. We made the right choice."

Mom's shoulders relaxed the slightest bit, then she smiled. "You're still cleaning up this glass and replacing that fixture, Kyle."

The family entered a grand hallway that opened up to a double staircase. Everything around them was made of fine, dark wood that had been carved and polished to look as soft and regal as marble. The sweeping banisters flowed from the upstairs to the downstairs like arms reaching out to hug Lucas. Even the floor had inlaid designs that were gorgeous and intricate. It was like his mom said, the builders really had been artists.

"Goodbye, tiny apartment," said Lucas.

"Hello, Great Gatsby's house," said Dad.

Mom was speechless. She walked around touching the walls, the banisters, peeking into the rooms set off to either side of the hallway. "Kyle, is this real?"

"If it's not, then we're all having the same dream," said Dad. "And I think that's impossible."

Lucas watched as his parents gasped at this and that: the chandelier, the lush furniture, the multiple fireplaces, the parquet floors (whatever that meant). As his parents moved from room to room, Lucas turned and closed the front door. From this side, the heavenly sunbeams in the stained-glass window were gone and the hooded figure returned. Lucas shuddered seeing the stranger again, but then he reminded himself that it was only glass. The hooded figure was all in his imagination.

He could still hear his parents' voices in the house but couldn't see them. They had moved on to other rooms deeper in the mansion.

"Mom?" Lucas called. "I'm going to take a look around, okay?"

"Fine, but don't go too far," her voice reached back to him. Then he heard her say, "Where's the kitchen? I need to see the kitchen."

Lucas roamed through the space, taking in everything from the widest rooms to the tallest ceilings he'd ever seen in his life. He walked up one set of stairs, running his hands along the banister railing. It was cold and smooth to the touch. The steps were deep, too—deeper than the hallway steps leading up to his old two-bedroom apartment in the city.

At the top of the stairs was a long, wide hall lined with closed doors. It was more like a hotel than a house. Lucas tried the first door and discovered a luxurious bathroom that was bigger than his old kitchen. The second door led to a bedroom with a four-poster bed. There was a giant white bowl on the dresser, too, and the two windows in the room stretched all the way up the wall.

The third door, though, was jammed.

As he pulled it, a small scratching sound came from behind the door. "Lucky?" Lucas asked into the empty hallway. "Did you follow us over here?"

Lucky was an escape artist. Lucas couldn't count the number of times he'd found his cat perched on the fire escape outside their locked window. If that cat could sneak out of their apartment, getting out of Eartha's cottage would be a cinch.

"Come on," Lucas muttered as he pulled harder at the door, but it wouldn't budge. The scratching became louder, then stopped. Lucas anchored his foot beside the door and pulled a third time. Violently, the door swung open and Lucas tumbled backward, clunking his head against the wall. It didn't hurt, but it was embarrassing.

"Why are you such a spaz?" he asked himself as he rubbed the back of his head. But when Lucas looked up, he was surprised. "That's weird."

The open door didn't lead to another bedroom. In fact, it didn't lead anywhere at all. Lucas sat face-to-face with a red brick wall that filled and blocked the doorway. He gave the wall a solid knock and the rough, uneven bricks scraped against his knuckles. Someone had built a door here, but no room. Lucas studied the back of the door he'd just opened. There was no doorknob on the other side.

Lucas shut the door and noticed a strange shape etched into the doorknob. He traced the shape with his fingers. It was a bone, and it was fashioned crudely into the brass knob, scratched like a kid had made it. Lucas wouldn't have noticed it on a regular door, but this door was . . . unexpected . . . he thought it was worth a second look.

As Lucas moved deeper into the house, the rooms became fewer and farther between. Dark green wallpaper lined the halls, casting a dull glow around him. Light fixtures hung like old lanterns on the walls. Lucas's shadow pushed in front of him, then swung behind him as he moved in and out of their light.

That's when he saw it. No—not *it*. Him.

Standing at the end of the long hall was a boy. Or at least Lucas thought it was a boy. The two of them froze in place, like they had caught each other doing something wrong.

Lucas smiled and waved, and the boy waved back.

"Oh, thank goodness! I was beginning to think I'd seen a ghost," Lucas said, not even wondering why there was a strange kid in his new house. "My name's Lucas. My family just moved in."

The boy didn't answer. He looked to be the same age as Lucas, though at this distance and in the murky light, it was hard to see anything. Slowly, Lucas moved forward. "Are you with the workers?"

The boy started to tremble nervously. Then the lights on the walls began to dim. Without thinking, Lucas jogged forward to meet the kid at the end of the hall as the lights flickered into a dull brown.

"Are you lost?" Lucas asked as he closed the gap between them. "Do you need help?"

The kid's head flicked up and down, then left and right, searching in all different directions—almost as if he was looking for a way to escape. Then the boy tensed up like he was about to run away.

"Don't run! There's nothing to be afraid of," said Lucas, but as he came closer, he could tell that the kid was about to bolt. Had Lucas caught someone breaking into the house?

Suddenly all the lights clicked off and the sound of heavy footfalls echoed through the hallway. The other kid was running right at him! In the darkness, Lucas braced himself and put his hands up to tackle the stranger, but then the footsteps . . . stopped?

Lucas called out, "I'm really just trying to help! Are you still there?"

His heart pounded in his chest as he strained to hear anything beyond its crazy thumping. That's when the footsteps ran away from him. Quickly, Lucas followed the sound, running with his hands outstretched and—WHAM! He crashed into the back wall at the end of the hallway and nobody was there.

Lucas jumped up as the lights flickered back on. A carbon copy of Lucas stared back at him through a mirror that reached from floor to ceiling. He let out a slow, deep breath. It hadn't been another kid in the house. It was only his reflection.

"Seeing things again," Lucas wheezed. He grabbed his inhaler and shook it before taking a deep breath. Once his breathing steadied, he stuck his tongue out at the mirror.

The doctors had told his parents that it wasn't unusual for Lucas to "mistake things" in his condition. That's how they said it: mistake things. It had to do with the amount of oxygen that reached his brain. Who knew that weak lungs could be so weird?

But this was one situation where Lucas was happy to be wrong about the other kid.

Lucas stared in the mirror. He didn't quite look exactly like himself. Lucas scratched his head. In the mirror, his reflection scratched its head, too.

But a different person stood in the mirror. The Lucas who lived in the city would have gone back to the safety of his room and his parents after a scare like that. The Lucas in the mirror had a chance for a new beginning in Sweetwater Manor. Wasn't that why his parents had moved him here?

The hallway split off into two directions from where Lucas stood. One headed to the left and one headed to the right. The way back was behind him. Lucas decided to go left.

CHAPTER 8

Every step in the new hallway echoed with a soft creak from the wide, wooden floorboards. Lucas was deep inside the house now, perhaps in an older part of the building. The wallpaper in the hall was a yellowish cream. Lucas imagined that it was once a bright white, but time had dampened its color. The sweet rose smell faded here, replaced by an earthier scent, like cinnamon. Lucas coughed as if grit was catching in his throat.

He wanted to go back downstairs. There was no need to discover all the secrets in Silas's house today. He was going to live here for years. That was plenty of time to find the lost gold or treasure maps or whatever else was probably hidden in this screwball place.

Lucas turned to leave, when he heard a clicking noise. It came from down the hall and sounded like someone typing slowly on a keyboard.

"Hello?" Lucas leaned in closer and listened.

Meow.

The call was faint, but Lucas knew it anywhere. "Lucky," he said with exasperation. "You crazy cat. Where are you?"

Meow, the cat answered from farther down the hallway. Lucas could barely make out a set of doors in the shadows. One of them slowly opened. "Stay there, I'm coming."

Meow-rrrr-ow-rrrRRREOW! The new sound sent chills down Lucas's spine. It wasn't Lucky's calm mew—it was the call his cat made when he was scared.

Lucas darted down the hall, but the door he'd seen drifted away from him. The walls stretched into the distance, like holding a mirror up to a mirror; the hallway was never-ending. Lucas closed his eyes tight. "It's fine, this place is normal. You're just not used to big houses," he whispered to himself.

Lucky's cries grew louder, and when Lucas opened his eyes, the door was suddenly in front of him. With each high-pitched whine, Lucas felt his heart pounding in his chest. "Lucky?" he whispered as he reached for the half-open door, but it slammed shut.

MRRREOWWWW-HISSSSSSSSSS.

The hiss cut off sharply and Lucas jumped back. The only thought in his head was *run*, but he stood his ground. If Lucky was trapped, Lucas was going to get his cat out. He reached for the knob, turned it, then slowly opened the door.

The room was a study. Lucas's eyes flicked from corner to corner, searching for Lucky's white-tipped tail or glowing green eyes. "Lucky? It's me."

Lucas rubbed his fingers together and clicked his tongue three times, just like when he'd give the cat treats to eat at home, but Lucky stayed hidden.

Shelves lined one of the walls. They were crammed with books. Lucky loved to squeeze onto shelves, so Lucas checked there first.

He ran his finger along the spines out of habit. For as long as he could remember, whenever he was near books on shelves, he felt the strange urge to touch them in this way. When he pulled his hand back, his finger had turned a dull gray from dust. The book collection was so old that most of the spines didn't even have titles written on them.

Suddenly something brushed against his leg. Lucas flinched backward and looked down, but nothing was there.

An old rolltop desk sat in the corner of the room with its pull-down shell closed like a balled-up armadillo hiding from danger.

"Lucky?" Lucas wandered over to look at the photographs on the wall.

Each one had a forest in the background, with people on horseback dressed up in fancy clothes with guns. The riders were surrounded by packs of dogs sniffing the ground for a scent. Lucas noticed writing on one of the photos, scribbled in the corner near the ornately carved frame. *Hounds Hollow Foxhunt, 1899.*

Beside the picture was an open window. Lucas watched for any movement in the room, but everything was still. He walked to the window and looked outside. A tree branch stretched from the nearest tree like a gnarled arm reaching for the house. At the edge of the branch, a squirrel stood on its hind legs, staring at Lucas.

"Did you brush against me?" he asked the squirrel. "Listen. You stay in your house and I'll stay in mine, okay?"

The squirrel squiggled up its whiskers, then turned and flicked its tail.

Lucas tried to shut the window down before the squirrel could get back in, but it wouldn't budge. Dad was not going to like a wide-open window where rodents could crawl in whenever they want. He made a note to tell his father about it later.

The squirrel, curious, inched closer.

"No," Lucas said sternly. "Remember our deal. You stay out there."

Then, with a crack, another creature sprang from the shadows and pounced on the squirrel with sharp claws and a heavy hiss. His own cat, Lucky, had pinned the squirrel to the floor and stood above it letting out a bloodcurdling hiss that Lucas had never heard before.

"Jeez, Lucky! Don't hurt it!" Lucas gasped as he snatched his cat off the trapped animal.

The squirrel's fluffy tail thrashed back and forth as it escaped to the tree and leapt from branch to branch. Lucky clawed out of Lucas's arms and landed in cat battle mode. His back was arched and his teeth clicked loudly, challenging the volume of cicadas outside.

Lucas had never seen his cat become a bloodthirsty hunter before. If Lucas hadn't stopped him, Lucky would have totally eaten that poor squirrel. What was crazier was how quickly and easily Lucky shrugged off the brutal attack. One second, Lucky was bristling with claws ready to slash; the next second he leapt gracefully onto the rolltop desk and purred for Lucas to come over. Then the cat casually licked his paws and nuzzled against Lucas's hand as if nothing crazy had just happened.

Lucas scooped up Lucky, and the cat curled in his arms like a baby. "C'mon, you psycho. Let's get out of here before that squirrel comes back with reinforcements."

As he held the cat, Lucas had a sudden urge to see what was hidden in the rolltop desk. He tried to lift the retractable top. It was locked. The tiny keyhole at the base of the desk stared back at Lucas. He traced it with his finger.

"I think we've found my inheritance," Lucas told Lucky as he started to pull the key out from around his neck.

Suddenly Lucky hissed again and climbed frantically over Lucas's shoulders, scratching to get out of his arms. The cat pounced to the floor and faced the doorway with a full and angry screech that gave Lucas a serious case of goose bumps.

He turned around to see the mysterious boy from earlier. Only he wasn't in a mirror this time. He was standing in the doorway. The boy's face was blurry and ashen and he wore a dull gray suit. It was like the kid had stepped out of the old foxhunting photos from a hundred years ago.

The boy stood still and slowly lifted his hand toward Lucas, but Lucky was not about to let anything happen to his master.

Hiss-Hiss-HISS!

At the cat's warning, the gray boy took off running. Lucky scrambled after him.

"Hey!" Lucas yelled, confused. "Wait, no, Lucky! Come back!"

Darting into the hall, Lucas could see the boy racing away. He was fast, but Lucky was fast, too.

Lucas didn't know what else to do, so he chased after them. The lights in the house flickered, but they didn't turn off this time. Lucas kept his eyes trained on the boy. The kid's suit made him look like a tiny businessman, but he might as well have been wearing a tracksuit. This kid was like lightning.

As Lucas ran, he couldn't believe what he was doing. Was he chasing a stranger in his own house, or was he chasing Lucky to make sure the cat didn't get hurt? Or to make sure the cat didn't hurt the stranger? Either way, doubt crept in on him. He wondered what people in chases do when they reach the end of the chase. Maybe he was going to find out today.

The floor started to slope upward, like he was running uphill. His legs began to burn, but he couldn't stop now, he'd come too far. At the top of the hall, Lucas rounded another turn just in time to see one of the doors slam shut. Lucky was caught completely off guard as the cat blew by the door and slid into a wall, leaving long scratch marks in the wood floor.

It took all of Lucas's energy to not fly past the door, too. How had the kid outmaneuvered a cat?!

Lucas huffed as he banged on the door. "I . . . I know you're in there. Just come out and I won't call the police."

Lucas had no idea what he was saying. Call the police? He was nowhere near a phone, and there was some strange kid hiding out in a room in Lucas's mysterious and comically large house. How was he going to call the police? It made sense at the time, though, and sounded threatening enough that it might get the kid to open up.

Lucas waited and stared at the closed door. The brass knob had a bone shape etched into it similar to the door that opened to a brick wall earlier. The bone wasn't ornate or beautiful like a decoration; it was scratched into place, quick and ugly, like initials in a tree. Lucas pounded on the door again, but there was no answer.

"If you're not coming out, then I'm coming in," Lucas warned.

He turned the knob and the door thrust open, pulling him violently inside. There wasn't a kid behind this door. There wasn't even a room. Lucas was facing the outside of the house, with nothing but air and trees around him. He peered over the threshold and looked down to the ground some thirty feet below.

Still clutching the doorknob, Lucas tumbled forward and lost his balance. He tried to pull back, but the door was being forced open like a spring-loaded trap. Lucas fell; he was going to hit the ground—and hit it hard. But at that moment, a blistering heat lit up behind him. It scorched like fire. Something caught hold of his shirt and lifted Lucas back to the hallway floor.

Startled, he tried to catch his breath and looked around for whoever had just saved his life, but no one was there.

A minute later, footsteps clumped and the same man in the green hard hat from that morning shuffled toward Lucas. "I've found the boy," the man announced into his phone, his voice a dry monotone. When he reached Lucas, he didn't say a word.

"I'm okay," Lucas said as he slowly rotated his right shoulder. His arm felt like it had nearly been ripped off. "Did you see the kid?"

"What?" the worker asked, almost in a daze. "Another kid? I was only looking for one."

"He ran." Lucas nodded to the open door. "He ran through there."

The worker looked at Lucas, then looked at the open door. Slowly, the man crawled over and peaked at the ground outside. "Anyone who goes through this door would be splat down there," the worker said. "I don't see any splat."

The worker's phone erupted in muffled screams as the man clicked it over to the speakerphone. "Yeah, he was by that third-floor trapdoor."

"How did he find the trapdoor already?" the voice over the phone said. It sounded a lot like Eartha. "Reset it and bring him back down before his parents flip out."

"Stay here," the worker said as he pulled the door shut. Then he looked at Lucas with almost dead eyes. "You must be careful. This place is dangerous."

"Yeah," said Lucas. "I just didn't expect that."

"That is why they call it a trap," said the worker as he helped Lucas up. "You are not supposed to expect it. You should stay downstairs. Your parents are worried."

The worker smelled like leather and sweat, but his hands were ice-cold. Lucas waved him off as if to show that he was okay, but he wasn't. As he went over to scoop up Lucky, he knew his parents were going to be mad. Not about the door, or his almost (for lack of a better term) splatting. They'd be mad because he'd wandered so far away.

CHAPTER 9

Eartha placed a bag of ice over Lucas's shoulder as he sat on the same couch he tripped over the night before. His mother sat next to him while his father paced around the small cottage den.

"Second-story doors that lead to nowhere, workers around every corner, that giant key ring alone," Dad sputtered in frustration. "What in the dickens is going on here?!"

"It was the third story, Dad," said Lucas.

"You are not helping, young man," Mom snapped. "Ms. Dobbs, I mean, Eartha, what can you tell us about this place?"

Eartha shuffled over to a heavily cushioned red chair with frayed edges that traced an outline of the old woman. She'd probably sat in that same chair for years now. "I told you that you could use a groundskeeper. Good thing I'm here. This property has been in the Sweetwater family for four generations. Y'all will be the fifth. It started as a horse farm."

"Respectfully," Dad interrupted, "horses don't explain anything about this place. Please skip ahead a few years and tell us why this mansion is built like a fun house."

Eartha nodded. "I understand your concern, Mr. Trainer, but I assure you, that house is safe. It's also just a little . . . quirky. See, after the horse farm, the Sweetwater family started adding on to the house. I asked Silas himself about it when I first came to work here. I said, 'Silas, y'all got all these workers building and building and building, but ain't got no one but you living in that old house. What gives?' And that's when he told me about the fire."

"There was a fire?" asked Lucas. The burn on his shoulder flared under the ice. He didn't mention anything to his parents about someone grabbing him before he fell through the door. He didn't tell them about the boy he saw, either. Not that they gave him much of a chance to talk. It was tight hugs followed by lectures about how dangerous it was to wander off. Sometimes he thought that might be the worst part about his sickness— that his parents treated him like a toddler who needed constant surveillance.

"Oh mercy, yes, there was a fire," said Eartha. "A mighty fire that swallowed up most of the house. Burned it to a crisp."

Dad's mouth dropped open. "You mean to tell me that this house is new construction?"

Eartha shook her head in a slow, kind manner. "Yes and no. Silas was just a young boy back then. It's a miracle the family escaped with their lives. They decided to build it back. Only this time, Silas told me, they never stopped building. First they built this cottage we're sitting in right now. They lived here while the house was reconstructed. They added new levels and additions to the old foundation. They added new houses in different styles, and then they connected all them houses. By the time Silas took over the project, he'd become obsessed with building."

"Obsessed?" asked Mom. "But why?"

"Because ever since they kept hammers swinging, saws sawing, and new walls going up on the house . . ." Eartha paused and both of Lucas's parents leaned forward. He saw her smile with big yellow teeth like a fisherman with a nibble on the hook. "Ever since then, nothing bad ever happened again."

Lucas considered what his family had done up to this point to protect him. The doctors, the bills, the tests, the medicine, and now the move. "Families do that," he said quietly. "They do the strangest things to keep each other safe."

His mom patted his leg. "Yes. Yes, we do."

"And now what?" asked Dad. "We're just supposed to take up Silas's obsession? We can't afford to keep people working on this house for the rest of our lives. Heck, we can't afford to pay them another week."

"Oh, don't you worry 'bout that," said Eartha. "The work's paid for. Silas made sure of that."

"Whoa, how rich *was* he?" asked Lucas.

"Not so much rich as dedicated," corrected Eartha. "He really believed that building the house brought him good luck. He was a superstitious man if I ever saw one."

The room went quiet and the cicadas' chirp-clicks took

over. Lucas's father was leaning on the couch. Lucas could feel his dad's hands gripping and releasing the pillow behind him like a stress ball. His dad was not the best-equipped person to handle these kinds of situations. When life handed him lemons, he usually threw a grown-up tantrum. His mom, on the other hand, at least tried to make lemonade.

"So the workers will keep working," she said, forcing an understanding tone in her voice. "We were in the house today and couldn't even hear them. I think as long as we live in the front original structure, we'll be fine."

"Holly," Dad said, "can we talk about this out back?"

As his parents left the room, the ice on Lucas's shoulder had turned to cold water in a ziplock bag. He felt it slush around as he tried to avoid listening to their not-so-quiet discussion outside.

Eartha stared coolly at him from her chair. "Need more ice?"

"Yes, ma'am," said Lucas. "But I can get it, thanks." He stood up to go the kitchen, when there was a knock at the front door. Lucas paused next to it and looked at Eartha.

"I ain't gettin' up outta this chair when a perfectly good young man is standing right by the door," she said. "Besides, it's not for me."

"How do you know?" asked Lucas.

"It never is" was all she said.

Lucas went to peer through the peephole and realized the

door didn't have one. His cheeks went flush. Eartha was watching and Lucas must have seemed like he had no idea how to use a door. With a deep breath, Lucas opened it.

Bess Armstrong was wearing jeans that had been cut at the knees, a black T-shirt, and a backward baseball hat.

"You coming out to play or what?"

"Play?" asked Lucas. "Did we have plans or something?"

"Yes." Bess nodded once. "Yes, we did. Well, not to play, but at least to hang out. You still got my basketball?"

"Sure, it's in the car," said Lucas. "You need it back?"

"Nah, not now," she said. Then she went stone quiet.

Lucas didn't know what to do, so he stepped outside. "Hey, Ms. Dobbs, will you tell my parents I'm just out here?"

"Em-hmmm," the old woman said from her chair.

As he shut the door behind him, Bess pulled the water bag off his shoulder. "Is this a new fashion thing that kids in the city wear?"

The question caught Lucas off guard and he laughed. "Oh yeah, definitely. But you can only wear one bag of water because if you wear two, then people think you're a real freak."

Bess smiled and Lucas felt warm all over, which was probably just from the sun. At least that's what he kept telling himself.

"How'd you get here?" he asked.

"Walked," said Bess.

"Wow, that's a long walk," said Lucas.

"Not really."

Lucas waited for her to say something more, but he was getting the sense that this girl was not a talker unless there was something that needed to be said. And sure, the last thing he wanted the night before was to hang out with her, but after this morning's weirdness, he was happy to be around another kid. Well, a normal, regular kid who wasn't hiding in his house, spying on him, and then disappearing.

"Let me see your back," said Bess. She lightly but insistently twirled him around. "Wow! Did you get a sunburn already, city boy?"

"What do you mean?" he asked, trying to see what she saw.

"Stop squirming," she said softly. "You can't look at your own back without a mirror. Necks don't work that way."

He instantly stopped and felt like an idiot, but Bess didn't seem to care. She picked at the back of his shirt gingerly and poked her fingers through four small rips below his collar that hadn't been there that morning.

"You oughta take better care of your clothes," she said. "Do city kids always cut up their shirts, or do you wanna tell me what happened?"

Lucas blushed at the feeling of her fingers on his back, so he pulled away and changed the subject. "I . . . uh . . . heard this place burned down."

Bess let go of his shirt and sat on the front steps. "Yeah, that's true. The Hounds Hollow Inferno, they call it round here. But that was a long time ago. You got a bike?"

Lucas sat down next to her. "No. Never needed one in the city."

"You'll need a bike," she said. "You know how to ride, though, right?"

"My grandparents taught me," he told her. "They live in the South. Every kid there has a bike."

"Sounds a lot like here," said Bess. "So we'll get you a bike. I know a guy."

"Do *you* have a bike?" he asked her.

"Of course I have a bike," she said. "What kind of a kid doesn't have a bike? I mean, besides you."

Lucas looked toward Sweetwater Manor. He didn't really know what to say next, so he asked, "Wanna go for a walk?"

Bess shrugged and tucked a wisp of black hair under her cap. "Sure. Where?"

"I haven't walked around the outside of the house yet. And I need to stretch my legs after the drive yesterday." He stretched his legs and arms in front of him dramatically.

"Okay," said Bess. "Let's go."

The cicadas still buzzed as the two kids followed the dirt road driveway beside the mansion. Lucas kept expecting to see work trucks parked along the house, but there were none.

Instead, Sweetwater Manor was surrounded by thick woods. Lucas stepped into the forest while Bess stayed on the path.

Inside, among the trees, the world felt different from inside the house. It was like the driveway was a moat protecting the home from the untouched wilderness around it. As he stepped deeper into the shadows, the sun disappeared and the temperature dropped a few degrees. Light strained through the branches, giving the surroundings an eerie, otherworldly glow. This was where monsters hid. It was like a Grimms' fairy tale, or a cursed forest level of a video game. Lucas shuddered and jumped back into the sunlight next to Bess.

"You okay?" It was the first thing Bess had said for a full ten minutes while they walked. "You're acting like something's chasing you."

"I'm not used to having this much nature around, I guess," said Lucas. "I mean, look out there. Anything could be hiding. Waiting."

Bess stood shoulder to shoulder with him and stared into the forest. "Hiding, maybe. Waiting, doubt it. What do you think's out there?"

Lucas realized he must sound stupid to her. Did he really want to tell her the truth? About the animal from last night? About the boy from today? About his sickness? Why did he have to say *waiting*? Bess was supposed to be the weird one, but now he was the one being wacky. "I don't know. Bigfoot? Bigfeet? What do you call, like, a group of Bigfoot?"

Bess pushed him away and laughed. She had a heavy laugh and a heavier push that surprised Lucas. He tripped over the dirt driveway but caught himself before he fell.

"You're funny," she said. "I've lived here all my life and the worst I've seen was a skunk. There's no monsters in those woods. It's just nature."

Lucas nodded. "I know, but, like, it's a lot of nature. I'm a city kid."

"Then stay out of the woods," Bess said. She tugged his arm and pulled him back along the driveway. "At least until I can teach you a thing or two so that it doesn't feel so strange anymore. Maybe we oughta go inside?"

"No." Lucas released the word before he knew what he was saying or how he was saying it. His tone fell like an iron wall between them, and whatever closeness they were sharing was cut off immediately.

Bess nodded, then reached into her pocket and tossed something to Lucas. Flinching, he managed to snag the object clumsily. Lucas opened his hand to find a triangle-shaped rock with smoothed edges. "What is this?"

"Duh," said Bess. "It's a rock."

"What's it for?" asked Lucas. He flipped the stone over and

and over in his hands. It was the perfect skipping rock and practically floated in his fingers.

"It'll protect you in the woods," she said. "Just keep it with you and you'll be safe."

Lucas laughed. "C'mon, so this thing is, what, magic? That's crazy."

"It's not crazy," Bess snapped back. Her eyes barreled into him, casting a glow of irritation, anger, and hurt. "It's not even weird, okay? It's lucky. Lots of people believe in luck, so why can't you think of it as a good luck charm? I thought you were different. I thought you might understand. I gave it to you because . . ."

But she didn't finish her thought. Instead, Bess turned her back and walked away, pulsing with an emotion that Lucas couldn't figure out.

"Sorry," he muttered, pushing the stone into his pocket and jogging to catch up to her. "I mean . . . thanks. Thanks and sorry."

She stayed quiet and Lucas didn't want to risk saying something wrong again, so they kept walking together without speaking. The house lumbered next to them the whole way, like some sleeping giant that was out of place in this world. The woodwork alone was mesmerizing. Balconies jutted out of the house, one after the other. Steeples rose above the treetops like churches, but they were just part of the Sweetwater Manor design. Every few steps, Lucas noticed another spotlight and camera. If Bess noticed them, too, she didn't let on. She was content to just walk with him.

"Did you, uh, know Silas?" Lucas asked when he felt enough time had passed.

"Kinda." Bess picked up a broken stick from off the ground and whiffed it through the air like a sword. "Did you?"

Truthfully, he had no idea who Silas Sweetwater was before his mom got the letter saying that her great-great-uncle passed away. The deed to the house was also in the envelope. Lucas's mom had no idea who he was and thought it was all a scam. But then Lucas's grandmother remembered Silas, though she had to dig deep through her family albums to find any proof of him. But he was there. She'd emailed them a grainy photograph of Silas. It was the only one his grandmother had, and she couldn't remember when or how she'd ended up with it.

Lucas stopped, thinking back to the photograph. The edges were uneven and worn away, almost as if they'd been burned. Silas was sitting on a set of steps in front of a porch. He was a kid in the picture, not much older than Lucas. Wearing a dark shirt and pants, Silas had wavy, black hair that stood in a tuft. He looked like he was from the Civil War days. Beside him were two dogs, a Rottweiler and a husky with all-black fur.

Neither Silas nor the dogs were looking at the camera in the picture. They were all staring off to the left and they weren't smiling at all. The photo didn't make Lucas any more excited about moving to where this weird-looking kid used to live.

The only thing Lucas's grandmother could remember was that the Sweetwaters moved and stopped talking to the rest of the family a long time ago, which is why everyone forgot about Silas until he died. Lucas wondered if the same thing would happen to him after he moved.

Bess snapped the stick suddenly in her hands, bringing Lucas back from his thoughts. "Well, did you know Silas or not?"

"No," he answered. "I didn't know him at all. Maybe that's why this place feels weird. You know, just moving into someone else's house with all their furniture and stuff still there."

"Wow, so his stuff is still in the house? Is it, like . . . everything?"

"How am I supposed to know?" asked Lucas. "I mean, maybe. There's a lot of junk in there."

Bess smiled after he said it. Then she grabbed Lucas by the shoulders and turned him to face her. For a moment, he thought she might try to plant one on him, but instead she asked, "Did you see anything out of the ordinary in there?"

Lucas let out a huge laugh. "Seriously? Look at this place. It's bigger than a museum and filled with way stranger things.

You might as well ask me if I ever saw any pigeons when I lived in the city."

Bess nodded and then broke their little huddle. "You'll have to show me sometime."

"Yeah, maybe. Just, not today" was all Lucas could get out. As Bess walked farther on, Lucas called out, "I didn't know you were a connoisseur of strange stuff." He didn't really know what the word *connoisseur* meant, but he'd heard his parents use it the same way. And for some reason, he wanted to impress this new, odd girl.

Bess stopped and kicked a clump of dirt before whipping around. "I'm friends with you, aren't I?"

A smile warmed on Lucas's face, the second one today. If he kept this up, he might be happy here. Then he remembered one thing about the house that he hadn't told anyone yet. "Hey, Bess. Have you ever seen, like, a boy—I don't know, like . . . hanging out with Silas before, I guess? Maybe someone who might know his way around the house?"

"A boy?" Bess froze a second before turning back around with a grin. "Hanging around here?"

Lucas knew that grin. It was a mask, just like his mom's— the one she wore whenever she knew more than she wanted to tell him. Bess had a secret.

"Yeah, no, I mean . . . now *I'm* sounding crazy," Lucas said.

"It was probably just a really young worker in the house or something. Forget I said anything."

"A boy?" she repeated, intrigued.

But then Lucas's mom pulled up the driveway in their car. A cloud of dust stirred in its wake. She rolled down the window. "Hi, Bess, it's good to see you again."

"Hi, Mrs. Trainer," Bess answered. "I hope you don't mind me snatching up Lucas for a walk."

"Not at all. New friends are always welcome." Lucas's mom gave him a wink. She loved winking and always thought no one else could see her do it. Problem was, everybody always saw it. She was horrible at winking. "Lucas, honey, I need you to come with me to pick up a few things in town. Bess, you're free to join us if you'd like."

"No, ma'am," Bess declined. "Thank you for the offer, but I should head home for lunch. I'll come back by later, Lucas. I can tell you more about Hounds Hollow and maybe you can show me around the house. Y'all have fun in town."

With that, Bess ran off into the woods. She was out of sight in seconds. Lucas stuck his hand in his pocket and palmed the rock she had given him. As he climbed into the car and clicked on his seat belt, he pulled out the rock and examined it. Bess must have been holding this rock for the whole time they were hanging out. She'd given it to him to protect him. Protect him from what, he had no idea. In fact, that Bess thought he needed protection at all kind of freaked him out. But if she was out to protect him, that meant she cared about him, which made Lucas feel good. Even if Bess might be a weirdo, Lucas was suddenly excited to see her again. He wasn't sure why, but he felt that he could learn a thing or two from her about his strange new life.

CHAPTER 10

Driving through downtown Hounds Hollow was like traveling back in time. There was a small, main street with a few buildings on each side. The sidewalks were mostly empty, but there were some people in the stores. First, Lucas and his mother passed a music store with a grand piano in the window. Next to that was a barbershop with one of those old-timey spinning candy cane–style poles out front. The men sitting outside watched their car suspiciously. They passed a diner with posters for banana splits, pies, and ice-cream sundaes. Servers in paper hats, and customers sipping coffee, looked up as they drove by. Lucas's mom gave them a neighborly wave, but they didn't wave back.

"Oh my goodness, look at that vintage clothing store," Mom said, ignoring the restaurant patrons' rebuke. The store didn't have a sign out front. Instead the words BUY SELL TAILOR WEAR were stenciled along the bottom flap of the faded green awning that covered the entrance. The windows were crowded with mannequins dressed like people from his mom's favorite movie, *Grease*. They wore white shirts, dark jeans, leather jackets, poofy polka-dot dresses, and skinny suits that made the plastic people look like they were frozen in time.

Across the street was a general store called Gale's, a bookstore called the Dog Ear, and lastly a movie theater called the Bijou. Seeing a movie theater gave Lucas a little hope that maybe this town wasn't as isolated as it seemed, but then he saw the marquee. The latest film they were showing was *The Great Muppet Caper.*

"It's like they built this place with barely enough stuff to actually call it a town," Lucas groaned.

After they parked, Lucas's mom hopped out first and saw the mud that covered the bottom half of their car. Their license plate was completely crusted over. Lucas kicked the front tire and a cloud of dust floated and surrounded the city-beaten Ford.

"There must be a car wash around here somewhere," said Mom.

"I think we fit in just fine." Lucas motioned to the other cars and trucks parked next to them that suffered the same dirt-worn fate. "I don't see one clean car out here."

"You're right," Mom said as she spun the keys in her hands victoriously. "See, we're fitting in already!"

Fitting in wasn't high on Lucas's list of things to do in his new town. Laying low would be much better. Some people thought that fitting in and laying low were the same thing, but Lucas was smarter than that. Fitting in was another code word;

it meant leaving the past behind. As his mom proudly crossed the well-painted crosswalk, she felt like a stranger to him. She was ready to let go of the city, to swap its dented bumpers for dirty tires and small-town unpaved roads.

But Lucas wasn't. He took pride in being a city kid.

Laying low, on the other hand, that meant biding your time. Going unnoticed by everyone around you, even your family, until you're ready to come up for air. And by the looks of this tiny town, Lucas might not breathe again until college.

"Hurry up, Lucas." Mom waved him on. "Your father needs the car this afternoon."

Lucas took a deep breath, then jogged into the road outside of the crosswalk before slipping back to walk right on the edge of the white lines.

From the outside, Gale's General Store looked like a fur pelt trading post from the 1800s. It had a porch with rocking chairs and hand-carved railings. Just off the porch, Lucas put his palm on a strange bench in front of the store. The seat came up to his chest and was round on top without a backside.

"What's with this bench?" he asked. "It looks more like a balance beam. How's anyone supposed to sit here?"

"That's not a bench," said Mom. "It's a horse post."

Lucas ran his hand over the smooth, round topside. "It doesn't look like a horse."

"Very funny," Mom teased. "When people used to ride horses for transportation, this is where they parked the horse. They'd tie the reins to those posts so the horse wouldn't run off."

"Wait, do people still ride horses here instead of cars?" Lucas quickly lifted his foot off the ground to make sure he wasn't stepping in anything gross.

His mom laughed. "It's supposed to be quaint. Don't you think this place is charming? I mean, I really feel like we've gone back in time."

"Yeah, but how far back?" Lucas followed his mom up the stairs to the porch. A rusty bell rang as they opened the front door.

"Be with you in a sec," a woman's voice came from the rear of the store.

Glass jars filled with hard candy like lollipops and peppermint sticks sat by the cash register. Shelves ran all along the walls, filled with canned goods, like stewed tomatoes or green beans, and condiments like pickles, mustard, ketchup, and mayonnaise. Rustic tables made up the center aisles. They were covered with loaves of bread, hot dog and hamburger buns, and a few bags of potato chips. Farther in the back were cleaning supplies, charcoal, and bottles of soda.

"This place is like an old-timey 7-Eleven," said Lucas. He studied the candy options. Each jar had a blue label with white letters on it announcing the flavor of the candy sticks. It started out strong with flavors like root beer, chocolate, and raspberry, but then it quickly veered into odd tastes like lavender, rose petal, and basil.

"Oh, look," Mom said from behind Lucas, "they've kept these sweets priced low! Ten cents for a candy stick? That's a deal. Can't find that back in the city."

An older woman with short white hair and chestnut skin came out of the door in the back of the room. Her green sweater was thick and unnecessary in the hot weather outside. As she toweled off her hand on a yellow floral apron, the woman smiled at Lucas and his mother.

"You must be the Trainers," the woman said.

Lucas and his mom exchanged shocked looks. How did she know who they were?

"Oh, don't look so surprised," the woman reassured them. "News travels fast round these parts. That and Mae Armstrong was in here already. Watch out for that one, by the way. She is a mighty talker—especially since her husband up and left her—but you didn't hear that from me."

Lucas was stunned. "How'd you know who we were? I mean, we could have been anyone. What if we were just passing through Hounds Hollow?"

The woman gave him a deep side-eye glance. "You could have been, but you weren't. And trust me, no one just passes through Hounds Hollow. Once you're here, you're home."

Lucas gulped, and the old lady cackled like an old lady.

"I'm Gale," she said. "I own the joint. Got my name on the sign and everything. As you can see, we're gearing up for the end-of-summer barbecue. Y'all are invited, of course. It's an annual town celebration."

She handed Lucas's mother a flyer.

"Thank you very much, Gale," Mrs. Trainer said. "The barbecue sounds wonderful, but we need some cleaning supplies first."

"Silas never did keep a clean house, did he?" Gale laughed at her own joke and showed a full, white-toothed smile. "Probably covered in sawdust. Follow me."

As Gale led them down one of the small aisles, Lucas's mom gave him the flyer. He looked at it, then stuffed it in his pocket.

"Did you know my uncle?" Mom asked Gale.

"As much as anyone could have known Silas," she said. "I grew up in Hounds Hollow, lived my whole life hearing stories about Silas Sweetwater and his manor. Half were just stories, but some were true. He's a local legend, so you'd be hard-pressed to find anyone in town who didn't know him."

"What was he like?" Lucas asked.

"He kept to himself mostly," said Gale. "Not much of a people person, but he loved animals."

"Really?" Mom chimed back in. "Wow. What kind of animals? Horses? Birds? Deer?"

"All kinds of animals is what I heard," Gale said. "But he had a special place in his heart for dogs."

"Huh." Mrs. Trainer nodded quietly. "It's so interesting to hear about Silas as a regular person. My family, we didn't know him that well."

"You knew him well enough for Silas to leave you his house." The sharpness of her comment caught Lucas and his mom off guard. Gale turned around immediately and her stance softened. "Oh my, that came out wrong. I'm sorry. I'm on edge with this barbecue coming up. I promised to help organize the event this year, but if it's not one thing, then it's another. Vern called today about one of my mustard bottles exploding. Well, I didn't pack the mustard, Vern, I told him—"

"No. It's okay," said Mom, cutting Gale off before she pulled them both into a conversation storm of epic small-town proportions. "We were surprised about the house, too."

"Of course, I was sad to hear of Silas's passing," Gale added. "We all were. Felt like we lost a part of the town's history."

They stopped in front of a section that reeked of detergent and cleaners. Lucas had to walk away from the aisle because the smell was so strong, it was about to send him into a coughing fit—and he was *not* about to let that happen. Gale did the same, leaving Lucas's mom to find what she needed.

Back at the front desk, Lucas watched out the windows as approximately zero cars drove by or left their parking spaces.

The town was so still, for a moment he thought he was looking at a painting.

On a shelf by the door was a stack of newspapers, the *Hounds Hollow Gazette*. The main headline read "End-of-Summer Festival Is Heating Up." Lucas picked up a copy and flipped it open to see what else was newsworthy in his new home. The paper was thin, only four pages long. Most of the articles were about local news, as if the outside world wasn't even there.

At the top of the second page, Lucas found the police blotter that listed all the police reports in the area. Mr. Marcotsis's garbage cans had been knocked over, probably due to a curious critter. Mrs. Sloan's prizewinning petunia garden had been dug up, probably due to a curious critter. But hidden in between the spicy tuna roll that caused Mr. Potter's allergic reaction and Ms. Blythe's heated debate over property lines with her neighbor (who was also her mother), Lucas found two lines that made him stop cold.

New resident William Turnkey still missing after three weeks. As yet no sign of foul play.

Tourist Shannon Bly still missing after five weeks. As yet no sign of foul play.

"Oh, you found the *Gazette*." Gale sounded proud as she rearranged the mustard bottles. "Go ahead and take one if you want. They're free for the locals. All the articles are written by the good people of Hounds Hollow."

Lucas nodded. "Thanks. Um, Mrs. Gale?"

"Just Gale, honey," she said with a smile.

"Okay, um, Gale." Lucas felt so strange calling adults by their first names. He held up the paper. "Did you know this Mr. Turnkey?"

Gale's smile fell. "I did and, oh, what a shame. I hope they find him soon."

"And this tourist, too? She went missing?" Lucas asked.

Gale shook her head and clicked her tongue three times. "Tsk-tsk-tsk, I tell you, Lucas. I never met that poor girl, but if you ask me, I'd wager anything that she was just traveling through. She's probably in Texas by now for all I know. But if you're interested in those types of police reports, check out the Hounds Hollow Update Wall at the *Gazette* sometime. You look like a little Sherlock Holmes. Anyone ever tell you that?"

"No, ma'am. Not really." Lucas folded the paper and placed it back on the stack. "But you said that once you come here, you're home. What about these missing people?"

"Oh, that was just a kind phrase, honey. It's not like everyone stays in Hounds Hollow forever like Silas or his family. Speaking of . . . ," said Gale as she went behind the counter and flipped through a notebook. "Well, I'll be. Says here that I'm actually holding on to a package for y'all."

"For us?" asked Lucas.

"It was for Silas," admitted Gale. "So it's for you now. He ordered it last month. Just came in today. Must've been held up somewhere."

Lucas was uneasy. "What is it? It's not, like, a coffin, right?"

"Ha!" Gale's strong laugh boomed through the store. "Coffin, that's a good one. Wait while I grab the box from the back."

As she left for the rear storeroom, Lucas's mom came up front with an armful of cleaners, brooms, mops, and dusters. "Where's Gale going?"

"Silas ordered something before . . ." Lucas paused. "It just came in, so she's giving it to us."

"What are we going to do with it?" Mom dropped everything onto the counter and went to grab paper towels.

"I don't know," Lucas said loudly while his mom searched the back of the room. "But I think we should take it."

"Mmm-hmm." His mother was balancing several paper towels and rolls of toilet paper in her arms and using her chin to stabilize the haul.

"Did you need some help?" he asked.

"Not anymore," she told him. "You can bring everything into the house. Deal?"

The squeak of an old wooden cart rang out as Gale returned pushing a large brown box on it.

"Wow, that's, um . . . that's going to take up a lot of space in the car," said Mom. "Good thing we unpacked."

"Yep, Silas and his dog food," said Gale. Then she smiled at Lucas. "You must be in puppy dog heaven with all those furry rascals."

"Excuse me?" asked his mother. "Dog food? For what?"

"Well, for his dogs, I'd assumed." Gale set the box down with a clunk. "He's been ordering this brand of dog food ever since I was a little girl and my parents ran the shop."

"There aren't any dogs," Mom said uncertainly. "At least I hope there aren't any dogs."

Gale threw up her arms, motioning toward the store. "Well, listen. It's a special order and Silas has paid up through the next few years, so as long as the kibble gets delivered, I'll need you to take it off my hands. I don't have room for it here."

An uncomfortable silence settled into the room, but Lucas broke the spell. "We'll take it. If that's what Silas wanted, then we'll take it. Right, Mom?"

His mom's worried smile crept back over her face as she nodded. The box was coming home with them.

After paying, Mom and Lucas filled the car with their supplies plus the extra surprise for Silas Sweetwater. It took Lucas several trips to carry everything out from the store, and on his last trip, he stopped in his tracks. Tied to the horse post in front of the bookstore was . . . a horse. The gray-speckled creature stared back at him and snuffed through its nose. Lucas searched up and down the street to find who the horse belonged to, but no one was there.

"Mom! A horse!" Lucas said as he ran to the car and climbed in.

"Well, look at that," she said. "A one-horse town."

She started the car and pulled back out onto the main road. Lucas kept looking at the horse and was surprised when a kid with a camera draped around his neck walked out of the book-store. He seemed to be Lucas's age but slightly smaller. As Lucas rode past him, the kid lifted the camera and took a picture of their car. Then he ran over to the post and unlatched the horse. Lucas's head swiveled around to see the kid hop on the horse and gallop off in the other direction.

Boxes of dog food, end-of-summer barbecues, and horse-back paparazzi. Laying low wasn't going to be easy in a place like this.

CHAPTER 11

As Lucas's mother drove along, the trees inched closer to the road. "Are you sure you know the way home, Mom?" he asked.

"Eartha gave me directions." Mom held up a sheet of paper like it was a hard-earned diploma. "Don't worry—we are *not* getting lost again."

Forty-five minutes and two three-point turns later, they were still looking for the house. His mother had given the directions to Lucas, but he couldn't help. "Turn right on Broucksou Lane," he said. "Okay, that would be easy to do . . . if there were street signs."

"I think we've passed that tree before." His mother pointed out the window. "Right?"

"I can't tell trees apart," said Lucas. "Maybe we could head back to town and get directions from Gale?"

"I'm never going to hear the end of this from your father," Mom said with a laugh. "He still talks about that time I tore our bumper off while trying to parallel park."

"I won't tell him," said Lucas.

"I'm not worried about you, I'm worried about gabby Gale telling the entire planet." Mom giggled at her own joke, which made Lucas snort. Then they both broke out into a laughing fit. Getting lost in Hounds Hollow was apparently easy, but escaping the ever-watching eyes of their neighbors would probably be impossible.

Even though it was almost one o'clock in the afternoon, the sunlight around the car dimmed as they drove. Lucas rolled down his window and checked out the sky. It was dotted with dark, gray clouds. A storm was coming soon. As they rounded a corner, his mom's cell phone rang. It was so unexpected that they nearly swerved off the road.

"That thing hasn't worked for so long, I thought it was broken!" Mom pressed the hands-free setting on the car. "Hello?"

Airy buzzing erupted over the car's speakers, followed by a man's voice. "Mrs. Trainer?"

"Yes," she answered. "Who is this?"

"This is the moving company, ma'am," the man said. "We've been calling you all morning. I'm glad we finally got through."

"Oh gosh, are you at the house already?" Mom asked. "I didn't think you were coming until tomorrow."

Static clicked through the line. "Bad . . . trying . . . accident . . ."

"What? I can't hear you, you're breaking up," Mom called out. Lucas saw her eyes flicker into the rearview mirror to meet his.

That's when he saw a shadow dart into the road. The world broke around them, starting with their car jolting backward and to the left. Lucas's head smacked hard against his window.

His mother screamed and turned the wheel forcefully, spinning the car while she slammed on the brakes. A ringing sound filled Lucas's head as the car bounced slightly after the abrupt stop. Then, just as quickly as it had appeared, the shadow was gone and the world became normal again.

The man on the phone clipped through like an angel. "Hello? Mrs. Trainer? Are you okay?"

Her white knuckles gripped the steering wheel, but Lucas's mom sat at an odd angle, looking straight at him. "Lucas? Lucas?"

"I'm okay, Mom. I'm okay," he said through heavy breaths. The seat belt had snatched his chest tightly, knocking the wind out of him. "Are you?"

She shook her head. "No . . . I think I hit something." Then his mother lowered her chin to her chest and started sobbing. "I can't—I can't look, Lucas. I don't want to look. You shouldn't look, either."

Too late. In the middle of the road, Lucas saw a black lump. It was hard to make out, since the storm clouds had rolled in and cast a gloom over the forest. Was it an opossum? A skunk? Whatever it was, the car had mangled it into an unrecognizable shape.

The hiss from the cell phone started up again. Inside the car, a heat began to bloom. Lucas wiped his brow as sweat dripped in his eyes. Whatever was in the road lay motionless. Then the black shape started to shudder. Lucas couldn't turn away; he was hypnotized by the shape's disjointed movements. As if it were made of clay, the mangled body began to adjust itself. Above the hissing, Lucas could hear the sounds of muscle and bone resetting like ringing out a wet towel in the sink. Hollow drips and cracks popped through the speakers, and as quickly as the animal had been dead in the middle of the road, it sprang to life and leapt back into the forest.

Meanwhile, the heat in the car boiled, fogging up the windows. Lucas felt his throat close up in the muggy air. He clicked open his inhaler and took a long, slow breath. Then he coughed, "It ran off, Mom. It's alive."

"Thank you, thank you, thank you," Mom whispered to someone. Lucas was pretty sure it wasn't meant for him because then she yelled, "Lucas Trainer, you weren't supposed to look! It could have been gruesome."

"Yeah," Lucas agreed. He was ashen and sick to his stomach. "It could have been."

"Mrs. Trainer!" The now frantic man on the cell phone cut through the static and hissing.

"Yes, sorry, we had a little accident," she told the mover as she leaned back in her seat. "My husband should be at the house to meet you."

"That's the thing, Mrs. Trainer," the man said. "We're not at the house. There's a slight problem. We won't be able to deliver your furniture for another week."

There was a long pause as Lucas and his mother expected the mysterious man to explain himself further. But he didn't.

"Hello?" Mom asked.

"Yes, ma'am, I'm still here," the man said. "We'll be in touch as soon as we know more."

Lucas's mom let out a deep sigh. "Okay." Then she ended the connection before the man could say another word.

"I'm sorry, Mom." Lucas wasn't sure why he was apologizing, but he felt like it needed to be said, that his mom needed to hear that from somebody right now.

"Not your fault, little man," she said. "Now, let's go look at that damage to our car."

They clicked out of their seat belts and opened the doors slowly. The day was sweltering with an ugly heat and thick with humidity. Walking to the front of the car, Lucas could see a dent in the right side of the bumper. White cracks and crinkles spiderwebbed out on the plastic from where they had struck the animal. Even the metal hood bulged upward, creating a ripple in the frame.

"What did we hit?" asked his mom. "This is too much damage for most animals to walk away unharmed."

Lucas shrugged. "Maybe it was a moose? It was hard to say." He wasn't lying. In fact, it was as close to the truth as he wanted to tell his mom. Any more truth and she'd take him to the nearest hospital for another round of tests. If he had to guess what the animal was, it looked sort of like a dog or wolf, but bigger. Way bigger and way creepier.

A ragged flash of lightning streaked overhead, followed immediately by a clap of thunder so loud and close that it caused a gust of wind to hit Lucas. Big drops of rain pelted the ground. Slowly at first, the shower speckled the gray pavement darker, and then it turned into a downpour. Lucas and his mother rushed back to the car, but they were soaked by the time they got inside. The storm pounded on their roof and blurred the windows with fog and buckets of water.

"Well, champ, it can only get better from here," Mom said as she started the car. Miraculously, it came to life, despite the damage. "See!"

Then she flicked on the headlights and shifted the windshield wipers on high. The black, skinny arms whipped back and forth trying to push the rain aside, but it was coming down sideways now. Lucas realized that they'd been stopped in the middle of the road for a long time without anyone else driving by. At least in the city, people gathered around an accident. Out here, help wasn't always around the corner. As his mother shifted the car forward, the headlights spotted a small wooden sign that had been hidden by branches until the storm had pushed them aside. It read BROUCKSOU LANE.

Lucas cheered. "Mom, look!"

"Ha! It seems we're heading in the right direction after all. Now let's get home before anything else crazy happens." His mother turned onto the road and deeper into the woods.

The car whimpered as they drove, no doubt from the wreck. Lucas looked back to where they had been in the accident. Through the wash of rain he could make out two red lights glowing at the intersection like brake lights from another car. Lucas wondered if someone had driven by as soon as they left, but then the red lights flashed. No, thought Lucas, that wasn't what they did. The lights didn't flash—they blinked.

And then they were gone.

CHAPTER 12

Walking into Silas Sweetwater's house—no, *his* house—for the second time took Lucas by surprise. It was exactly as big as he remembered it. Never before in his life had this happened. Usually the first time he visited a place—school, a library, a doctor's office—everything felt larger-than-life. But by the second visit, he knew what to expect, there were no more surprises. And knowing what to expect made everything feel smaller. After living in his room at their old apartment, Lucas couldn't imagine going back to a place so cramped and tiny.

His new house, on the other hand, seemed every bit as gigantic and overwhelming as it had the first time he stepped foot inside. The massive cathedral ceilings were enormous, and the oddly shaped furniture sat like wild animals watching him. And even with the dark storm overhead, the stained-glass windows glowed and spun color around the room with each lightning strike. This house was filled with surprises. And Lucas suddenly had an itch to uncover them.

But first he needed to change. He was soaked to the bone from helping Mom carry in the groceries. Wet paper bags of cleaning supplies and food sat in the entryway.

"That's the last of it," Dad said as he clunked down the oversized box that Silas had ordered. "What's in here, anyway?"

"Dog food," said Lucas.

"Of course, it's so obvious," Dad joked. "But remind me *why* we need so much dog food when we don't have any dogs?"

"It was Silas's last order." Lucas ran his hands over the clear packing tape that glazed the box. Raindrops rolled down the sides of the seemingly waterproof tape. How much did his family really know about the man whose house they were living in? Not much at all.

"Well, then, I'm glad you delivered it in one piece," said Dad as he swept Lucas and his mom into a soaking-wet group hug. "I'm also glad you two are safe. Crash the car, lose all of our earthly belongings, I don't care as long as you're both here with me."

Mom snorted. "The movers will get here eventually, but I don't know how to fix you sounding so incredibly cheesy!"

Dad squeezed them once more and let them go. "Listen, I went ahead and found bedrooms for us, keeping to the front of the house like we talked about. This place . . . this place is practically a museum! I mean, look at these paintings! They're probably worth money, don't you think? Come with me!"

Dripping-wet Lucas was dragged to a room to the left side of the stairs. The wood door had circular designs etched into its surface that looked like moons laid on top of other moons. Each circle intersected the other, creating a wave of lines that almost vibrated. Lucas wasn't sure whether to be amazed or seasick.

"This is your room, son." With a twist of the crystal knob, his father opened the door. "Well? What do you think?"

It was blue. Like stepping into the ocean, Lucas held his breath. The murky wallpaper cast an underwater sensation over everything. The four-poster canopy bed was like a ship docked against the back wall with a well-cushioned chair next to it like a lifeboat. There was a dresser with claw feet, like a strange sea serpent with seven hungry drawers waiting to eat his clothes. And there was one full-length mirror against the far side of the room. But the strangest thing Lucas noticed was the five square spaces on the wall that were a lighter color than the rest of the room.

"It's . . . is it missing some pictures?" Lucas walked over and placed his hand on the mysterious spaces. "I mean, it's cool. I like it."

"I took the paintings down," his father explained. "I would have taken the mirror down, too, but it's on there pretty good. Stronger than your old bed, even."

"Why did you take down the pictures?" Lucas asked.

His father nodded. "Yeah, they felt, I don't know, intrusive."

"Intrusive?" repeated Lucas.

"Creepy," Mom said. "Your dad means that they were creepy."

Dad nodded. "They were all portraits of . . . well, of dogs. I was making your bed and suddenly it felt like I was being watched. It was the paintings. All those dog eyes, I don't know. I figured you'd want a room without animals staring at you all the time."

This time Lucas nodded. He'd been to Disney World before. He'd ridden the Haunted Mansion ride, though he freaked out the first time and made his parents leave. On the ride, there were statues of people's heads where their eyes followed you wherever you went. Lucas shivered thinking about it. "But the pictures . . . what about Silas's rules?"

"Huh? Oh, what Eartha was talking about?" Dad smiled and waved off Lucas's worry. "This is our house now. I think bending the rules a little bit will be fine. They're just pictures, right?"

The room was like a palace compared to Lucas's old room in the city. Then he saw his backpack sitting on the bed with Lucky curled up next to it. Lucas couldn't explain it, but having his backpack there was like planting a flag in the ground. This room was hereby property of Lucas Trainer. He was home.

"Thanks, Dad."

Mom clapped and gave her husband a hug. "Okay, now I'm excited to see our room."

"This way," said Dad as he guided her out the door.

Alone, Lucas squeaked over to the well-cushioned chair by his bed. He sat down and pulled off his wet shoes and socks. There was a towel next to his backpack. His dad must have left it for him. He dried off and grabbed his *Haunted History* book to read about haunted houses. Sweetwater Manor definitely fit the bill. Then he flipped through the pages, looking for any stories about the forest. There were well-documented histories of gnomes, fairies, witches, and even a thing called the New Jersey Devil. But he couldn't find anything that matched what he had just seen in the car accident. Maybe his doctors were right. Maybe he was starting to blur the real world with his imagination.

Lucas shut the book and pulled out his tablet to start playing one of his favorite games, Wolf Life. In the app, you lived a wolf's daily life. Hunt. Eat. Fight. Run. Live with your pack. That's all. Still, he loved it. Roaming through the digital forest, pouncing, stalking, even howling, it relaxed him. Maybe that was because he had never really lived in the woods before. But even now, in the heart of the forever forest of Hounds Hollow and in the underwater world of his brand-new room, the game cheered him up.

An hour blew by before Lucas knew it. Standing up, he realized he was still in his wet clothes. Pulling out the middle drawer from the dresser, Lucas was surprised to find his own clothes, neat and folded. A note was on the top shirt. It was from his father:

Here's to finding a new home that fits like your favorite shirt. Love, Dad.

Lucas put the card back in the drawer and closed it with a thump. The dresser was sturdy, but it was also heavy and the drawers had been warped by time.

Another thump echoed behind him. Lucas whirled around to see Lucky on the floor, stretching as if he'd just woken up from a nap.

"Lucky." Lucas exhaled. "Stop sneaking up on me like that."

The cat looked at him a moment, then padded over and nuzzled against his leg. Lucas petted the cat's back, then went to examine the lighter squares of wallpaper. He wondered how long a painting had to be on the wall before the color change was so visually different. Without the pictures he could tell that something was missing in the room. He wished his dad had just left the dog portraits hanging and followed Silas's rules, even if they were bizarre.

Lucas caught sight of himself in the mirror. His shaggy hair had been made worse by the deadly combination of the rain and sitting in the chair for an hour playing video games. He patted at his cowlick, but it was untamable.

Suddenly his reflection shook. It was a small tremor, but Lucas noticed it right away. He stopped and stared at himself in the mirror. It shook again, just slightly. Lucas touched the reflective surface with his palm and felt the glass. As soon as he did, the mirror pulsed again, sending a jolt through his arm like a shock of electricity. Lucas expected to see a burn mark as the feeling of pins and needles surged in his fingers, but his hand was fine. He clenched his fist until, slowly, the sense of feeling came back. Trying not to touch the mirror itself, Lucas felt around the wooden frame, pulling on it, but it was glued to the wall just like his dad had said. Then, carefully, Lucas touched the mirror again, but this time there was no shock. He leaned and pushed against it. With a click, the mirror opened toward him. It was another door.

A breeze of heated air blew in Lucas's face. It smelled awful and rotten. Lucky curled between his legs, sniffed at the darkness, and skittered into the new hallway.

"Hey, no, bad cat," Lucas said. "Get back here!"

Without thinking, he stepped inside, too. A light dangled overhead with a beaded chord attached to it. Lucas tugged at the chord and the bulb popped on. The hallway was shorter than he thought, but it led to a bigger room. Even with cracks of light stippling through the slat board walls and tall roof above him, Lucas had no chance of finding Lucky in the shadows. He searched for a light switch by the doorway and found a large, brass knob. Instinctually, Lucas turned it and a hissing sound erupted. The smell of gas replaced the rotten stench. Seconds later, light fixtures against the walls flickered to life.

"Whoa, gas lamps?" Lucas shook his head. "This place *is* old."

Gas lighting wasn't new to Lucas, but he'd never seen *actual, working* gaslights. Before the invention of electricity, people depended on candles for light. Then came the concept of lights that could be run by gas. At first, the streetlights used gas, but after a while, buildings in the city adapted the new technology. Tubing was placed in the walls to run the gas directly into the lights. Then, when the world switched over to electricity, many of the old gas tubes were used to run the electrical wiring. He'd learned all about it while living in the city. His own building had been wired that way and it drove his mom crazy. She constantly thought that she smelled gas when she turned on the lights in their apartment. She called the gas company at least once a month to come check for leaks. Their solution always pointed back to gas tubes used in old buildings.

But this was real gas. The lights on the walls flickered a bluish flame. Of all the things to have in a house that burned down, working gas lighting was the last one Lucas expected to find. He stepped farther inside.

The new room was a huge barn with vaulted ceilings. It echoed the hissing from the lights like a chamber of snakes. There were small stalls running along both sides of the barn. They looked like horse stalls, but smaller. Each spot had a copper number plaque nailed to wooden gate doors that were waist high. Lucas clicked one of the black bolts that held each stall shut. The metal hinges turned smoothly as the gate swung open. Above the doors, black bars rose up to create a tiny jail cell for whatever had been stored there. He'd seen bars like this before. They were just like the wrought-iron fences outside fancy brownstones in the city. The bars curved upward, creating a beautiful design. Lucas ran his hands over them. They were still smooth, as if they'd been polished recently.

"Lucky!" Lucas whispered, his tiny voice bouncing around the room.

He walked up and down the row of stalls, searching for his cat. There were fifteen empty stalls. Lucas counted and read the numbered plaque above each one.

Mmrreow. Lucky poked his head out from the top of a stall.

"How did you get up there?" Lucas found a stool and used it to reach Lucky, but the cat jumped back from him. "It's all right. C'mon, it's just me here. Let's go. I'll give you a treat."

As soon as he touched Lucky's back, Lucas could feel the vibrating fear inside his cat. Lucky's tiny cat heart pounded against his rib cage like a mini time bomb ticking toward a massive hissing fit. And then it happened.

Lucky bared his teeth and narrowed his eyes, heaving out a hissing warning that sizzled over the gas lanterns. Lucas jerked back his hands just in time as the cat's claws came out with a swipe. Then, gracefully and furiously, Lucky bounded down the top of the stall railings, leapt to the ground, and darted back into his room.

Lucas wheeled around to see what spooked the cat so much, and a bright flash went off from the other side of the barn.

"Who's there?!" Lucas hollered as he jumped down and ran to the large closed doors. His heart thumped harder in his chest with every step. Lucas crashed into the doors, but they didn't fly open like he thought they would. Instead they buckled and pushed him back to the ground.

From under the slatted doors, Lucas could make out a shadow of someone running so fast that they slipped first, then scrambled back up, kicking dirt that puffed into the barn. Whoever it was, Lucas must have scared them.

By the time Lucas found a knot in the wood to peek through, the stranger was gone. A chain was locked around the barn doors' handles, holding them tightly shut. Lucas wished he'd noticed the chain before he tried to crash through the barn like the incredible Hulk. As he sat there, his heart steadied, and Lucas wondered what he would have done if the chain hadn't been there. In a huff, he turned and went back the way he entered, through his mirror. But not before he turned off the gaslights, dimming the barn into the darkness from which it came.

Safe in his room, Lucas shut the mirror door and pushed the heavy dresser in front of it. Moving the giant piece of furniture left four deep scratches in the wood floor. Lucas sat against the dresser, breathing hard and feeling his muscles burn all over. Under his bed, a set of eyes glowed. It was Lucky.

The cat jumped onto Lucas's lap and curled up into a ball. Both of them bristled with the same nervous energy.

"It's okay," said Lucas, even if he didn't really believe it. He stared at the mirror, waiting for it open. Lucas held his breath. It was one way to stop his wheezing. He felt the silence all around him, but stayed focused on the mirror. Then Lucky launched from his lap with a hiss and scrambled out of the room. Lucas heard the cat's claws sliding along the wood floor in a frantic escape. But escape from what?

He looked back toward the mirror. It rattled in its doorway, shaking the reflection of the entire room. The sound of heavy breathing was muffled behind the thin glass. Whatever was hidden there had come for Lucas.

He slowly backed away from his room to the front of the house. Lucas told himself there must be a logical explanation for this. Maybe one of the workers was adding a fountain back there? Maybe they were taking down a wall somewhere that was causing the mirror to shake? But the "better not be too logical if you want to stay alive" side of Lucas wanted to get out of Sweetwater Manor immediately. He reached the front door, pulled it open, and stumbled backward with a gasp.

Bess was standing in front of him with her hand raised, about to knock. She didn't jump, but instead smiled. "How'd you know I was here? Were you spying on me?"

"It was you, wasn't it?" Lucas snapped. His cheeks started to burn. "Is this all a joke to you? Are you trying to scare me out of here?"

Bess's eyebrows rose. "What's that now?"

Lucas cut her off. "In the barn. Did you, like, take a picture of me or something? There was a flash and the doors were chained and the mirror shook."

"Slow down, city boy." Bess raised her arms gently like she was trying to calm a frightened animal. "I don't know anything about a barn and I'm not taking pictures of you. What kind of weirdo do you think I am?"

Lucas wasn't sure if she really wanted him to answer that. "Then what are you doing here?"

"I brought you a bike." She pointed behind her. "Like I promised."

"What?" Lucas shook his head. A black BMX bike with dark blue tires leaned against the porch railing. "You came over? With a bike? In the rain?"

"Rain? It's not raining." Bess was right. The evening was clear, and the sun was dipping just beneath the trees. "It hasn't rained all day."

Lucas patted his shirt; it was still damp from the sudden storm that afternoon. "Yes, it did. My mom and I, we were in an accident. We hit some animal with our car. Then there was a thunderstorm, rain everywhere. We barely made it back here."

Bess gasped. "Whoa. You hit an animal? What did it look like?"

"Big? I don't know. Big enough to bounce off our car and then run into the woods." Lucas nudged past her out onto the porch as he closed the door.

"Hmm," Bess said. "It sounds like you had a wild day. Maybe if we just go back inside, then—"

"No," Lucas interrupted her. "I have a better idea." Then he grabbed her hand and pulled her down the stairs. They raced around the house in the direction of Lucas's room.

"Where are we going?" asked Bess.

Lucas waved off her question and motioned for Bess to keep quiet.

Bess dug her heels in the dirt and stopped immediately. Then she shook her hand out of his. "No, you can't tell me to shut up," she snapped. "Either you tell me where we're going or you're on your own. I don't do the sidekick thing."

"Okay, okay," he said. "Sorry. Like you said, it's been a wild day."

Bess kept him locked in her stare. "Yeah, Hounds Hollow will do that to you. Where are we going . . . and why?"

Lucas's eyes skittered around in his head as he tried to think of the most sane way to tell her what had happened. "I'll tell you everything, but you have to promise to keep an open mind."

She nodded. "I promise."

"Right, well . . ." Lucas paused before launching into the long-winded replay of his day. The secret room, the stalls, the rain, the accident, the flash, the shadow, Bess listened to all of it without saying a word.

"So you want to see if someone's spying on you?" asked Bess.

Lucas nodded.

"You should have said so in the first place," said Bess as she took the lead and started running again. "He could be any-where by now."

Lucas rolled his eyes and darted after her. "You should have said so in the first place," he mimicked under his breath.

Bess made it to the barn doors first, but no one was there. "Looks like they're gone now. You said there was a flash?"

"Yeah, like a camera, but it was super bright," Lucas huffed as he caught up to her. He bent down and put his hands on his knees, trying to catch his breath. Running wasn't exactly what the doctor ordered. Neither was running to catch potential maniacs. Suddenly he realized exactly how crazy and dangerous it was to run after this stranger.

"And you didn't see them?" asked Bess. "Was it a worker? Was it the boy in the suit you saw earlier?"

"I don't know, but—" Lucas spit into the dry dirt underneath him. "Wait a minute. I didn't tell you that the boy was wearing a suit. How'd you know?"

"Sure you did, didn't you?" Bess said. "I thought you did. So it *was* him."

Lucas was certain he hadn't told Bess anything about the suit. "All I saw was a pair of legs and a bunch of dust kicked up near the barn doors." He walked over and studied the ground. "Hmm."

"*Hmm* you found something or *hmm* I haven't run in years and now I'm going to keel over and have a heart attack?" Bess joked.

"It wasn't a worker," Lucas confirmed.

Bess joined him as they both knelt close to the ground. "How can you tell?"

"The dirt," said Lucas as he pointed to a set of footprints that danced in the dry ground. "It tells us three things. One, whoever was here was a kid. Look at these Nike shoe prints. Workers wouldn't wear sneakers like that on-site, and they definitely don't have feet this small. Two, look at how the prints are repeated in the dirt. That means it's only one kid."

"You can tell that from a shoe print?" Bess looked impressed. "But what if it were two or three kids all wearing the same type of shoes?"

Lucas considered it, then shook his head. "No. The patterns of the shoes are almost always facing in the same direction. If it had been multiple kids, the toes and heels would be pointing in lots of different directions. Plus, these prints are only in one area. We're looking for one kid."

"Three things," repeated Bess. "You said the dirt told us three things."

"Yeah," said Lucas as he looked at her. "That's the part that freaks me out a little. The dirt back here is dry."

"So?" asked Bess.

Lucas stood up and pushed on the barn door from the outside this time. It rattled but didn't open. "So, you were right. Dry dirt means it didn't rain. And that's impossible. I was caught in the storm right by the front of the house. It rained everywhere. This dirt should be a muddy mess."

Bess remained crouched on the ground and rubbed over the shoe prints, erasing them while Lucas wasn't looking. "You're right. The dirt is dry. It didn't rain at all today."

Lucas followed the foot scuffs in the dirt where the stranger ran back into the woods. He stopped at the edge of the forest. "Bess, what's really going on in Hounds Hollow?"

She got up and peeked through the knothole into the barn before facing Lucas. Her face was pale. "It's a long story. And if I tell you, *you'll* need to keep an open mind."

"Tell him what?" Both kids jumped at the sound of Mr. Trainer's voice.

"Whoa, Dad! Don't sneak up on us like that!"

"Sorry, champ, it's time for dinner. I called but you couldn't hear, I guess. Your mom saw you run off the porch in this direction, so I came to get you." His dad waved to Bess. "Of course, Bess, you're invited, too, if you'd like to join us."

Lucas expected her to jump at the opportunity to get inside Sweetwater Manor, but Bess shook her head.

"No, thanks, Mr. Trainer. I'd better get home, too. See you tomorrow, Lucas?"

"Yeah, sure" was all Lucas could say as Bess pushed past him and ran into the woods—in the same direction as the stranger.

CHAPTER 13

Lucas wasn't hungry. He spent most of the meal pushing mashed potatoes, grilled chicken, and green beans around on his plate. His parents didn't seem to notice. They talked about getting the car fixed and making school arrangements for Lucas.

"What do you think?" Mom asked him.

Lucas straightened up in his seat, snapping to attention. "Sorry, what?"

"Did you seriously not hear what I just asked?" Mom smiled and rolled her eyes with her buoyant laugh. "The school bus, we need to sign you up for the route. You're okay taking the bus to school, right?"

"Do I have a choice?" Lucas forced a bite of food down while his parents were looking at him. "Maybe I could ride my bike?"

"Since when do you have a bike?" asked Dad.

"Oh, Bess is letting me borrow one," said Lucas. "She brought it by today. I can totally use it for as long as I want. She said it was cool."

His parents fell silent and looked at each other. Then his mom took the lead.

"Cool or not, I'm not sure you should be riding a bike." She held her fork in front of her with a piece of chicken dangling from the edge. "I've seen my fair share of bike accidents in the city."

Lucas knew she wasn't worried about bike accidents. She was worried about whether he was healthy enough to ride a bike. He could see it in her eyes. She was picturing Lucas fallen in a ditch and unable to catch his breath. She saw him winded and gasping for air when he should be putting on the brakes. She saw her sick son trying to ride away from her. That's why she stared at her food and not at Lucas.

"This isn't the city, Mom," Lucas pointed out. "I'm not going to get doored by someone getting out of a parked car."

"What about a parked moose?" joked Dad.

"Too soon, Kyle," Mom said.

The reminder of the car accident set another hush over the room, like the dinner table had been covered by a glass top. Everyone was quiet for a moment.

"Your father and I will talk about the bike." She gave Lucas a weak smile. He knew that *Your father and I will talk about the bike* was code for *You'll never ride that bike in your life.*

"Thanks, Mom." Lucas set down his fork with a clink against the plate. "I'm tired. Is it okay if I go to bed now?"

"Of course," said Mom. "You had a big first day. Go get some sleep. We'll pick up the bike versus bus debate tomorrow."

Lucas nodded and headed back to his room. As the door

creaked open, the blue walls were hidden in shadows. The sun had set during dinner, casting a deep darkness across the house.

He hadn't been making up an excuse to leave dinner. Lucas was really exhausted. His eyelids weighed a million pounds. They itched to be closed. He clicked on the overhead light and stumbled over to where his dresser had been, then remembered that he slid it across the room in front of the mirror. He thought about changing out of his clothes, but even the three extra steps to the mirror seemed too far to make it. He fell into bed.

Lucas grabbed the edge of the heavy, green comforter and pulled it over him. As he drifted to sleep, Lucas heard the padded footfalls of Lucky running and leaping from the wood floor. Then he felt the cat's familiar weight on his blanket.

"Good night, Lucky," he said, then turned off like a light.

The next morning, Lucas woke up crammed into a tiny corner of the giant bed. A warm body snuggled against his back, breathing peacefully. Lucky never slept like this in the city.

"Hey, Lucky, are you a cat or a bed hog?" Lucas asked as he flipped the covers over the sleeping animal. It was playful revenge, but the cat sat still, a lump on the bed.

Lucas coughed and sat up to find bits of dried mud and grass all over the sheets. The clothes he'd slept in were dirty, too. Climbing out of bed, he changed into clean clothes. Then he walked back to get the cat. "Time to rise and shine, Lucky."

But the lump under the blanket didn't stir. It just breathed, lifting the covers up and down.

"Well, don't say I didn't warn you." Lucas grabbed the comforter and flipped it back over, expecting Lucky to jolt awake. But there was nothing under the blankets.

Behind him, the door to his bedroom nudged open and in strutted his cat.

"Lucky?" Lucas asked as the cat walked past him, then jumped on the bed, sniffing and exploring like it was brand-new territory. Lucky stretched and sank his claws into the mattress, plucking them back up to make a half-scratching, half-popping sound. Dust puffed into the air with every pop. Then the cat curled up and settled down to sleep.

Lucas backed away from the bed like it was cursed. *Breakfast*, he thought, *that must be it*. He needed to eat. Lucky must have been in his bed last night. There was no other explanation.

Lucas walked through the main hallway on his way to the kitchen, when he saw the bike that Bess had given him leaning against the stairs. There was a helmet hanging from the handlebars.

"You should thank Eartha." Mom was sitting on the stairs, drinking a cup of coffee. "She saw the bike on the porch and happened to have a helmet. Try it on."

"Really?" Lucas asked. "Like I'm not asleep and dreaming right now, am I?"

"Yes, really," said Mom. "Now try on the helmet before I change my mind."

He lifted the helmet up to study it like a precious ruby. It was pitch-black with silver reflective strips that looked like lightning all around it. It was also enormous. Unlike the bike helmets he'd seen kids wear in the city, this one was like a motorcycle helmet.

He tried it on and it covered his entire head. It made his breathing sound like Darth Vader. "Can I go for a ride?" His voice rattled around the inside of the helmet.

His mom held her own breath dramatically, then heaved out a long sigh followed by a smile. "Yes. But don't go far, okay?"

"Thanks, Mom!" Grabbing the handlebars, Lucas pushed the bike outside and down the steps. He climbed on and began to ride. At first his tires skidded in the pebble driveway. Lucas wobbled, but he didn't fall. Then he picked up speed and rode the bike by the side of the house. A few workers walked past him. Lucas waved, but they didn't wave back. He wasn't sure if he could get used to having them around all the time, even if Eartha insisted that he would.

He pedaled on behind the house to the back doors of the old barn. He braked and kicked up dirt. There were no more signs of strange footprints, only his and Bess's from the day before. Lucas paused and listened. The barn was quiet, but the woods behind him were rustling. Bess had run into the woods here the other day. She'd said she was heading home. The only problem was that Bess's home was in the other direction. Where had she gone?

He needed to see for himself.

Lucas scooted the front wheel of the bike around to face the forest. Then, after a deep breath, he rode straight on. Lucas felt the tires of the bike dropping down and rising up to meet the forest's uneven ground. Roots, pinecones, and natural dips made his ride anything but smooth. There wasn't a clear path, either. He pushed on as the branches from small trees and bushes brushed against him. If he were walking, it wouldn't have hurt, but on his bike, the small slaps from nature stung his arms, legs, and chest.

The faster he pedaled, the louder his breathing echoed within his helmet. Over his Darth Vader–style gasps, Lucas could also hear the whiz of the bike gears and the scattering of small animals from the underbrush around him. The wind pushed against his chest as he pedaled harder and the bike bumped and bucked like a bronco. Lucas felt every kick rattle his hands on the front grips.

He looked around the forest as he rode and saw something close to him. It was a shadow, tracking him and keeping up with his speed. A light blast of hot air nudged him from the side, and Lucas felt the bike turn left, away from the shadow. He leaned hard against it, fighting to keep going straight.

There was a clearing up ahead. The shadow seemed to be racing there. Peeking from the corner of his eyes, Lucas tried to make out what the shadow was. It was smaller than him and moved incredibly fast. For a moment, it looked like a large cat—no, maybe a small dog. Either way, the race was on, and the hot air coming from Lucas's right side became stronger and stronger the closer he came to the clearing. It felt like the sun was beaming directly on him with heat so intense that he worried about getting a sunburn.

Lucas had never pedaled so hard and with so much determination in his life. Looking at the shadow, it was as if he was chasing something and running away from it at the same time. It thrilled him and made his heart beat out of his chest.

Then the shadow darted into the clearing, and Lucas stood on his bike, pedaling at top speed. Nothing was going to stop him now.

Nothing except the boy who suddenly stepped out from behind a tree and tackled him right off the bike.

"Aaagh!" Lucas cried.

His head rattled in his helmet as he hit the ground. The bike, which had felt so steady underneath him, flopped over Lucas like a wounded animal. It clung to him awkwardly as the rear tire smacked his back. Lucas's hands fumbled into the dirt as he tried to catch himself.

A second after the crash, Lucas looked for the shadow he'd been racing, but the dark streak was gone.

"What were you thinking?!" The boy's white shirt was dirty from the ground and there was a stick in his hair. "You could have been killed!"

"By *you*, maybe!" screamed Lucas as he flipped off his helmet. He could feel the scrapes on his elbows and knees start to burn, but his anger burned brighter. His mom was not going to like this. Not one bit. Lucas jumped up and shoved the bike aside. "What's your deal? Do you always tackle other people in the woods?"

The kid swatted a leaf out of his hair and searched the ground instead of looking back at Lucas. He was black and skinny and wasn't the least bit concerned that Lucas was upset. His once dark jeans had been sun-washed gray with rips in the knees, and the gray pants made the kid's neon-yellow Nikes glow. The only sound was the rustle of the kid searching through the underbrush of the forest. Quickly, he found what he was looking for—a brown loop like a belt next to Lucas's wrecked bike. The kid snatched it and threw the loop around his shoulders. It was attached to an old camera, one of the kinds that prints pictures instantly. The kid clicked it open and inspected the camera before mumbling under his breath, "You have no idea, new kid."

Then it hit Lucas. He'd seen this kid before. "Hey, I know you. You were the one riding the horse in town the other day. What are you doing out here? Are you following me?"

Lucas stepped forward, but the kid pointed at him accusingly. "Watch where you're going next time. I might not be here to help."

Then the kid snapped his camera shut and took off running into the forest. He was fast. Lucas lost sight of the strange horseback kid after a few steps into the trees, neon Nikes and all.

"Like I needed help!" Lucas's scream echoed in the woods. He really hoped camera boy had heard him.

Lucas shook with bubbling energy as he walked back to his wrecked bike. He thought he'd crashed deep in the forest away from all signs of life, but that wasn't the case. Picnic tables with long benches were mixed into the trees, spread out like they'd been abandoned in the middle of the woods. How had Lucas not noticed them while he was riding? Stepping over his bike, Lucas jogged to the wide-open clearing where the shadow had been leading him. At least he felt like the shadow had been leading him there. Or was it running away from him? Or had there not been a shadow at all?

As he stepped to where the forest ended, the adrenaline coursing through him washed away and a different sensation took its place. Lucas's stomach lurched and his knees buckled. What he'd thought was a clearing wasn't a clearing at all.

An old wooden sign lay on the ground. It must have been knocked over very recently, because Lucas could see the fresh splinters and the almost white wood at the base of the sign where it had been snapped apart. The sign read WARNING: DEVIL'S DROP AHEAD.

The ledge was steep and sudden. Even if the sign had been intact, he would have never seen the drop in time. Lucas shifted onto his hands and knees to peer over the edge. The jagged rocks below stuck out in all directions, like flames frozen in stone form. At the bottom, Lucas could make out a deep, black sliver of a hole. It looked like the entire ravine had exploded open from that one spot. The rest of the forest around the hole was thick, lush, and green, but in this one spot, nothing grew other than stone.

Lucas didn't want to admit it, but if it weren't for the camera kid, he would have been buzzard bait at the bottom of that pit.

Carefully, he backed away from the cliff and went to his bike, which was covered in mud. Lucas went to rub it off, but jerked his hands back quickly. The frame was scorching hot. The bike fell sideways again, and Lucas leaned in to study it. The sour smell of melted metal almost knocked him out. The bike hadn't landed in mud; it had been charred on the right side.

Lucas stepped back, then saw something against the tree where the horseback kid had been hiding. Duct-taped to the lower branch was a Polaroid camera. The front was open. Lucas reached for it and the camera flash went off right in his face. He reached toward it again and the flash erupted a second time. Annoyed, he tore it down from the tree. *D. Lindsay* was written in black marker on the back of the camera. Wires spilled out of the camera, too. They were connected to a smaller lens. Lucas waved his hand in front of it and the flash went off for a third time.

"Motion-detecting cameras in the forest?" Lucas leaned down, trying to make sense of it all. "But why didn't it take any pictures?"

He ran his hand over the leaves on the ground, and a white corner peeked out from the foliage. Lucas grabbed the corner and picked it up. It was a photograph with a fresh Nike footprint stomped on the back. He'd seen this print before . . . it was the print from behind his barn—the one that had mysteriously disappeared. It looks like he'd discovered the stranger. But why was the horseback kid—this D. Lindsay—spying on him?

Lucas flipped the picture over angrily. It was a photo of the forest. He followed where the camera in the tree had been pointing and saw the exact same scene in real life. He held up the photo. Seeing a picture of the forest next to the actual thing was oddly unsettling. Lucas thought for a second, then scattered away more leaves on the ground. Sure enough, he found other photos. Each one was the same image of the forest with very little changed. Some were taken during the day. Some at night. He combed through the photos until he found what the camera kid must have been looking for.

The picture was hazy, taken at night. Still, the sight of the photo made Lucas's neck hair stand on end: It was the shadowy blur he had been chasing—and it stared back at him with glowing red eyes.

Quickly, Lucas stuffed the picture in his pocket and ran back to the bike. He held his hand over it, testing for heat, but the metal frame was cool now. Lucas looked around, then picked up his helmet and set it on the handlebars. There was no way Lucas was going to ride the bike again that afternoon. So instead he walked it back toward Sweetwater Manor.

As he traveled, the forest shifted around him. He had felt so free and excited during his bike ride out there, but now he realized just how lost he was. Nothing looked familiar.

Suddenly a howl moaned in the distance. Even though it was the middle of the day, Lucas picked up speed. Another howl answered, and this time it was closer. The forest around him went quiet and still. Lucas felt like he was being watched and called out, "Hey, horseback kid! If you're trying to scare me, it's not funny."

Then, to Lucas's right, a third howl shattered the silence, and that was three too many. In an instant, Lucas was on his bike and pedaling away from the noise. His helmet dangled from his handlebars as Lucas pumped faster. Howl after eerie howl erupted, forcing Lucas to swerve left and then right to escape the strange calls. Maybe his dad was wrong. Maybe there weren't bears in the woods. Maybe there were wolves.

In the distance, Lucas saw a black iron fence with an unhinged gate that hung open. Beyond that, the castle-like turret roof of Silas's house peeked through the treetops. Lucas was almost home. But the howling chased him still. He glanced behind him to see if any wolves were on his trail. Nothing was there except the forest, thick and mysterious.

When Lucas whipped back around, a gray angel had appeared from out of nowhere and stood directly in front of him, arms outstretched. Lucas screamed and gripped his brakes hard, pulling the bike into a skid as he narrowly avoided crashing into the statue.

"Great," Lucas mumbled to himself. "Of *course* Silas had a sculpture garden, too."

In his panic, Lucas had ridden in between several statues of angels that now surrounded him in a large circle. They faced one another, frozen in different poses. The angel in front of Lucas was reaching down with its palms open, as if it were ushering him to fly away with her. He wheeled his bike around. Two of the angels were slumped over, as if crying, while the others bowed solemnly or gazed upward with the slightest smile etched onto their stone lips. But every angel statue stood on a pedestal, and chiseled on that pedestal were names.

Lucas gritted his teeth when he realized what he'd ridden straight into. "Not a sculpture garden. This place is a graveyard!"

Carefully, he got off the bike and walked it outside the circle. He shivered at the thought of standing on top of his long-gone Sweetwater relatives. Generations of family—at least ten members, judging by the final resting places—were buried six feet beneath him, with the giant tombstones arranged like Stonehenge.

From outside the circle, the wings of the angels blocked his view. It was designed this way, Lucas thought. Anyone within the circle was part of the family. They could see the statues' emotions and actions. But anyone outside the circle was left out of this private moment. They were given the coldest of stone shoulders.

Lucas pushed the bike around the outside of the angels' circle when he saw a dead patch of grass on the ground. A path of small stones wrapped around it like a border, and while the patch was close to one of the weeping angels, it was definitely not included within the circle of graves. The grass outside the rocks was green and lush, but the grass inside the rocks was yellow and dry. It looked lonely and sad, and suddenly, without knowing why, Lucas wanted to be as far away from that pale grass as possible. He almost wished the howling would start again, just to take his mind off the strange site. Because the patch looked like more than poor yard work . . . it looked lonely. It looked like death was seeping up through the ground.

CHAPTER 14

When Lucas reached the house, there was a note from his mother on the front door.

Hi, hon. Out running errands. Back in a few. Ms. Dobbs is home and workers are everywhere if you need anything. Sandwich stuff in the kitchen, I'm sure you're hungry. Hope you had a good bike ride. —Mom

It hadn't been a good bike ride, not by any stretch of the imagination. Lucas dumped the bike and helmet on the front porch and slipped into the house. He was actually relieved that his mom wasn't there. Mostly because he had no idea what he was going to tell her about his morning adventure. That he'd almost ridden off the edge of a cliff? That some strange kid had knocked him off the bike to save him? That some strange kid was spying on him? That he'd found a creepy picture? That he scraped his elbows and knees? That he'd found the Sweetwater family's graveyard? None of it seemed like the correct answer to her inevitable question, *How was your bike ride?* Lucas breathed easier because he didn't have to explain any of it to her yet, and his sigh echoed through the huge front parlor.

That's when Lucas realized he was basically home alone. He

patted the key still hanging around his neck. He hadn't gone back upstairs since the trapdoor incident, but he was certain that this key would open whatever was hidden in the mysterious rolltop desk.

A clock chimed eleven times. It must have come from deep within the house, because Lucas looked around and couldn't see a clock anywhere. The solemn bell rung soft and distant like the clock itself was whispering. Eleven o'clock in the morning and Lucas had the whole spooky place to himself. But then, louder than the chimes, came the gurgles and grumbles from his stomach. Sandwiches were definitely necessary. His inheritance—whatever it was—would be fine waiting until after lunch.

The kitchen was a mixture of updated and outdated. Stainless-steel appliances sat next to hand-carved cabinets with decorative twists and patterns chiseled and smoothed out of woodwork. Brass handles lined the rows of drawers under the gleaming granite countertops.

In the middle of it all, two focal points competed for attention: On one side, there was an antique stove. It was black with brass trim and looked very alien to Lucas. Never in his life had he seen a stove that stood on clawed legs like this one did. The other kitchen oddity was the fireplace built into the wall. It must have been older than the old stove and it totally creeped Lucas out. First of all, hooks still dangled underneath the flue, and when a breeze blew in, the hooks rocked slightly on their hinges, letting out a horrible creak. There was also a black, charred mark at the back of the fireplace. Lucas's dad said that this was where the family cooked their meals, did their laundry, and maybe even heated water for their baths a long time ago. To Lucas, though, the smudge looked like a witch had been burned at the stake in there. He shuddered at the mental image.

Lucas walked over to the fridge. Puffs of steam rose out when Lucas opened it. He leaned in and heard the glass bottles clink in the door shelf. The cold air felt amazing against his face. Lucas hadn't realized how hot it had gotten in the kitchen. He grabbed the turkey and cheese along with mustard, mayo, and bread, then kicked the door shut. Dropping the food on the island in the middle of the room, Lucas found a plate and pulled a knife out of the drawer.

A bead of sweat dripped down from his nose, plopping on the dark granite countertop. Lucas wiped his forehead across his upper sleeve. He'd ridden and run hard through the forest, but he didn't realize just how gross he'd gotten. As he reached for a folded towel by the sink to wipe himself off, the package of turkey fell to the floor.

Plap. The wet sound made him jump. Then he shook his head and leaned down to get it. As soon as he did, a long scraping noise from the top of the island made Lucas cringe. He stood back up to see his plate on the opposite end of the counter, far away from where he'd placed it.

"That's not good." Lucas studied the empty kitchen as he held the turkey slices. "Eartha? Was that you? Did I do something wrong again and you're trying to teach me a lesson?"

No one answered.

Then, suddenly, the cap on the mustard exploded and a stream of yellow sprayed violently into the air. The mayo fell on its side, too, splattering all over the counter. Lucas froze, waiting for the cheese to start boiling or whatever kitchen catastrophe was coming next. But the room went still again.

He picked the mustard bottle up from a thick yellow puddle and studied it. Instantly it erupted again, spurting even more yellow all over his face and the floor.

"So *that's* what Gale meant about exploding mustard," he said to the empty room. Lucas grabbed a few paper towels nearby and cleaned his face.

His stomach whined loudly. Lucas reached for the mustard bottle again, but thought better of it. With a shrug, he scraped the butter knife against the mustard on his shirt, then swiped it across the bread.

Plap. The cheese smacked against the floor this time.

"C'mon, world, I just wanna eat!" Lucas sighed as he bent over to pick it up.

But there was something else on the floor that hadn't been there a minute ago. Stains. *No, not stains*, thought Lucas. *Paw prints.*

A trail of mustard-yellow paw prints led out of the kitchen and into the living room. Lucas touched the closest mark and it smudged. The trail was fresh.

"Lucky?" he called, but these paw prints belonged to something bigger than his cat.

Lucas took a bite of bread, then put it down to follow the strange, new tracks. The steps seemed to hover above the dark wood floors, and they didn't stop or wander. Whatever made the marks knew exactly where it was going.

The prints led up a flight of stairs Lucas hadn't seen before. This staircase was thinner than the one in the front of the house, but it was every bit as strange. When he reached the second floor, the staircase kept going up. Only instead of reaching the third floor, they dead-ended at the ceiling. "Why would anyone build a staircase to nowhere?" he asked aloud.

The paw tracks jumped down from there and onto the second floor. Lucas hopped down, too.

Thoughts swirled in his head as he hypnotically followed the prints. He had no idea what kind of animal he was trailing. The prints were big, but the stains didn't seem to land with much force on the floor. Each mark showed four pads at the top with a fifth, larger pad at the bottom. The inside of each pad mark was crisscrossed with dots that came together to look almost like fingerprints.

As he stepped carefully around the yellow impressions, the silence of the house pressed down on Lucas. Suddenly his stomach growled again and he wished he'd brought at least some bread with him.

Soon he reached an unfinished wall that must have been new construction. Lucas ran his hand over the pale white drywall that glowed soft like a night-light. Fresh chalk came off on his hands, and Lucas wiped them against his pants. The tracks turned right around a corner, down another hallway. The new construction continued down this way, too. After ten steps forward, they turned right again and down another unfinished hallway. Another ten steps later, the prints turned right *again* . . . down a *third* hallway. After ten more steps, Lucas looped back to the original hallway, where the tracks finally ended.

"No way," he whispered. He retraced his steps in a square again, making sure that the animal wasn't hiding anywhere. Again and again, there was nothing to be seen.

A scraping sound made Lucas jump. It was urgent and seemed to come from behind the drywall. He put his hand against the hallway and felt a pulse with every scratch, like something was pawing from inside the wall. Frantically, Lucas retraced his steps, looking for a door to let the animal out, but there was no door. The scratching followed him to each wall. Lucas knocked against the wall and the scratching grew more insistent and anxious, moving up and down.

"Hello?!" Lucas called out. "Anyone? Help! There's an animal trapped in the walls!"

A construction worker appeared around another corner. He wore a blue flannel shirt and carried a bucket of plaster with a trowel. His tired eyes stared flatly at Lucas. "You are not supposed to be here."

"Yeah, well, neither is the animal trapped in this wall," said Lucas.

The worker shook his head. "There's no animal. Just you. Go back downstairs."

Instantly the scratching stopped and the hallway went silent once more.

"Oh," Lucas said. He wasn't sure why, but having the worker there didn't make him feel any safer. "Okay, I'll get outta here, but please check that wall. And look out for a stray animal. I followed these paw prints up here, and—"

"Paw prints?" the worker interrupted.

"Yeah, tracks. Like, paw prints on the ground." Lucas pointed down, but the yellow paw prints were gone. Just like the scratching, they'd disappeared.

"You need to leave," said the worker. "We have rules in this house. Do not go where you are not supposed to go."

"But I swear! There were tracks and a scratching!" Lucas said as he knocked against the wall. "Something's inside here. Can't you hear it?"

"We. Have. Rules. In. This. House." The worker's tone grew angry as he dragged himself forward. His movements were irregular, like watching a puppet on a string try to walk. He seemed to float in the light of the hall. "Now get back to *your* side of the house."

"Hey, I wasn't doing anything wrong," Lucas argued as he retreated the way he came. He needed to tell his parents about this, even if it meant he'd get in trouble. Keeping an eye on the worker, he watched the man dip the trowel in the plaster and begin to smooth the wall with it.

All signs of the mustard-yellow paw prints on the floor were gone. Looking around, Lucas realized that without the prints, he had no idea how to get back to the kitchen. After a few wrong turns, Lucas found the strange steps that led back downstairs. The island in the kitchen was still a mess, but now his plate was smashed on the floor and the food was strewn about.

As he bent down to clean up the plate shards, a thump echoed from the other side of the room. Lucas stayed hidden behind the island. "Eartha? Mr. Worker Guy? Any chance that noise was Mom or Dad?"

Thump. This time Lucas flinched at the sound. It was like a body hitting the floor. Slowly, he peeked over the island. Everything was still. Then the giant box from Gale's moved on the table, causing Lucas to jump up, too. Lucas and the box stood stone-still, waiting to see which one of them would make the next move.

Thump. Thump. Thump.

The box shifted back and forth on the table like someone was trapped inside. Suddenly the top of the box exploded open, spilling tons of dog food onto the floor. Lucas let out a shriek so high-pitched that it could have cracked every window in the house, but he didn't care. In that moment, the only thing he cared about was getting out of the house as fast as humanly possible. He bolted for the front door, ripped it open, and stopped in his tracks.

Bess was on the front porch. Again. "You okay, Lucas? We were coming over and heard some lady screaming inside your house."

"No, that was me." Lucas nodded as he huffed and puffed and pointed at himself. "I'm the screaming lady and before you tell me I'm crazy, let me just say that you'd scream, too, if you saw what I just saw."

"What's going on?" Bess asked. "Should we come inside?"

Lucas moved from nodding his head to shaking it. "All I wanted was a sandwich and now the box of dog food is alive, the walls are alive, there's a worker who is totally out to get me, and the mustard paw prints just disappeared—"

"Did you say mustard paw prints?" A new person was standing off to the side of the porch next to Bess.

"Yeah, the mustard blew up. It was the kind we got from Gale's in town, and I guess these mustard bottles had been . . ." Lucas stopped rambling when he looked at the new kid. It was the horseback boy from the forest who'd knocked him off his bike. "You? What are *you* doing here?"

"He's with me, Lucas." Bess stepped between them. "We need to talk."

Lucas pointed over her shoulder. "Do you have any idea what he did to me, Bess?"

"I saved your life," the kid answered. "You're welcome."

Remembering the cliff's edge, Lucas yelled, "Darn right, you did! Thank you!"

Bess scrunched up her face as she patted Lucas's arm back down. "Why are you yelling at Lens if he helped you?"

"Because I'm really weirded out by everything right now," Lucas hollered. "And you bring this guy over to my house who was spying on me yesterday, by the way, and he saved my life, but he also royally messed up your bike, by the way, and then I found a graveyard."

"Stop," Bess commanded. Her hair flipped around as she faced the other kid. "Lens? You hurt my bike?"

"No," the kid said stubbornly. "I kept him from riding it off the Devil's Drop."

"By tackling me," snapped Lucas. "That really hurt, by the way."

"It would have hurt worse if you'd fallen to your death."

Lucas nodded. "Yeah, I guess you've got a point there. Oh, and I found your special forest camera, too, Mr. Lindsay. If that is your real name."

"His name is Deshaun," said Bess. "But everyone calls him Lens."

Lens held up another camera that was slung over his shoulder and, with a quick smile, took a picture of Lucas. The bright flash popped and made Lucas wince.

"Fastest photographer in the South," Lens bragged over the camera's mechanical whining. A white square pushed out of the plastic case and Lens gave it a strong shake. "That's why they call me Lens. Like a camera lens. It's kind of my thing."

Bess rolled her eyes. "That and your last name is Lindsay. You made us all start calling you *Linds* at first to try and be cool. Then you got into cameras later, so—"

"Okay, okay," Lens said with a nervous laugh. "We don't have to tell the man my life story." He handed Lucas the picture he'd just taken. "Here."

A ghostly image rose from the white center of the photo. Lucas watched as the picture started to develop into full color, then looked down at his shirt. "Awe, man. I forgot about the mustard stain."

"Look," said Bess. "Go change your shirt and show us what's going on in Silas's house. You said a worker was out to get you?"

Lucas stared at Bess. She stood in the doorway like a kid about to jump off a diving board. She was ready to plunge inside.

"No," he told her. Then Lucas pulled out the picture he found in the forest. "Not until you tell me the story behind *this*."

Bess closed her eyes and raised a fist to her forehead. "You had *one* job today," she said, turning to Lens. "One job! I asked you to get all the pictures."

"I thought I did!" Lens said with a shrug. "Apparently, I didn't."

Lucas nodded as the shadowy photo hung between them.

Bess pushed Lens backward with an angry grunt before she turned to Lucas. "Okay, Lucas Trainer. We'll tell you what we know, but you've got to come with us." Her voice became suddenly grave. "'Cause you'll need to see it to believe it."

CHAPTER 15

The hedge maze was overgrown. Roots pushed up through the uneven ground and the bushes were wild, with tiny limbs reaching out to scrape Lucas. Still dressed in his dirty shirt, he followed Bess and Lens into the bizarre place he'd seen the night he arrived at Sweetwater Manor. A stone archway entrance was the only part of the maze that had kept its original shape. The hedges hadn't been trimmed in years; they were pear-shaped in the middle and scraggly at the top. The manicured glory of the maze had become a weed garden and the walking path barely existed.

As Lucas swatted through bushes, the bushes swatted back. "Gah, isn't there an easier way to get where we're going?"

"Nope." Bess smiled.

"Don't worry, we're close now," said Lens from somewhere ahead of the group. As soon as one body pushed through the hedges, the deep green shape bounced back into place.

"I'm not worried." Lucas stumbled over a knotted patch on the ground. He had to kick his foot to get free from the plant's grip. "But are you going to tell me where we're going?"

"See for yourself," said Bess as she disappeared through a small opening that closed like a portal of greenery.

Lucas tried to find the same gap she'd taken, but the limbs were locked thick wherever he put his hand. "Guys? A little help?"

A hand shot out of the bushes and grabbed Lucas by the shirt only to drag him forward through the pointed leaves that grazed his entire body like thousands of fingernails. Once he made it to the other side, Lucas stood in a hedge-walled clearing. Bess clutched his shirt collar while Lens stood in front of an old, wooden shack. The tiny house was covered with vines. The walls and roof were made of weathered, wooden slats that had rotted to a pale gray. *Rickety* was the nicest word that sprang to Lucas's mind. Lens had set up cameras all around the interior of the maze, pointing toward the shack.

"You brought me all the way out here to see a haunted shack?" Lucas wiped his hands over his arms and face to cool his skin where the branches had scraped him.

"No," said Bess.

"We brought you all the way out here to see what's *inside* the haunted shack," said Lens.

"Uh-uh, no way, I decline your invitation," snapped Lucas. "I'm sure you can understand. I mean, one, I hardly know either of you. Two, it's a haunted shack. Three, there are enough cameras here for you to just take a picture and send me the photo of whatever you were going to show me. And four—and I can't stress this enough—it's a haunted shack!"

Bess waved Lens over to Lucas. "Tell him. Tell him why the town is called Hounds Hollow."

Lens stared at her, then recited a speech that he'd clearly memorized. "Hounds Hollow used to be famous for foxhunting. That's a sport where people ride on horseback chasing a fox through the forest. Dogs—hounds, to be exact—were trained to sniff out the foxes."

"So?" asked Lucas.

"Really? You don't think chasing foxes with dogs while you ride on horseback is weird?" asked Lens. "I think it's kinda psycho. Anyway, foxhunts eventually died out."

"Why?" Lucas shifted away from the shack, which slumped in the midday sun. "Did people finally realize that chasing foxes while you ride on horseback was ridiculous? Or did the world invent video games?"

"The beast." Lens's voice was flat and matter-of-fact.

"The beast," Lucas repeated skeptically. "Like that explains everything. What are you talking about? Does this have something to do with the picture I found in the forest?"

"For a long time," Lens began, "like before we were even born, people here have told the story of the beast. It's a Hounds Hollow legend. There's a creature out there haunting the town. Every night it goes into the woods, searching."

Lens stopped talking, lengthening the silence.

"Drop the dramatic effect, man," Lucas begged. "Searching for what?"

"We don't know," said Lens. "But the beast scared all the foxes away. He scared all the horses, too. And he definitely scared off all the hunters."

Lucas took another step back and pointed his finger at Bess. "No, this is like some practical joke, right? Like scare the new kid to death. I'll bet you stashed those photos for me to find. Ha ha, very funny."

"It's not funny, Lucas," said Bess. "Some people think the beast is a campfire story, but we've seen it. And you know what?" Bess walked toward Lucas until they were eye to eye. "I think you might have seen it, too."

"W-what makes you think that?" asked Lucas, suddenly flashing back to yesterday's car accident.

Bess looked around. "Let's go inside and talk about it."

Lens entered the abandoned shack. Bess followed, leaving Lucas outside by himself. The day was sunny and bright and nothing felt right about it. Lucas took a deep breath and stepped inside.

The smell of musty, damp wood and mold made Lucas cough. Light shone through the broken windows and cast jagged shafts that cut through the single room. There was a small table with tiny chairs inside that Lucas almost stumbled over.

Drawings of stick figures covered one of the walls. They all had misshapen heads and drooping eyes that stared back at Lucas. Some figures were running, some were jumping, and some were having picnics, but the stick figures did everything in pairs. There were two human stick figures in each scene, surrounded by lots of four-legged stick figures. Lucas traced the drawings and felt the bumps along the old wood walls.

"This was a kid's fort, wasn't it?" asked Lucas. "But Silas didn't have kids."

"We think this was Silas's fort when *he* was a kid," said Lens.

"That's not what we wanted to show you, though," Bess explained.

Lens gave her a pleading glance. "Are you sure we want to do this?"

Bess nodded. "We can trust him. And I think we need him."

"Trust me? Need me? What's going on?" asked Lucas.

"Have a seat." Bess sat at the tiny table and nudged another chair out with her foot.

Lucas sat down and his knees were practically in his chest.

From a dark corner, Lens retrieved a thick, black binder. He carried it over and placed it in front of Lucas.

Bess covered the binder with her arms. "Before you look at this, I want you to think about your boy from the house story.

I believed you when you told me. Now I need for you to believe me."

"Okay," Lucas agreed with a slight waver in his voice.

Bess slid the binder over. "This is the beast."

Lucas opened the book. Slippery plastic pages bent in his hand. Each one had four pictures in slots like a Pokémon card collection. The pictures were all taken outside in the woods at night—a collection of shadows. "What am I supposed to see?"

Lens hovered over her shoulder. "Look at what's right in front of you."

Lucas flipped through several floppy pages before one photo caught his eye. It was a hazy smudge. He leaned closer and felt his chest tighten. The smudge floated like a mistake in the picture, something that wasn't supposed to be there. But it had a distinct shape: four legs, a tail, and two glowing, red eyes—not unlike the eyes he had seen the day before. He quickly closed the book and opened it back up, scanning every photo. Over and over again, the same ghostly shape was hidden.

"I've . . . I've seen this thing." Lucas looked up at Bess.

She nodded. "I know. We've seen it, too. Tell him, Lens."

They sat quietly for a moment. Then Lens broke the silence.

"It started last year. I was riding through the forest on my horse, Bolt, when something spooked her. I'd never seen her turn so scared in my life, and I've been riding her since

I was six. She threw me from the saddle and took off in the other direction. I landed on my back, knocking the wind out of me. I couldn't catch my breath, but then I turned and saw a shadow with glowing, red eyes hiding in the trees. I tried to get away from it, but it just watched, turning its head like it was studying me, or sizing me up. I screamed to try and, I don't know, freak it out and make it run off. But this thing wasn't scared."

"And then what?" Lucas was mesmerized by the story.

"I ran for my life," Lens continued. "That's when it pounced."

Lens crossed his arms nervously, and Lucas could see the boy was still frightened.

"But . . ." Lucas paused, trying to gather his words in the nicest way. "You're, um, you're . . ."

"Alive." Bess finished his ugly thought. "Lens was lucky. I found him and scared the beast away."

Lucas shook his head. "Wait. How did you scare the beast away?"

Bess held up another smooth stone. "Let's just say I'm lucky, too."

Looking back down at the table, Lucas touched the photo album. "And all these pictures?"

"You don't live through something like that and forget about it," said Lens. "I told my parents, and they talked to Silas. He said he'd been having problems with wolves in the area.

That I'd probably stumbled on to a pack out hunting and was lucky to make it home in one piece."

"There aren't any wolves in Hounds Hollow," said Bess. "And even if there were, this thing wasn't a wolf. It was a beast."

Lens nodded. "So we started hunting for proof, and you're looking at it."

Lucas stared at the binder, then glanced up at the camera Lens was wearing. "Why did you take a picture of me in the barn yesterday? That was you, right?"

Lens held up a photo. "I wasn't taking a picture of *you*, necessarily. I was trying to take a picture of *it*."

The photograph showed Lucas in the barn, but he wasn't alone. A ghostly smudge ran toward him, frozen in the white frame. But unlike the other images of the beast in Lens's book, this hazy figure had a more realistic shape. It looked like a giant dog. Its gleaming white teeth were bared in a snarl about to snap into Lucas. His breathing became heavy and fast.

"I was chasing the beast through the forest," Lens explained. "Took me by surprise because I've never seen it out during the day. I was collecting footage from the night before when, *poof*, the beast was right in front of me. It was so close, but it took off. I ran after it and nearly slammed into the side of your barn in the process."

Lucas couldn't take his eyes off the picture. "How'd it get inside my house?"

"It's a ghost, man, I dunno," said Lens. "It went right through the wall. I snapped the picture, then heard your voice, which freaked me out. I thought you were a worker, and if I got caught lurking around Silas's place again, my parents would turn me into a ghost, too."

"What does it want?" asked Lucas.

Bess slowly took the photo from his hand and gave it back to Lens. "From the look of this picture? It wants to get inside your house. That's why *we* need to get inside your house."

Lucas shook his head like he was trying to wake up from a nightmare. "We can't do this alone. That's crazy. We've gotta tell someone about this . . . this . . . this *thing*."

"No," whispered Bess, and the silence of the hidden shack in the hedge maze suddenly stifled Lucas.

"No?" he repeated. "Why not?"

"Did you tell your mom about the beast from the accident?" Bess reached over and took Lucas's hand. "Even with pictures, even with proof, it's not the kind of story that people want to believe. It would be easier for everyone to say that we were crazy."

"There are legends from all over the world," said Lens. "Witches, werewolves, vampires, and yeah, they might seem cool in books and in movies. But this isn't a book, it's our lives."

The feeling of Bess's hand in his felt good, like Lucas had a connection to the real world again. She was attempting to pull him back to reality before he floated away into fear. "Okay. So if we don't tell anyone, what are we supposed to do?"

Lens looked down to Bess, but she didn't take her eyes off Lucas. "We're going to search for what the beast is after in your house and make sure it never finds what it's looking for. I think that's why you're here. That's why Silas gave you his house. We've got to kill the beast."

As soon as she said it, Lucas jerked his hands out of hers. "Whoa, I'm . . . I'm not a killer."

"Neither are we, man," said Lens. "Plus, I'm not sure you can technically kill a ghost, but we've got to do something to stop it."

"Stop it from what?" asked Lucas. "You guys have all these pictures of the beast, you've got your freaky stories, I get it. But what if this thing just wants to be left alone?"

Bess snatched the picture back from Lens and slammed it down on the tiny table in front of Lucas. "Are we looking at the same picture? This isn't a thing that wants to mind its own business and live its own life. It's coming for something inside Sweetwater Manor. Maybe it's coming for you."

"Or maybe Lens chased it into a random house and I scared it," Lucas offered.

"It doesn't look scared to me," insisted Bess as she tapped the picture. "It looks determined."

Lucas stood up from the tiny chair. "I don't care what it looks like. Does the beast freak me out? Yes. But so do jelly-fish and sharks. I'm not going to hunt them down and kill them, and I'm not going to stop swimming at the beach, either."

"Then what do you suggest we do?" Bess asked.

"I don't know. We find out what it is. We find out what it wants. And . . . maybe we can help it." Lucas looked at the stick figure drawings on the wall again. "Ever since I moved here, this entire place has been a mystery. But mysteries aren't meant to be hunted. They're meant to be solved."

"So let us into the house already!" snapped Bess. "Let's start tonight. Maybe if we find what the beast is after first, then it'll go away."

Lucas patted his chest and felt the small key hanging under his shirt. The desk, the key, what the beast was after—Lucas sud-denly knew what he had to do. He was about to invite the others back with him when a high-pitched screech ripped through the maze and the small shack. It was so loud that the windows rat-tled, birds startled from the bushes, and Lucas's face dropped.

"W-what was that?" Lens jumped back, knocking over a tiny chair, which clacked against the floor.

A brief silence spread over the room again, followed by another sharp scream in the distance—one that sent chills down Lucas's spine and made him wonder if he might be better off with the beast: "Lucas Ward Trainer!" a woman yelled. "Get back here right NOW!"

CHAPTER 16

With a loud crack, Eartha Dobbs opened the front door to Sweetwater Manor. Her full frame blocked Lucas from coming into his own house.

"Oh no!" she cried as she glared down at him. "First you mess up the entire kitchen, then you disappear, then you make me come into this house from all your momma's hollerin' like the manor's on fire, and now you're tryin' to sneak in the house? And I thought no-flushin' was bad!"

"I'm not trying to sneak back in—I'm walking through the front door, like a normal person!" Lucas tried to squeeze past her, but Eartha wouldn't budge. Lucas sighed. "Sorry about the kitchen and about the mom alarm. I just don't see why a little exploding mustard and some spilled dog food is such a big deal."

"Mustard?" Eartha called out from the doorway. "Dog food? If you think mustard and dog food caused that mess, then heaven help you."

Lucas gave her an odd look, but Eartha shuffled him along as she went back to her cottage. "Don't make me come in here again. You understand?"

"Yes, ma'am." Lucas jogged to the kitchen. "Mom, I can explain. Remember the exploding mustard and the—"

"Not. A. Word," Mom said in her coolest, calmest voice, which was parent code for *There's not a volume loud enough for how much trouble you are in.* She stood in the middle of a wreck that used to be their kitchen. All of the chairs were knocked over, and some were even broken. Every door in the room was open, from the cabinets to the fridge to the dishwasher door. The food they'd just bought the day before was scattered across the floor. Tomatoes, broccoli, apples, grapes, raw meat, and potato chips were crushed, smashed, and stinking up the room. Uncooked chicken was even stuck to the ceiling. No food group had been spared.

"I . . . ," started Lucas, but he was silenced by the death stare coming from his mom. The kitchen was a culinary crime scene. "This wasn't me! You believe me, right?"

"Then who could it have been?" asked Dad, walking in with a broom. "I suppose this mess just magically appeared."

"Maybe," suggested Lucas. "Stranger things have happened."

But his father held out the broom's handle. "Well, then maybe *you* can make this mess magically *dis*appear."

Lucas was about to beg his mom to listen to him, but she had her arms crossed and was turning a particularly angry shade of red.

"Tonight." Her voice was strained and measured, a perfect recipe that told Lucas she meant business. "If this room isn't spotless tonight, we will have a problem. Am I clear?"

"Yes, ma'am." Lucas leaned the broom against the wall and began picking up the plastic bags.

His parents left him to clean on his own. Piece by piece, Lucas picked up the trash. Empty soda cans littered the floor next to sticky spills. A sideways bottle of olive oil poured down the lower cabinets and glowed in the kitchen light. Lucas ran towels over everything, mixing the smells together in a rotten, sugary horribleness that made him gag. There was even milk dripping from the ceiling.

Lucas went to get a chair so he could reach the milk stain, when he noticed that the large box from Gale's had been shredded open. The thick brown sides of the box looked like strips of confetti. Remembering how the box had moved on its own, he ran his hands over the paper. It was wet. Inside, Lucas found four giant, empty bags of dry dog food that had been chewed open. Extra pieces of kibble were scattered across the floor, too. He didn't want to think about what could have made a mess like this, or why.

Four trash bags and two hours later, the kitchen was back to normal.

When his mother came back in, she gave him a hug. "I know it's hard, moving to a new place. Especially to a new place as strange as this. But I'd rather you talk to me about your feelings instead of acting out."

"I didn't . . . ," Lucas started, but how could he tell his mom the truth? He didn't even know what the truth was yet. "I didn't want to bother you."

"You're not ever going to bother me, Lucas," she said. "You couldn't if you tried." Then she added with a smile, "Although this came close."

"Thanks, Mom. I feel better now." And Lucas meant it. "Since we're talking life in Hounds Hollow, Bess and her friend wanted to come over tonight. Is that okay?"

"Hmm . . ." His mom was already shaking her head. "Seems a little late for guests to visit, don't you think?"

"Well, the sun stays out longer here," Lucas rationalized. "And it would be good for me to make new friends before school starts."

"That's true," said Mom. "Okay, but it can't be a late night. We moved here for the cleaner air, but that won't help unless you pace yourself, Lucas. I don't want to scare you, but the doctors were very honest about your condition."

"I know," Lucas said with an awkward smile. He hated thinking of himself like a ticking time bomb, but that's how the doctors had described him—in kinder words, of course. But he knew what they meant. His lungs weren't made like normal lungs. One day, he'd most likely just stop breathing. Lucas didn't like to think about it, so instead he just told his mom what she wanted to hear. "I'll take it easy. Patient's honor."

After leaving the kitchen, Lucas started to sneak up the

stairs, determined to find the rolltop desk again, but his mom stopped him. "Hey, Mr. Patient, where do you think you're going?"

"Umm." Lucas paused. He'd hoped his mom would stay behind in the kitchen, but she was apparently a little suspicious of him, too. Quickly, Lucas snapped his fingers and pointed back downstairs. "Oh yeah, my room's that way, isn't it. Gosh, this house, huh. It really gets me turned around."

His mom smiled. "I don't know what you're up to, but for now, let's stick to the main areas we already know. Okay?"

"Sure, Mom," Lucas agreed. "That sounds like a good idea . . . for now."

Back in his blue room with the missing picture frames, Lucas tumbled onto the bed face-first. Then he flopped onto his back and pulled out the tiny key that hung around his neck. It was old. The original brass color was almost gone, tarnished into a sea of grimy brown spots. He'd stared at it tons of times in the city and thought it was nothing but a collector's item. Lucas couldn't imagine what kind of lock would ever need a key this tiny and old. Now that he was living in Silas's house, it was clear that this key could potentially fit lots of the locks here. But Lucas was certain it matched the desk.

He tugged the key back and forth along its chain as he stared up at the ceiling and wondered what could be hidden under the rolltop. Gold, jewels, cash, a map of the house, or even treasure . . . or maybe nothing. Maybe just old paperwork or taxes like the usual stuff people put in desks.

Lost in his imagination, Lucas heard a small scratch at the door. Without looking he said, "It's open, Lucky, just come in."

The cat leapt onto his bed and stood on the pillow next to him. Lucky's fur bristled as the cat tensed his shoulders and crouched angrily.

"What's your problem now?" Lucas asked, but Lucky remained focused on something opposite the doorway.

Another scratch moved slowly through the room. This one was louder and made Lucas sit up and take notice. If Lucky was on the bed, then what was scratching? He followed his cat's gaze straight to the full-length mirror that he'd blocked with his dresser. Only now, the dresser was back to its normal place. A large note was folded on top.

Lucas carefully inched off the bed as quietly as possible and picked up the note.

Whoa, crazy design scheme, mister! Don't worry, I moved the dresser back into place. Now you can use the mirror to actually comb your hair every once in a while. Love, Dad

"Oh no, Dad," whispered Lucas. "What did you do?"

As soon as he spoke, the scratching started again, this time repeating itself faster and faster. The mirror door rattled. Whatever was behind there wanted out. Lucas stared as the scratching got louder.

Then Lucky let out a low hiss-growl from the bed, snapping Lucas out of his trance. He knew in his heart what was lurking behind that door. It was the beast, come back to finish the job.

"Mom! Dad!" Lucas screamed, but his voice sounded muffled, as if he were underwater in the deep blue room. The scratching grew louder and faster at the sound of his voice, but Lucas wasn't going to stick around to find out what was going on.

He grabbed Lucky, who had his claws dug deep into the pillow, and started to run from the room, when the scratching stopped. That's when Lucas heard a new sound.

A small whimper came from behind the mirror door. Lucas was transported to a memory of the city, listening to people walking their puppies as he sat outside his building. They whimpered the same way when they passed him, pulling away from their owners as they tried excitedly to reach Lucas. The puppies would always burrow happily into his hands before the owners apologized and continued on their way.

The whimper behind the mirror held the same kind of excitement. But this time, it was Lucas who turned around and walked toward the whimper. He held Lucky in front of him, and Lucky still wielded the pillow in his claws like a shield. As he stepped in front of the mirror door, he felt where the sharp-edged needles from the maze had scratched his arms earlier. He wondered if this was how it felt to be a ghost walking through a wall, like the act was both natural and unnatural all at once.

Aside from the whimper, everything in the house had gone quiet. The chorus of saws, hammers, and distant creaks from walking workers was gone. Even the cicada buzz was gone. Lucas clicked the door with his free hand.

The mirror swung open and revealed a small puppy sitting still and staring at Lucas. When their eyes met, the dog's tail waved back and forth with excitement. It was a fluffy white mutt with a funny nose and matted ears sprouting out of its peanut-shaped head.

Lucky scratched over Lucas's shoulder and escaped the room completely.

The puppy tilted its head curiously at the cat as it ran. Then it took a few steps toward Lucas.

"You are not what I expected." Lucas bent down and the puppy squirmed up against him, twirling in circles and letting out babyish yips and barks that sounded like nervous coughs.

Its whole body was shaking. Lucas tried to give the puppy his hand to smell, but the dog merely nuzzled against it with instant warmth and happiness.

"Are you lost, little guy?" asked Lucas as he sat on his knees. The dog stopped, as if considering Lucas's question. Then it dove onto his lap, spinning with a dizzy kind of joy.

Lucas rubbed the small dog and looked past it, down the hidden hall that led to the dark barn. He could feel the puppy's backbone and ribs with every pat. When he was sure the coast was clear, Lucas frisked the pup. "No dog collar, eh? Hmm, and no yellow mustard paws, either. That's good. And you're certainly no beast. Did you sneak through the gap in the barn door?"

The mutt snorted as if to say yes and then crawled into Lucas's arms, pawed at his shirt, and tried to lick his face. Warmth radiated through Lucas as he picked up the pup.

"Mom is not going to like this," he warned the dog. "At least tell me you're potty trained."

The dog turned its head, giving Lucas a quizzical look. The mysteries of Hounds Hollow melted away for a brief moment and Lucas actually smiled.

"Okay, okay, I didn't mean to offend you," he said with a laugh as the dog yipped. Its voice was very quiet and hoarse. "Well, then, if you know how to go to the bathroom outside, this might be the beginning of a beautiful friendship. Just one question, though: What do *you* think about the beast?"

Yap-yap-yap-yap-yap! The question ruffled Lucas's new friend as the pooch broke into a barking fit and reared back with surprising strength. Flipping out of his arms, the dog landed gracefully and stood at attention.

"Whoa, boy! I get it. You're not scared of anything, are you?" Lucas stood up and patted the dog's back. The brave mutt almost broke into a smile. "That's good, 'cause I've got a mystery to solve before either the beast or Bess do something stupid."

Lucas had never had a dog before. At first his parents said they weren't allowed to have pets in the apartment, but then they took in Lucky. Apparently, cats were allowed, but dogs were forbidden. He later found out that one of his doctors had been concerned that having a dog might be too energetic for Lucas. It might bring on an incident, she had said. That's what the doctors called it when he couldn't breathe. An incident.

The dog barked again and Lucas put his finger to his lips. "*Shh*, now, keep quiet and let me do all the talking to Mom and Dad when the time is right. Oh, and one more thing. Do you like cats? Never mind, even if you hate cats, this house is so big, I'm sure there's room enough for you and Lucky. So follow my lead. Deal?"

As if it understood every word, the dog nodded, or seemed to nod. Lucas held his hand out and was met with a soft, warm paw.

"Wow, you can shake hands, huh?" Lucas smiled. "You must have a home somewhere. We'll find where you belong. But first, you're going to meet my new friends."

CHAPTER 17

The sun was setting when a chorus of chimes announced the visitors. The melody was so loud that it shook the entire house. Each note made Lucas feel like he was inside a church with bells ringing out for the entire countryside to hear. The white dog in Lucas's room howled along woefully.

"Quiet!" Lucas covered the pup's mouth, but the mutt still wailed along with the music. Then, as suddenly as it had begun, the song was over, replaced by silence.

"Well, ladies and gentlemen, it's official," said Mom from the front hallway. "We have the doorbell to end all doorbells."

The front door creaked open and Lucas could hear his mother talking to someone, then she called out, "Lucas, you have company."

"Be right there," he answered.

The dog followed him to the door, but Lucas knelt down to block the entry. "No, no." As he said it, Lucas's necklace fell out from his shirt. The small key dangled over the dog, and the dog sat at full attention as if Lucas were offering it a treat. Clutching the key, he gave the dog a smile.

It wasn't the right time to tell his parents that he'd found a stray dog. Or that there was a mysterious beast haunting the area. Or that his newest friends in Hounds Hollow who'd just popped over for a visit wanted his help to kill that same mysterious beast. Or that the key he inherited might be the key to stopping the beast. These things took expert timing and attention to detail to explain to parents.

Looking at the dog, Lucas tucked the key back under his collar and then pushed both hands through the air. "You . . . stay . . . here. I'll . . . be . . . back . . . okay?"

Surprisingly, the dog didn't move. Instead, it lay down right in the middle of the room and kept its eyes on Lucas.

"Good dog," he said as he scrambled out and closed the door behind him.

Lucas could see Bess already casing the front hallway while Lens was talking to Mrs. Trainer.

"Lucas, you didn't tell me that Lens's mother owns the bookstore *and* runs the local newspaper," Mom said cheerfully. "A media mogul in our house, huh?"

Lens held up his camera and pretended to take a picture of Mrs. Trainer, who smiled and struck a pose.

"Well, that's *news* to me," Lucas said.

The others groaned at the horrible joke.

"Don't worry, I've heard it all before," said Lens. "I'll bring you to the printing press sometime, Lucas. You'd love it. Maybe we can do a story on the new kid in town?"

A low laugh escaped Bess as she walked around the hallway,

casually peering into rooms. "It's a hand-crank printing press, Lens."

Lens nodded sincerely. "It's historic. That press has been printing issues for Hounds Hollow since . . . I don't know. Since Hounds Hollow started, I guess."

"Well, I think that sounds cool, Lens," said Mom, which made Lucas wince. It wasn't her fault, but his mom had a way of making something cool sound so uncool.

Seeing her son's reaction, Mrs. Trainer clapped her hands and began backing out of the hallway. "Okay, I'll let you guys do your thing. Call if you need me, Lucas."

Lucas nodded. As soon she left, Bess dropped her casual snoopy routine and broke into a full-fledged spy-a-thon. She even started knocking on the walls.

"What are you doing?" asked Lens.

Bess moved from one side of the hall to the other, gently rapping every surface with the back of her hand. "Looking for a secret room. If Silas has all those cameras set up around the house, then he's got to have a surveillance room, right? We find that, then I bet we'll find real footage of the beast. And that footage might tell us what he's after. Have you seen a room like that, Lucas?"

"A room like what? Filled with TVs and computer stuff? I haven't seen anything like that here."

"No," said Bess. "We're looking for a room that doesn't make sense."

With the crystal chandelier above them, a larger-than-life staircase behind them, and ornate velvet chairs beside them, Bess's question seemed crazy. None of the rooms in Sweetwater Manor made sense. Lucas didn't know where to start.

"Why don't we start with the barn?" Lens suggested.

As Lucas opened the door to his bedroom, he warned the others. "Oh, just FYI, I had a stray dog sneak in today. My parents don't know about him yet, so if you could . . . you know."

"Relax, Lucas," said Bess as she pushed past him into his own room. "Your puppy secret's safe with us."

Lens patted Lucas on the back. "Sorry about her. She's kind of . . . well, let's just say she doesn't always realize she's being blunt."

"Yeah, I picked up on that," said Lucas.

Inside the room, Bess made her way over to the bed and grabbed the mask from Lucas's CPAP machine. "What the heck is this thing?"

Lucas blushed. It had been a long time since he'd had to explain his equipment to new friends. Usually his friends' parents had that conversation with them before they came over to his house.

Bess went to place the mask over her mouth, and Lucas lunged forward.

"Please don't," he said, louder than even he expected. "That's my CPAP machine. I use it at night to help me breathe."

"Sorry," Bess said, setting the mask down on the bedside table. "So why are we in here if we're going to the barn?"

"Look behind the mirror." Lucas pointed to the secret door. Then he did a quick scan of the room, looking for the small white dog. It was nowhere to be seen.

"Did you lose something?" asked Lens.

"The dog," said Lucas. "He's . . . gone. Did you see him when you came in, Bess?"

She ignored his question and walked straight for the mirror. Instinctually, she clicked it open and smiled. "See, now, *this* is what I mean when I ask about a room that doesn't make sense."

"Maybe the dog is in there?" suggested Lens.

Bess turned on the first light in the dark passageway. "Only one way to find out."

Lucas followed her, calling out to the missing dog. "Here, boy! Here, boy!"

"You know, I've never seen a stray dog in Hounds Hollow," admitted Lens as they walked. "Then again, I've never seen a secret mirror door, either." He raised his camera and took a picture as they reached the main barn. The flash burst, shedding light over the black, wrought-iron gates and weathered wood that filled the room. The whine of the instant photo rang out in the heavy silence.

Lucas flipped the gas lamps on and the warm light spread over them with a hiss. The chained door had a small gap at the bottom where the dog must have squeezed through. "Oh man, I think he's gone."

Bess grabbed hold of the bars and tugged at them like a prisoner testing how strong the cell was. They didn't buckle at all. She let go and the bars let out a low-toned *brung* like a solid, metal harp. "Sorry about the pup," she said as she kept exploring. When she reached the end of the barn, Bess announced, "This isn't the room we're looking for. Next."

Lucas watched as she left the odd, hidden barn behind as carelessly as leaving a bathroom. "But wait, the dog . . ."

"We don't have time for that, Lucas," Bess's voice echoed from the passageway. "We're looking for what the beast is after, remember? Not some silly, lost mutt."

Lens clicked another photo and jogged over to Lucas. "She's kinda right, dude."

Lucas bent down and peeked under the barn doors, but there was no sign of the dog. He sat back on his knees and sighed. "Why us? Why do we need to find out what's going on? Why can't the police handle this?"

"Yeah, um, do *you* want to be the one to call the cops and tell them there's a ghostly beast wandering the woods of Hounds Hollow?" asked Lens. He reached down and helped Lucas up. "Now come on. There's got to be another room around here that's as off-putting as this barn."

Dusting the dirt off his pants, Lucas realized that he knew just the spot.

Quietly, they walked upstairs and down the hall with the large mirror at the end. The lights stayed on this time and Lucas watched his own reflection carefully, making sure it wasn't the ghost boy.

"Where are we going?" Bess huffed. "We passed like fifteen doors already without looking in the rooms."

"Shhh," Lucas whispered. "Please keep it down. If my parents hear us up here, we're toast."

Bess opened her mouth to say something, but then closed it and nodded. The action was so un-Bess that Lucas was slightly shocked.

Lens waved his hand in front of Lucas's face to bring him back. "Lead the way."

Lucas walked cautiously over the old, wood floors, managing to avoid any possible creaks. The others followed him to the room with the locked rolltop desk.

"Dude, this room is totally not what we're looking for," said Bess. She went over and tipped the books on the shelf as if she were looking for another secret passage. Nothing happened. "Congratulations, Lucas, you brought us to the most boring place in the house."

"I don't know, Bess," said Lens, studying the foxhunt photos on the wall. "These are pretty wild. Check it out. This is old-school photography."

As they admired the pictures, Lucas slipped over to the desk. He lifted the chain from around his neck and thumbed the tiny key he'd inherited. "Watch the door, will you?"

"For what?" asked Bess.

Lucas didn't answer. He didn't want to talk about the boy he'd seen and chased, in case it was just his imagination running away with him. That's what his mom liked to call his visions. "Just, like, for anything," he finished.

Then Lucas fit the key slowly into the rolltop's lock. Part of him was worried it would break or get stuck in there forever. There was no guarantee that it would match the desk, but Lucas felt deep in his gut that it had to. He turned the key and the latch gave way. A light but satisfying click sounded in the room. Bess and Lens moved next to him, looking on with interest.

Gently, Lucas rolled the arched cover of the desk open. The desktop was bare except for a single notebook. At the back of the desk, there were rows and rows of small drawers, each with a different number on them.

He opened the notebook first. The pages were yellow and old. Lucas could smell the musk of age rising with every turn. There were five words written in cursive at the top of each page: *Scout*, *Shadow*, *Dakota*, *Duke*, and *Casper*.

Bess read over his shoulder. "Are those names?"

"No idea," Lucas murmured. "Maybe?"

Underneath each of the names were indecipherable notes that had smudged over the years. The blue ink leaned right and was written almost in code or shorthand. The words that Lucas could make out didn't help him understand what the journal had been used for.

Feeding. Walking. Bitten. Muzzled.

He closed the book and handed it to Bess, then moved on to the drawers. The first one had a heavy, red ball inside. Lucas took it out and held it in his hand. It had a stripe on it and the surface was covered with rough, tiny nicks. He bounced it on the floor and called out to Lens. "Wanna play?"

Lucas gently tossed the ball, but Lens jumped back, acting like he'd been tossed a poisonous spider. The ball rolled to the corner of the room. "Come on, man. Not cool! This place is creepy enough, and I hate surprises."

"Well, now we're even for knocking me off my bike," said Lucas.

"Hey, I was saving you from Devil's Drop, Mr. X Games Extreme."

"Stop it, you two," said Bess as she set down the notebook. "This thing is useless. What's in the next drawer?"

Lucas opened it and found an old newspaper clipping. He unfolded it, feeling the brittle paper threaten to tear with every crinkly move. When he flattened it out on the table, the header read *Hounds Hollow Gazette.*

"Think your mom wrote this?" asked Lucas.

Lens pointed to the tattered edges of the brown paper. "No way. This looks so old I don't even think my mom was alive back then."

Lucas's eyes traveled down to the headline and the article underneath:

Fire at Sweetwater Manor

On Friday, a fire destroyed Sweetwater Manor. The cause is unknown, but James and Martha Sweetwater survived the blaze along with their son Silas. Local residents could see the inferno for miles, and the blaze almost spread to the neighboring woods. Luckily the volunteer fire brigade was able to contain the damage, saving the town and the countryside from the threat of wildfires. If not for their dedicated work, the danger to Hounds Hollow would have been unimaginable. Unfortunately for the Sweetwater family, this fire wasn't the first tragedy to strike, after

The article stopped there. Lucas flipped the paper over, trying to find the rest of the story, but the back was just an advertisement for baking flour. "After?" he asked. "After what?"

Bess shut another one of the small drawers with a *clack* that made Lucas flinch. "There's nothing here," she announced.

"Unless you think this is going to help solve the mystery." She held up a cream-colored, rubber clown and squeezed it. A surprisingly piercing squeak sounded from the toy. "Total waste of time. Where else can you check, Lucas? We need to find that control room."

"It's a big house, Bess," said Lucas. "We'll find it, but it's gonna take time."

Frustrated, Bess shook her head and walked to the window while Lucas refolded the article carefully, returned it to its original place, then slid the drawer shut with a quiet thud.

"Aw, jeez, what is this?" Lens sounded seriously creeped out. He reached into a drawer and pulled out a ratty, old stuffed animal. The fur was matted down in clumps, and one of its plastic eyes was missing. Lens tossed it to Lucas, who caught it and instantly wished he hadn't.

"Ha! *Now* we're even," snapped Lens.

"Gross, it smells like wet dog." Lucas put it back where it came from and sniffed his hands. "Oh, great, I smell like it."

Lens sniffed his hands, too, and gagged. The two friends laughed.

Lucas searched through the other drawers. Each one hid a single item. There was a knotted rope, a torn-up tennis ball, and some real bones with sharp teeth marks notched into the edges. One drawer made Lucas stop completely. He picked up a charred triangular object and showed it to Lens. "Is this dried mango?" he asked.

Lens's face screwed up as he jumped backward. "Nah, I've seen that before. It's a pig's ear."

Lucas threw it back in and wiped his hands against his shirt. "Why would Silas keep a pig's ear? And why lock it in a desk drawer?"

"Maybe it was a good luck pig," said Bess, and Lens cracked up.

"It's not funny." Lucas felt the back of his neck get hot. He pulled at his shirt collar and realized that he was sweating a little. "How do you know what it is, anyway, Lens?"

"They sell them at pet stores now." He grimaced at the thought. "They're by the front register, just this box of crispy pig's ears. I think dogs like to chew on them. So gross."

"Why's that any grosser than bacon?" asked Bess.

"I don't know," said Lens. "It just is."

Lucas tried another drawer, but it wouldn't open all the way. He pulled harder, but it kept its hold. Whatever was inside was packed tight. Lucas worked his finger into a thin opening at the top. The drawer suddenly clamped against him, pinching his finger, and Lucas had to wiggle it back out. He shook his hand and sucked in sharply, trying to chase away the sudden bite of pain.

"Mime mo-kay," Lucas said through his gritted teeth. He put his finger in his mouth and bit at the sides of it, like he was forming it back into its normal finger shape. "What are you hiding in there, Silas?"

Leaving the stubborn drawer, Lucas opened the last one. There was an oddly shaped whistle inside. Its chain rattled as he lifted it out of the desk. Instinctually, Lucas put the whistle to his mouth and blew softly. There wasn't any noise. He tried again, harder this time, but the whistle still didn't work. "Must be broken."

Bess reached for the whistle. "It's for dogs." She blew into it as hard as she could. Lucas flinched, expecting a loud shriek, but only a light wheeze came out of the tiny whistle.

"Told you it was broken," Lucas said.

"Oh, it works, but only for dogs," Bess explained. "See, the sound is too high for humans to hear, but to dogs it's really loud."

"Cool." Lucas smiled nervously and wondered if the small stray dog might hear the noise and start barking.

Bess took the whistle and put the chain around Lucas's neck like it was an Olympic medal. "Listen, this room is a bust, but I'm awarding you a dog whistle for participation. Now, is there another place we can check?"

"Yeah, like one that isn't so hot?" asked Lens. Beads of sweat were forming on his brow as he tried to close the window. The evening heat was suddenly sweltering.

"That window doesn't close," said Lucas as he went to grab the red ball that had rolled across the floor. "Guys, I think Silas might have been a big dog person. The whistle, the notebook, all these toys. I mean, it's weird to lock this stuff up, but I'd better put everything back the way we found it, just in case Eartha comes snooping. There are rules in this house, after all." Lucas leaned over to get the ball, and the whistle around his neck dangled in front of him. Without thinking, he put the whistle in his mouth and breathed through it while he reset the desk.

Then he heard a chilling howl echo from the world outside. Lucas dropped the red ball and froze with the whistle clamped between his teeth. He'd heard that howl—that baleful howl that defied nature itself—too many times before in his nightmares. "What was that?" he whispered.

"Y'all . . ." Bess pointed out the window. Her tan skin looked pale white in the rising moonlight, and her breathing became quick and shallow. "We're not alone."

CHAPTER 18

A dull, dark glow shifted through the forest. The idea that a shadow could be luminous confused Lucas's mind. He blinked and blinked again, thinking that each time he opened his eyes, the glowing shadow would fade away, like a mirage. But with each blink, he realized that it was real. The shadow moved quickly, then paused, as if it were considering where to run next. And then . . . it howled.

"The beast," Bess said in a swallowed whisper.

"No way." The dog whistle fell from Lucas's mouth. He'd *maybe* seen the beast in Lens's pictures. He'd *maybe* even seen the beast hit his mom's car. But looking out the window from his house, Lucas never imagined that the beast could be so real. He rubbed his eyes and began to panic that he was imagining things again. Lucas grabbed his inhaler and breathed deeply. "No. There's a perfectly normal answer here. Maybe that's a hunter with a lantern and he's tracking a deer. Maybe the pictures you took weren't the beast. Have you ever stopped to consider that it might *not* be a monster haunting us? There's always a good explanation for spooky legends. It's, like, a wolverine or a skunk."

But as soon as he said those words, Lucas didn't believe them. The beast emerged from a clearing and its two red eyes gazed directly at the house. For a second, Lucas thought it might even have seen him.

"We gotta go," said Bess.

Lucas stood stone still. "I like that idea," he said without moving his lips. He dared not do anything that might risk catching the beast's attention.

"Wow, I really didn't think you'd see it my way," said Bess as she climbed out the window onto the tree branch. "I thought we'd need Silas's cameras to spot the beast, but there he is, right now. Let's go!"

She shimmied down the tree and landed on the ground before Lucas realized what was happening. "Wait, what?!" he gasped.

Lens pushed past him onto the tree, too. "Come on, Lucas. We need your help."

"*My* help?" Lucas repeated. "Are you out of your minds?"

Lens nodded and jumped from branch to branch until he was next to Bess on the ground. Then he called back up, "Okay, but good luck telling your parents what happened if we go missing, 'cause they'll have to explain it to our parents."

"And to the police," said Bess with a smile that reminded Lucas of the first time he met her—the smile that apparently said *This person will chase after demonic beasts.* Instantly she pulled two glow sticks out of her pocket and snapped them. A green light came to life as she handed one to Lens. "You moved here for a reason, right, Lucas?"

Lucas leaned out the window. "Yeah, to breathe easy and stay alive. Please don't do this," he begged. "Can't we play video games or Dungeons and Dragons? Normal stuff where the monsters aren't real?"

Instead of answering, Bess and Lens took off running, chasing after the glowing shadow. Lucas could see the beast make odd shifts. Bolting forward, then stopping. Jolting to the left, then stopping again, as if it were tracking something that Lucas couldn't see. The heat in the room was suddenly suffocating. Wiping the sweat from his eyes, Lucas went to grab the ball he'd dropped to put back in the rolltop desk, but it was gone.

"Where in the world . . . ?" Lucas mumbled, then he locked the desk. Sure, his only two friends in Hounds Hollow were going to be eaten by an unknown animal, but Lucas still didn't want anyone else snooping around the desk. Silas had given him the key for a reason, so Lucas tucked it and the whistle into his shirt, then looked out the window. The beast was gone, but he could still see two glow sticks racing through the woods.

"This is stupid," Lucas told himself, but he still stepped out onto the branch. They didn't have trees like this in the city. He kept saying "This is stupid" over and over again as he made his way down the tree slowly. Those were the only three words he was capable of stringing together. The tree bark scraped against his arms as he slid from branch to branch. Once on solid ground, Lucas raced after his friends.

The forest was impenetrably dark under the canopy of leaves. The moon and stars above disappeared, replaced by shifting shadows that danced on top of him.

"This is stupid," he repeated under his breath as he ran, searching for the green glow sticks. The trees moved closer and Lucas tripped over the wild roots.

As the dark land shifted, Lucas recognized exactly where he was heading: straight for the Sweetwater cemetery. The silhouettes of statues stood black in the clearing as the moon cast its light over the unsettling scene. Lucas slowed down and whispered for the others. "Bess? Lens?"

Suddenly a hand reached out and yanked Lucas into the bushes. Bess covered his mouth and made her eyes so wide that he could see her pupils, like tiny islands in a sea of white.

"Listen up, city kid," she whispered. "When you go to the zoo, do you jump in the tiger cage and try to pet it?"

Lucas shoved her hand away and adjusted his necklaces. "What? No, that'd be stupid."

"Well, so is calling out when you've seen the beast!" Bess said. "This isn't a nature hike, and we're not leaf peeping, Lucas. Staying hidden is the first rule to staying alive."

"But you're the ones who jumped out of a window to chase it!" Lucas complained.

"First of all, we didn't jump, we climbed down a tree," said Lens as he shuffled next to them. "Jeez, dramatic much? Second, we didn't walk up and introduce ourselves to the beast like you almost did."

"The beast is gone," said Lucas. "I saw it disappear."

Bess shook her head. "It always comes back."

Lucas shuddered. He'd seen the beast vanish into the woods. He'd assumed that the coast was clear and that he was simply going to get his friends so that he wouldn't have to explain to his parents why they weren't in the house anymore. But now, Lucas was in way bigger trouble.

"What's our plan, then?" Lucas asked. He tried on his bravest voice, but even he could hear it crack.

Lens held up his camera and pointed to the flash. "Here's what we know. The flash doesn't bother the beast. He never even flinches when one goes off."

"We're working on a theory that the beast can't sense light," said Bess.

"Or maybe it can't even see at all," added Lens.

"So what, it just roams through the forest bumping into trees?" asked Lucas. "I mean, there's got to be an answer for what this thing is. Maybe the beast is an animal that people thought was extinct, but it's the last of its kind and we should probably just leave it alone to live out the rest of its days in peace?"

Bess huffed. "There's only one way to find out."

Lucas was getting tired of hearing her say that. Nothing good ever came of it.

They stayed low in the bushes as the moon cast a soft haze on the forest. A thick fog rolled in. Thin wisps like tendrils reached out of the trees and swirled around the graveyard statues. The air sizzled with a heat that hadn't been there before. It reminded Lucas of the hissing radiators in his old apartment when the high temperatures swallowed him whole. It was like being caught in a furnace, but there wasn't a single flame in sight.

Leaning forward, Lucas peered through the bushes. A shadow moved near the woods, and the image made him hold his breath. The animal, standing on four legs, had a gray glow shining around it. The beast was more like a smudge of an animal brought to life. One look at this creature dispelled Lucas's hopes that it was really just another legend. This beast was very, very real. Fiery red eyes darted back and forth, searching either to make sure the coast was clear or to find what was hiding in the night. Lucas silently prayed it wasn't looking for him.

With a quick pounce, the beast shuddered into the cemetery of statues. Watching it move made Lucas sick to his stomach. The beast walked in jarring, ragged angles. It was like looking at a broken mirror—Lucas saw one reflection from millions of shattered points of view. It gave him vertigo and car sickness all at once.

The beast faced only one of the family plots. The statue watching over this grave was unlike the others. It wasn't a winged angel sent down from heaven but the statue of a man in a robe surrounded by animals. A deer, a lamb, a dog, and birds—all made of stone—huddled around the character with a halo of hair chiseled around his stone head.

"This is crazy," Bess whispered. "The beast has never stood still!"

Lens's camera flashed and Lucas almost jumped out of his skin. "A little warning next time!" he hissed.

Lens shifted closer to get more pictures. With every flash, Lucas started to see a shape beneath the pulsing dark smudge. The high-pitched whine of Lens's camera was loud, but the beast didn't react. Instead, it remained in the circle of graves, like an animal waiting for its owner to return.

"I'm going in," whispered Bess.

"Don't . . . ," Lucas pleaded, but she was already up and running to the next bush. Lucas rolled his eyes and finished his thought. ". . . do anything dumb."

A trail of pictures lay in the dirt. Lens let them fall, keeping his eyes targeted on the beast.

"Stop it," begged Lucas. "It sees us. It knows we're here."

"Nah, we're good," whispered Lens as he gave Lucas a thumbs-up.

Bess was ahead of them and moving closer to the dark shadow. As she stepped forward, a branch rustled against her arm. It made a natural sound, like an animal scurrying to safety. Lucas steadied his breath and studied the forest around him. He pressed his fingers into the dirt and dug his feet into the ground. Lucas had walked directly into his recurring nightmare. He'd never turned around in his dreams to see what was chasing him, but now, he was staring right at it and hoping maybe the beast wouldn't notice. *Please bolt away*, he thought. *Please, beast, bolt away anywhere but here.*

Suddenly the eerie serenity of the beast cracked. Without moving its body, the beast's head swiveled around like a demon and snarled. The low growl rumbled through the graveyard, and Lucas felt it bubble up from the ground below him. The sound was unnatural and unsettling. Lucas was about to spring forward, but it was too late.

The beast pounced toward Bess like a living video glitch, moving in fast-forward and rewind at the same time.

Bess didn't scream. She didn't even flinch. She held as still as one of the graveyard statues. The beast circled her curiously, its red eyes like heavy embers.

Lens made the next move, clicking a strobe effect on his camera. The night became a burst of light that held the ghastly beast in a world of stop-motion horror.

FLASH. The beast rose up on its hind legs and laid a paw on Bess's shoulder. Lucas saw real terror in her eyes.

FLASH. The beast's head turned, looking directly at Lens, and dropped back on all fours. Bess stood alone in the forest and screamed, "Run!"

FLASH. The beast was running toward Lens! Lucas leapt out and blew the dog whistle.

FLASH. The beast froze and two smudged ears lifted at the top of its ashen skull. It roared at the noise with a new rage.

FLASH. The gray shadow turned to red flames rising off its body. Lucas stumbled backward and blew into the dog whistle again.

FLASH. A smaller, white creature appeared in front of the beast. It howled and snarled, digging its tiny paws into the earth. The fiery beast and the new creature paced around each other.

FLASH. Bess and Lens dragged Lucas into the dead patch of grass on the other side of the cemetery. They slumped down, once inside the stone border.

FLASH. The beast lurched closer toward the kids, but stopped at the edge of the dead grass. The small white creature pounced on the beast and bit into its neck, making the beast howl.

FLASH. The small white creature scrambled into the forest as the beast chased after it.

FLASH. The world was as normal as if nothing had ever happened except for—

FLASH.

Lens fumbled with his camera and turned off the strobe light. The forest went dark again. Bess stood up in the dead grass. She looked like a zombie just risen from the grave. Lucas was gasping and wrestled to find his inhaler, the bright lights from the strobe still burning in his eyes. Pulling his pockets inside out, Lucas drew in the medicine until his breathing steadied.

Lens rubbed his forehead and gave Lucas a wide-eyed stare. "What just happened?"

"I'll tell you what happened," said Lucas between deep breaths. "You both have a death wish! Normal kids don't come out to a graveyard at night to take pictures of some crazy, haunted beast that may or may not want to rip them apart!"

Bess's face glowed in the now-dark night. She breathed in short, quick breaths, and still held her arms up in a defensive stance, as if she was trying force the beast away.

"Bess!" Lens gently pushed her hands down. "You're shaking. Are you okay? Did it hurt you?"

"I'm fine," she said slowly, as if she were trying to convince herself. "Did you get pictures?"

"Pictures? We gotta get out of here!" urged Lucas. "If it weren't for that other animal, we'd be beast chow. Let's go. That thing's gonna come back."

"I'm counting on it," said Bess. Her voice turned solid as a rock. "Wanna do this again tomorrow? Same time?"

Lucas shook his head and started back toward his house. "I'm outta here."

"Wait!" It was Lens who spoke up. "Lucas, we've been hunting the beast for months, and we've only seen it once or twice. You move in and our sightings are suddenly off the charts."

Lucas pointed at him angrily. "You say that like it's a good thing."

"No, it's just that if you hadn't been here . . ." Lens paused. "If you hadn't acted so fast, then Bess . . ." He didn't finish the sentence, but Lucas knew what he was going to say.

Bess stood still, refusing to look at either boy.

A rustle in the forest broke the silence and set the three of them on edge. Lucas was about to run to the house, when Eartha Dobbs shuffled out of the darkness with a lantern.

"This ain't no playground," she announced. "This here is a place to be respected. And I know that three kids your age at this time of night ain't up to doing no respecting."

"We were just leaving, ma'am," said Bess.

"I'm sure you were, missy." Eartha gave Bess a slow stare. "Your mom will be wondering where y'all are. Best head home now."

As they walked away, Lens turned and asked, "See you tomorrow, Lucas?"

Every muscle in his body said no, but Lucas's mouth had a mind of its own. "Maybe."

Sure, Lucas had just almost been shredded by a creature with fangs and claws, but he realized that life in Hounds Hollow would be really lonely without his bizarre new friends.

Lens nodded as he and Bess headed down the hill back toward Bess's house.

"You, too, mister," said Eartha. "Do your parents even know you're out in this mess? They don't strike me as the let-my-child-go-running-around-at-night-in-the-wilderness type of parents."

"They're not," agreed Lucas.

As they walked back, Lucas thought about the small white creature that challenged the beast. He knew he'd seen it before. It looked exactly like a tiny white mutt. And that made Lucas smile.

"I don't know why you're grinning, boy," said Eartha. "Caught you in the middle of a graveyard—on a grave, no less. What were y'all doing up here anyway?"

Lucas wiped the smile off his face. "Nothing really. Just kid stuff."

CHAPTER 19

Sleep was the last thing on Lucas's mind as he tossed and turned in bed. He played the night over and over in his mind. Lucas wasn't sure which freaked him out more: the beast or Bess's willingness to become its bait. He stared at the ceiling, listening to the sound of Silas's old house creak and moan alongside the hiss of his special mask. The house had made noises every night since he'd arrived. This time, though, Lucas kept imagining that the sounds were coming from something inside the house and not from the house itself.

Unable to close his eyes without seeing the beast, Lucas pulled back the covers and eased out of bed so as not to disturb Lucky. The cat gave him a tired glare, then settled back in.

He left the mask running on the side table, then picked up the key and the dog whistle.

Walking through the house at night wasn't as frightening as Lucas thought it would be. The dark furniture just looked like furniture. The corners hid nothing behind them. If anything, the house that made him so uneasy before had grown on him. He couldn't put his finger on why, but tonight, Lucas felt safe inside these halls.

Upstairs he flipped on the light in the study and the room was just as he had left it. Lucas unlocked the desk and picked up the journal. Scout, Shadow, Dakota, Duke, and Casper. They did sound like names. Then Lucas opened one of the small drawers again and pulled out the pig's ear.

"Dogs. I was right," Lucas mumbled as he went back to the journal. In every column, there were notes on each animal. *Fed. Walked. Playtime. Cleaned stall.* But under one entry, there was a longer paragraph. Running his finger under the faint writing, he read it out loud to the empty room.

Weeks since A. left and Shadow is not doing well. Tried to walk today, but body and spirit are not right yet. Still suffering. Shadow lingers near A.'s room. We should not have let them into the house, but empty halls can play tricks on a mind. Sometimes even I can still hear A. Shadow does, too, I think. Brought him to the plot the night after to pay respects. May have been a mistake. Shadow's stolen out into the night ever since. Can't find how he's escaping, but he's always in the same place. Right by A. The other animals have tried to help, but Shadow has broken from the pack. I have a plan that could help, but it's not natural. And it's dangerous. Heaven help me if I'm wrong.

This was the final entry in the book. Lucas set it back down on the desk and tried the stuck drawer again. This time, he used the small key instead of his finger to wedge down whatever was blocking the drawer. It took a few tries, but finally gave way and slid out.

A stack of photographs tumbled over the lip, sliding into Lucas's hands and onto the desk. Lucas picked up the first one. It was a photo of Silas as a young boy. He looked eerily familiar in a way that sent a shiver down Lucas's back. He was suddenly very aware that another kid had lived his entire life in this same house. Did that mean Lucas was going to turn into Silas one day?

In the picture, Silas hugged his arms around a Rottweiler's neck, and the dog happily had its mouth open with its tongue hanging goofily off to the side.

The next photo was of a husky with black fur. Its piercing crystal eyes glowed in the black-and-white picture. "Hey, you must be Shadow," Lucas said. "That's what I would have called you."

In picture after picture, the dogs and Silas seemed so happy together. The sight put Lucas at ease; the joy in those photos was infectious. There had been love in this house. But at the same time, the pictures carried a loss with them. Silas had locked them away for a reason.

A cool breeze from the open window blew more of the pictures onto the floor. Lucas bent over to pick them up as a wave of exhaustion finally crashed over him. Each blink became longer and longer, until he was sure the next time he shut his eyes, he'd be asleep. Lucas carried the pictures with him. He wasn't sure how they played into the mystery of Hounds Hollow, but he was developing a theory.

He gazed out the window again. The night was clear. Moonlight cast the forest in its otherworldly light. Lucas searched the trees for the beast's glowing red eyes, but the woods were calm and empty. The wind made the branches sound like the ocean.

With heavy lids, Lucas sleepwalked back to his room and was dreaming before his head hit the pillow. He dreamed the photographs were alive and heard the sound of Silas's laughter as his distant relative ran back and forth with dogs. Silas held a ball high above them and hurled it out the front door. Suddenly their paws pitter-pattered on the wood floor as they scrambled after it. The simple act repeated itself over and over again in Lucas's dreams until he felt a wet, rough tongue lick him right on the nose.

The slobber was real. Lucas could smell the awful breath of the dogs as their tongues lapped his cheeks. He pushed them away, but the dogs kept joyfully nuzzling and licking him. Then, from behind his dreams, a loud, snapping bark ripped through everything. The dogs whimpered and darted back, cowering in fear. Lucas felt a different steaming breath huff down his neck as he jolted awake.

The bedroom was silent. Lucas expected to find the beast waiting for him, but he was wrong. It was just a dream. Stunned, Lucas pulled off his mask and pressed his palms to his face. When he pulled them away, wet drool dripped from his hands like he'd been slimed.

Then Lucas felt something bound off his bed and heard the clicking of claws leaving the room.

He jolted up, thinking it might be the cat, but Lucky was curled up, quietly sleeping, full of his own cat dreams. Morning light poured through the window.

"Just a dream," Lucas told himself as he wiped his face off with his pillow. When he was finished, he pulled back, horrified. "Gah! That's a lot of drool. Stupid mask. I must have put it on wrong last night."

He turned off the CPAP machine and stretched. Underneath the blankets, grit and dirt rubbed against Lucas's legs like tiny, annoying bugs. He kicked off the covers, but still didn't manage to wake up Lucky. Running his hands down the sheets, black and brown specks flicked off the bed and onto the floor. Lucas shrugged the mess off as his own dirt and grime from the previous night. The forest, after all, was not a clean place.

After a warm shower, Lucas dressed, made the bed, and started a plan for the day. First he was going to find the little white dog. If it had stood up to the beast, then it probably needed help.

Next, Lucas wanted to explore more of Sweetwater Manor. Maybe Silas had left other clues about the beast. Maybe Lucas could even find the control room for all of Silas's cameras. Maybe there was even video footage from the night before.

As Lucas walked into the front hallway, though, he realized his morning plans would have to wait. Lens stood next to

Lucas's mother, waiting for him. He gave Lucas a slow wave and nodded his head as if he was trying to send a signal.

"You didn't tell me that you were going out today, Lucas," Mom said.

"Oh, yeah, uh, I totally forgot," Lucas said, catching on in time. "We had a—"

"Bike ride," Lens finished, which was good because Lucas had no idea what crazy excuse he might have come up with on his own.

"Yeah, Lens wanted to show me . . . the thing with the . . . thing." Lucas watched as Lens rolled his eyes.

Mom gave a confused smile. "The thing . . . with the thing?" she asked.

Lens swooped in to help. "I told Lucas that I'd take him into town to meet a few other kids. You know, since he's new, it seemed like a good idea."

"I love that, Deshaun." Mom clapped her hands and leaned toward Lucas. He'd seen her act this way before, but it was usually in front of his teachers when they met at a parent-teacher conference. "Thank you so much for helping Lucas with the transition."

"Yes, Lens. Thank you so much for thinking of little old me," Lucas said through a gritted smile. "Before we get this party started, can I talk to you outside?"

"Sure." Lens waited as Lucas led the way onto the porch. The two of them sat on the front steps. Lucas waved to his mom as she peeked through the window and gave him a thumbs-up.

Once she was gone, his mood shifted. "What in the world are you doing showing your face around here again?"

"It's good to see you, too," said Lens, who acted as if nothing strange or monumental had gone down between them last night. "And you're wrong about Bess."

"Wrong?" Lucas laughed. "Okay, tell me, which part do I have wrong? That she wants to risk her life being a ghost hunter? Or that she doesn't care who she puts in danger to get what she wants?"

"She cares," said Lens. "Trust me. She cares. She's just after something bigger than the beast."

"What could be *bigger* than the beast?" asked Lucas. "Especially if it means risking her life?"

Lens looked over his shoulder to make sure they were alone. "Look. Last year, Bess's dad went missing. She's convinced that the beast took him."

Lucas swallowed. He wasn't sure how to say what he wanted to say without being rude. "Actually, I heard a different story. Gale from the town store told us that Bess's dad left . . . on purpose."

Lens shook his head. "Gale said that? Hah! Listen, you can't believe a word that old crow squawks. She's always in everyone's business."

"So you think Bess is right?" asked Lucas. "That the beast took her father? What would it do with him other than . . ." Again he trailed off, not wanting to think about the answer.

"I don't know," Lens admitted. "But Bess thinks the beast is connected to this house, and I do, too. I don't know how or why, but it can't be a coincidence that most pictures of the beast are from the cameras I hid here."

Lucas thought back to the old photos from the desk. "Speaking of pictures, I did find something that you should see."

The two friends went to Lucas's bedroom. Lucky was lying in bed again. The cat stretched out its front paws before leaping to the floor and circling Lens, sniffing his legs.

Lucas handed over the pictures. "Look, these used to belong to Silas. Do you think they're connected to the beast?"

Handling the photos carefully, Lens looked through them for any clues. He lifted some up to the light. "Whoa, these are crazy old, but the quality has lasted. They must have been taken with a pretty good camera. What's with the dogs?"

Lucas took out the notebook and pointed to a photo with the boy in it. "See, that's Silas. I think that he used to take care of stray dogs. If you look in this journal, there are lists for dog care. Walking. Feeding. See?" He flipped through the pages, pointing out the repetitive notes.

"You know what's weird about these pictures?" asked Lens. "Silas is in a lot of them."

"So, that doesn't seem weird," said Lucas.

"Yeah, but this is way before selfies. And if he's in so many of these shots, then *who's* taking the pictures?" Lens stopped at one of the photos that showed Silas. The black-and-white boy was squinting and shading his eyes with his hand, almost like he was saluting. Lens pointed to the bottom of the picture, where a long, thin shadow stretched into the frame. "Someone took these pictures. Here's the proof."

Another shudder went down Lucas's spine. He'd been so focused on what was in the photos that he hadn't thought about who was taking them. "It must have been his parents, right?"

"No way," said Lens. He spread the pictures out on the bed. "Look at the angles of each shot. These pictures were taken by someone short—maybe even another kid."

But Lucas wasn't listening. His mind was on another clue they'd found inside the locked desk. "Hey, your mom runs the paper. Do you think she has copies of every issue ever printed?"

"Knowing my mom, I bet she does," said Lens. "Why?"

"That article we found, it was about the fire that burned down this house. But it's just the first page. There's got to be more to the story!"

Lens smiled. "That's brilliant! Feel like taking a trip into town?"

"Yeah, my mom could drive us," said Lucas.

"No," said Lens. "You've got your bike, right?"

"Sure," Lucas said with a smile. "Let's go for a ride."

CHAPTER 20

Riding a bike next to a galloping horse was something Lucas never imagined he'd do, yet there he was, riding his bike next to Lens and his horse. The dirt road thundered and erupted in a cloud of dust next to him with every hoofbeat.

"Bolt's not an ironic horse name, huh?" Lucas hollered through his BMX bike helmet. His legs burned as he pedaled hard to keep up with Lens.

"Nope!" Lens leaned in closer to Bolt and pulled ahead of Lucas.

They traveled a back path that was hidden away from the main road. When they'd started riding, Lucas was worried that they might come across the beast again. But with trees crowding the way and roots pushing up through the dirt, Lucas spent most of the ride trying not to crash.

Taking the path was a surprisingly faster way to town because it cut a straight line through the forest instead of following the winding, paved roads. Lens and Bolt were trotting down Main Street in no time. Lucas wobbled on his bike just behind them.

Lens pulled up to the hitching post in front of the Dog Ear bookshop and slid off his horse. A car stopped alongside him and rolled down the passenger's-side window. Gale from the local general store called out, "Deshaun Lindsay! What have I told you about riding that horse in town?"

"Good morning, Ms. Gale," said Lens as he tied Bolt up to the hitching post.

"I will take this to the council again," Gale threatened. "It's not normal."

Lens exhaled deeply. "Neither is having hitching posts in front of your stores. I've told you, Bolt isn't hurting anyone, and my mom is fine with the way I ride."

"Well, *I'm* not fine with it," snapped Gale. "I'm not fine with it at all. And if you think you can ride your horse over to our end-of-summer barbecue, I'll give you and your little friends the boot."

Lens smiled but didn't look at the older woman. Instead he patted Bolt's neck and the horse whinnied. "No horses at the barbecue, Ms. Gale. I hear you."

Lucas cruised to a stop with his thin breath wheezing through his helmet. The bike almost fell over as he was getting off, but Lucas held it upright. He reached instinctually for his inhaler, but decided to give it a second to see if he could catch his breath without the medicine.

"What's wrong with your friend?" Ms. Gale complained. "Is that the Trainer boy from Sweetwater Manor? Are you sick or something? Can't barely stand up. Or have y'all been—"

"He's fine, Ms. Gale," said Lens, who came to Lucas's rescue and helped him get off the bike. "We'll see you at the picnic."

"Without that horse!" Gale yelled as she drove away.

Lucas leaned his bike against the post. As he steadied his breathing, he pulled off his helmet. "What was that all about?"

"Oh, that's just Ms. Gale," explained Lens. "She likes life to be nice and orderly, which sounds awful and boring to me."

"Yeah," Lucas said. "She was nice and kinda mean at the same time."

Lens snapped his fingers and pointed. "Yes! Exactly! That's her style. Now come on in before she comes back."

In front of the store, Lucas noticed a corkboard filled with pictures of people. Some were having picnics with their family, some were at the lake, some were out hunting, and some looked like mug shots from the police. Lucas wasn't sure why, but even though the pictures seemed normal, they made him feel nervous. "Did you take these?"

"Nah." Lens seemed uncomfortable. "These are the people who've gone missing from town. My mom thought that maybe if she posted pictures, someone might recognize them."

"Whoa," said Lucas. "I didn't know. That seems like a lot of people."

"Yeah" was all Lens said.

In the photographs, most people were smiling. Suddenly a sense of dread fell over Lucas. These people lived in houses. They had families. They were alive once . . . and maybe they still were, but for their families, it was like they'd walked out of the picture frame and disappeared.

Lens motioned for Lucas to follow him and pushed the front door open. A small bell chimed. "Mom, it's me."

The Dog Ear was crowded with books. Handwritten notes hung under the shelves marking each section: poetry, history, fiction, literature, mystery, horror. Every stack of books had another stack of books directly behind it. Lucas felt at home instantly. The narrow aisles, the closeness of the room . . . it was like he was back in the city.

Behind the counter in the back of the store, a woman was reading. Her short, braided hair bounced as she looked up and smiled. "Hi, Deshaun. Did I hear Gale's motormouth running outside?"

"Yes, ma'am." Lens motioned behind him with a nod of his head. "But that's not why we're here."

"We?" asked Mrs. Lindsay. "Oh, you must be Lucas! Deshaun has told me all about you. I feel like we already know each other."

"Nice to meet you, too, Mrs. Lindsay," said Lucas.

"Mom, we need to look up some old issues of the *Hounds Hollow Gazette*," said Lens. "Can you help?"

"Of course," she said. "What are you looking for?"

After a brief pause, Lucas spoke up. "I'm hoping to find some history about Silas and our house."

"Well, then, you've come to the right place." She pulled out a laptop computer and opened a search window. Her long fingers danced over the keyboard as she continued. "Everyone who knows me knows that I love history."

Mrs. Lindsay's hands flashed in front of the screen like a magician as a program opened up. It read "*Hounds Hollow Gazette* Archive" across the top. "This was one of my favorite projects. I even worked with the local librarian to collect all of the past issues in one place. Do you know the date you're looking for?"

Lucas closed his eyes and tried to picture the folded, old paper in his mind. "August 12, but I don't know the year." His face fell. "I'm sorry."

"It's fine!" she cheered. "I developed this to be foolproof." Mrs. Lindsay typed in *August 12 Silas Sweetwater.*

One entry flashed with that date on the screen. "Here you go, Lucas. You do the honors and I'll leave you both to your research." Then Lens's mom walked to the front of the store and started shifting books in the rows so that the spines were all even and flush on the shelves.

Lucas moved the cursor with the trackpad until it locked onto the link and clicked it. Almost instantly a digitized article appeared—the very same front page as the newspaper from the rolltop desk. The two friends read the article together.

Fire at Sweetwater Manor

On Friday, a fire destroyed Sweetwater Manor. The cause is unknown, but James and Martha Sweetwater survived the blaze along with their son Silas. Local residents could see the inferno for miles, and the blaze almost spread to the neighboring woods. Luckily the volunteer fire brigade was able to contain the damage, saving the town and the countryside from the threat of wildfires. If not for their dedicated work, the danger to Hounds Hollow would have been unimaginable. Unfortunately for the Sweetwater family, this fire wasn't the first tragedy to strike, after

Lucas scrolled down the page in search of the next passage. There were ads for toothpaste, medicines, and tonics he'd never heard of, each one promising longer, healthier lives. They reminded him of the pop-up ads he always saw online, usually about zit cream.

"There it is," said Lens.

their son Abel died the week prior.

Abel, Lucas thought. *That must be A. from the notebook!*

"Whoa, Silas had a brother?" Lens pointed to the screen and continued reading.

The Sweetwater brothers were known in town as the hound collectors. For years, Silas and Abel took in stray dogs and nursed them back to health. Unfortunately the animals under their care did not survive the fire. Neither did the house. When reached for a comment, the Sweetwater family vowed to rebuild their home and their life as best they could. The authorities have ruled out foul play and claim that the fire started due to a gas leak within the home.

"What happened to Abel?" asked Lucas. He felt a pain in his chest. "What else does it say?"

"That's it," said Lens. "That's the end of the article. Poor Silas. He lost his brother, then he lost his house."

Lucas's stomach turned at the thought of the notebook and the photos he'd found. His eyes itched as he blinked. "He lost his dogs, too."

"I know," Lens whispered. "What now?"

Lucas clicked on the search bar again and typed *Abel Sweetwater*. Several links appeared. The first article was about the brothers beginning their animal shelter. It started with two dogs, Scout and Shadow, both found wandering through

Hounds Hollow and picking through the town's gardens. The sheriff had wanted to put the animals down, but Silas and Abel promised to take care of them. After that, whenever someone in town found another stray, they delivered it to Sweetwater Manor.

He exited the article and clicked the next link, "The Sweetwater Brothers Grow Their Hound Pound."

"Hmm, they sure loved their stray dog news," said Lens.

That made Lucas laugh. It was only a snort, but it felt good, like his sadness was slightly diffused. He closed the article and looked to the next link.

"Sweetwater Brother Dies."

The headline winded Lucas worse than the bike ride into town.

Abel Sweetwater has passed away as a result of tuberculosis. He was twelve years old. The famously kind and loving Abel had always been a local character. Best known as one-half of the Hound Pound, Abel was happiest at home with his brother, Silas, and their pack of stray dogs. During his final days, though, much of the person Abel had been began to change, according to friends and family. As the sickness took hold, Abel's physical appearance altered. He became thin and emaciated, and lost pigment in his eyes and hair.

"Hey, Mom, what's it mean when someone loses the pigment in their eyes and hair?" asked Lens.

"Color, dear," said his mom. "It means that a person's hair and eyes turned white."

Lucas grabbed his inhaler and took a deep breath.

"You okay?" Lens asked.

"Yeah," said Lucas. "It's just that tuberculosis is what the doctors thought I had at first. They put me in quarantine and wouldn't even let me near my parents. Turns out I didn't have it, but it was scary, like being in jail."

"That's crazy," snapped Lens.

Lucas nodded. "Yeah, tuberculosis is no joke. It used to be called consumption a long time ago because if someone had it, they seemed fine on the outside, but their insides would break down. Then they'd stop eating and lose so much weight that it looked like they were consuming themselves. In fact, some towns thought that consumption victims were actually vampires or that they were cursed."

"No way!" Lens's jaw dropped. "For real?"

"Yeah," Lucas continued. "It's highly contagious, so people who had it were usually separated from everyone else around them . . . and probably died alone."

"You know a lot about this, huh?" asked Lens.

Lucas didn't answer. Instead of reliving every doctor's

diagnosis, he scrolled through the article about Abel. A picture appeared and Lucas fell out of his chair.

"Are you okay?" asked Mrs. Lindsay as she rushed to help him back up.

"Yes, thanks. Don't know what happened," he said quickly. Then Lucas snapped the laptop closed and backed away from Lens and his mother. "Sorry about that, Mrs. Lindsay, but thank you for your help. I think we've learned enough about my family for one day."

"You're welcome, Lucas. Come back if you need help with anything else."

She put her hand on Lucas's shoulder, which made him flinch; it reminded him of how the doctors used to treat him just before another test. Lucas walked to the front door, tracing his fingers across the book spines until one fell off the shelf. "Sorry, Mrs. Lindsay!"

"That's no problem." She smiled. "It's easy enough to pick up."

Lucas grabbed it from the floor and turned the book over in his hand. "Hey, it's *Goosebumps*," he said, trying to play it cool. "I loved these stories."

"Not me," whispered Lens. "I've got enough scary in my life with a certain you-know-what."

"Wow, so you like haunted stories?" Mrs. Lindsay asked.

"More like ghost histories, I guess." Lucas's mind was racing. Reading the articles about his distant family gave Lucas another keyhole into the strange happenings in Hounds Hollow. The more he peered through, the more seemingly random events were coming into focus.

"Well, then take the *Goosebumps* book, Lucas," offered Mrs. Lindsay. "It's on the house."

"Oh no, I couldn't," Lucas said, but Lens insisted.

"Just take the book, man. If you don't, I'm going to have to dust it for eternity."

Lucas relented and smiled. "Okay, thank you."

Once they were outside, Lens turned to Lucas. "What was *that* all about? You seemed legit spooked at something."

"There was a picture of Abel Sweetwater," said Lucas as he climbed on his bike. "And I've seen him before."

CHAPTER 21

Bess was sitting by the side of the road with her basketball. As they approached, Lucas realized how ridiculous they must have looked—Lucas on his bike, wearing an outdated helmet, and Lens riding horseback with a Polaroid camera slung over his shoulder. But if they did look outrageous, it didn't faze Bess. Lucas had a feeling that nothing would.

She rolled the basketball back and forth from her right hand to her left hand. "I suppose you're here to apologize?"

"No," said Lucas. "I stand by my theory that you're crazy. But crazy is what we need right now." He jumped off his bike and sat next to her. "Do you believe in ghosts?"

"No," said Bess.

Lucas nodded. "Then what do you think the beast is?"

Bess raised an eyebrow. "You think the beast is a ghost?" The sound of the basketball rolling on the dirt echoed in the afternoon. "You're wrong. The beast is a real-life monster."

"What if we're *both* right?" Lucas slipped off his backpack. "There's something you need to see."

After explaining about Silas, Abel, and their Hound Pound, Lucas and Lens watched as Bess studied the photographs.

"Well, what do you think?" asked Lucas.

"You're saying that the beast has something to do with the Hound Pound and the fire." Bess wrinkled up her face. "How?"

"I don't know," admitted Lucas. "It sounds crazy, and I don't know how to explain it, but they're connected."

"I need more than a feeling," said Bess. She stood up and bounced her basketball. "See that? I throw the ball, it hits the ground, and then it comes back. I see it and I feel it. I experience it. Gimme something like that. Gimme proof." She shoved the ball against Lucas's chest to emphasize her point.

Lucas thought back to all of the suspicious moments he'd had since moving to Hounds Hollow. Except for the car accident, they'd all centered around one place.

"Sweetwater Manor," he said with certainty. "Silas's house is the proof. You don't build a place as weird as that without a reason. Let's find the control room and start the hunt."

"A ghost hunt?" Bess wore a grimace of doubt.

But Lucas could see a spark of interest in her eyes. She was dying to get back into that house, he knew it. "I can't say if we're dealing with ghosts or not, but whatever the beast is, it's not normal. And I think it's reaching out to us for a reason. You can't tell me that it roams through the same woods night after night without having a connection to that place. The beast could have gone anywhere in the world. Why does it stay in Hounds Hollow?"

Bess took the ball and bounced it once more. "I'm in."

"I'm in, too," said Lens, who was still on horseback. "Let's go check out your creepy old house again. But this time, maybe let's not jump out a window."

The trip through the woods was short, but Lucas still couldn't get used to traveling next to a horse. Bess took the lead since she knew the paths like the back of her hand, so Lucas kept close to her as Lens galloped in and out of the trees beside them.

When the woods opened up, the house lay before them. Lucas pedaled faster, hoping to reach his home before something dangerous woke up. Once Lens had tied his horse to the porch, the three friends went inside.

"Mom, I'm back with friends," Lucas called out, but no one answered. "Mom? Dad?"

The house was absolutely still.

"I'm sure they're here," said Lucas. "The car's parked outside."

"This place is huge," said Bess. "Maybe they're exploring the house, too."

"Yeah, must be," Lucas agreed, but he felt like something was missing. His parents usually left notes if they went anywhere. Actually, they left notes even if they were just watching a movie in their room.

"Where should we look first?" asked Lens.

"Most of this place was burned down because of a gas leak, according to what we know," said Lucas. "But I think at least one room survived—the barn."

As they went to his room, Lucas felt the house around him. It was as if the air was pushing against him, like walking through a swimming pool dressed in all his clothes. His arms and legs treaded heavily through the hallway.

Lucas pushed the mirror and clicked it open. A rush of wind blew through the room as if the heavy air had been uncorked. He turned on the lamps and small flames flickered to life.

"I still can't get used to those gaslights," Lens noted. "Isn't that what started the fire?"

"I'm not so sure about that," said Lucas.

"What do you mean?" asked Lens as he traced the metalwork around the stalls. "The article said that the fire was due to a gas leak."

"That is *exactly* what the article said," Lucas confirmed as he pulled out the journal. "But if that were true, then why would a room with gas lighting be the only space that didn't burn down?"

The black bars danced in the hazy light. Lucas walked down the aisle, staring into each stall.

"What's going on? Did I miss something?" asked Bess. "We know the control room isn't in here."

Lucas ignored her and tugged at the straps of his backpack. "Silas's journal mentions that the dogs slept in stalls, not pens like a normal kennel. This was their home. The Hound Pound."

Bess cleared her throat. "So what are we doing, looking for ghosts?"

"No, we're looking for *proof* of ghosts," Lucas corrected her. "The Hound Pound was made up of real dogs, and something really bad happened to them."

"So?" Bess said. "The dogs in the pictures you found don't look anything like the beast."

"Of course not," Lucas argued. "When bad, unthinkable things happen to good people—or good animals, in this case—they don't come back the same."

Bess made a farting noise with her tongue. "This is ridiculous. Have fun with your doggy ghost dreams. I've got a beast to catch."

As she walked toward the connecting hallway, the gas lighting hissed louder. The lights brightened intensely, then dimmed to a low, almost blue flame. Clicks echoed through the room, and Bess stepped back with the boys. Something was walking toward them.

"What's going on?" she asked.

The room became a playground of dull shadows from the gates flickering in the dim light. As the darkness moved around them, Lucas felt a sudden tug on his pant leg and jumped. He looked down and saw the white mutt again.

"Whoa, boy," said Lucas. "You scared me. Guys, this is the stray dog I was telling you about. Maybe he snuck back in through the door?"

The dog yipped and the small, sharp sound made the stall bars ring in the room. Lucas tried to pick up the wiggly puppy, but it squirmed out of his arms. With another yip, the white dog bit at his pant leg again and pulled him with surprising force. Lucas flopped forward and almost fell into the final stall.

"C'mon, this isn't the time to play," he complained.

Bess walked back and knelt by the dog, inspecting it like it was a brand-new form of life that she'd just discovered. "Why does this dog look familiar?"

Lucas nodded. "Last night, with the beast. I think this little guy jumped out and scared it off."

The dog yipped again. Then, with a skittering of its claws on the wood floor, the dog darted into the last stall and out, running back and forth in a small loop. Lucas, Bess, stall. Lucas, Bess, stall. Over and over again.

"That little dog sure is full of energy," said Lens. "Or he's trying to tell us something."

Lucas walked into the last stall. There was hay on the ground, three solid walls, and a lone gaslight at the back that had burned out. Lucas walked up to the light, which was set lower than the others in the room. It hung crooked and off-kilter. He leaned close and gave the light a strong sniff.

"What are you doing?" Bess asked.

"The light," Lucas said. "It's out. That's bad if you've got a gas leak. But I don't smell anything."

He sniffed it again. Then Lucas grabbed the light fixture like a doorknob and turned it upside down. A creaking sound filled the room as the back wall slowly slid open.

"No way," whispered Bess as she ran next to Lucas. "Creepy secret passageway alert. Where do you think it goes?"

Lucas peered inside the gap. A glare of dull light flashed from within the darkness. "Only one way to find out," he said, channeling his inner Bess.

"Maybe we could say we checked it out, but then really we don't?" asked Lens. He was keeping his distance, yet still took time to snap a picture.

The white dog tilted his head curiously at the boy with the camera. Then it trotted ahead into the secret door.

Bess smiled. "Come on, Lens. Even the scrappiest dog in the world isn't afraid."

"That's not fair. Do dogs even *get* scared?" asked Lens.

There was another room inside, lit up by twelve black-and-white screens. They were mounted to the wall and stacked on top of each other like an epic game of tic-tac-toe. Each screen showed one room inside Sweetwater Manor, and then the image would disappear, only to be replaced by a picture of a different room in the house. A lone chair was positioned in front of the screens. It was facing a control panel with silver knobs and sliders.

"I thought Silas only had cameras set up outside of his house," said Lucas.

An image of the kitchen flickered to life on one of the screens. His parents were drinking coffee and talking.

"Apparently not," answered Bess as she sat down in the chair. She leaned over and studied the board. It was dirty, covered in a thick layer of white dust. As if she were blowing out candles on a cake, Bess blew hard onto the board and a cloud of grime lifted into the air. The kids swatted and coughed at the mess.

"I'll bet these control the volume," Bess said, pointing to the sliders. She moved one up and Lucas's parents' voices were suddenly audible.

"He's not getting better."

"Give it time, Kyle. We've only been here for—"

Click. The feed switched again to another part of the house and the speakers went quiet. Lens and Bess looked at Lucas. He felt like he was back in the doctor's waiting room, when his name was called to finally go inside. How all the other kids there gave him that same look as he stood up with his mask and air tank on wheels. He used to drag it behind him like an underwater diver, exploring a world in which he didn't belong. Lucas didn't need the air tank anymore, but his friends' gazes still said the same thing: They were scared to know what Lucas knew, and hearing it, seeing it, made them realize that life wasn't a game. With nothing more to add to what they'd just heard, Lucas broke their stare and shifted his attention to the screens.

Bess did the same. She clicked a few buttons and the screens reacted, jumping from scene to different scene.

"If the buttons swap out camera feeds," said Lens, breaking the silence, "then I'll bet these knobs make the cameras swivel."

Bess turned one of the knobs and the view moved in the same direction. It was like playing a video game, but times twelve screens and times who knew how many points of view. This house was wired with some serious technology.

"So, are people spying on us?" asked Lucas.

"Not on you, I don't think," said Bess. "But Silas was spying on something."

An old, yellow strip of tape ran across the bottom of the board, closest to the chair. Bess ran her finger over it lightly, lifting up more dust and lint. There were names written on the tape that aligned with certain control sets. Bess read them aloud and looked at Lucas and Lens.

"Scout, Dakota, Duke, Casper."

"He named cameras after his dogs." Lucas moved beside Bess to see for himself. It was the same handwriting from the journal, but written with more confidence—the kind that only comes with age and practice. "Why would Silas do that?"

The screens continued clicking through empty room after empty room, until one screen landed on a feed showing workers in the house. The movement caught their attention. Bess pressed another button and the scene held this time without switching to a different camera. She turned up the volume.

"What are you doing?" asked Lucas.

Bess shushed him and focused on the screen. At first glance, the workers were doing their jobs. Putting up drywall, carrying boards, or laying down the hardwood floor. But the more the kids watched them, the stranger it seemed.

"They're not talking to each other," said Lens.

Lucas nodded. "They barely even notice each other. It's like watching a beehive. They're busy, but there's almost nothing human about them."

Yip, answered the tiny white dog. It was sitting behind the kids. With a small whine, the skinny puppy nuzzled forth a ball that rolled across the wooden floor. Lucas picked it up. The small nicks from teeth marks rubbed against his palm.

He held up the red ball with a single stripe on it. "Where did you get this, boy?"

Yip. The dog's tail patted excitedly against the floor. Lucas tossed the ball lightly and the dog darted after it into a dark corner. Lucas and Lens watched the corner, waiting for the dog to return, but nothing happened.

After a few seconds, Lucas said, "Boy?"

The ball rolled out of the shadows slowly, as if it had just dropped from the dog's mouth. Quickly, Lucas picked it up. The ball was so wet and slobbery that he had to shake off the dog spit. As he walked over to the corner, he found a chain dangling from the roof, like the other lights in the barn, and pulled it. The light came on, illuminating the room, but the white dog was gone.

"No, no, no," said Lens. "Where's the dog? He was just there a second ago!"

"I don't know," Lucas answered. "Bess?"

"Huh," Bess said without turning around. She was still playing with the cameras and had found several other feeds of workers in the house. Each of them played a similar scene, as if the workers were zombies going about their boring building tasks.

"What's the name under the cameras closest to my room?" Lucas asked.

She studied the screens until a familiar image popped into view. It was Lucas's room. And there was something new there. A small white mutt sat on his bed, looking straight at the camera.

Bess whispered the name on the tape, "Casper."

Lucas ran like a bolt of lightning into his bedroom, but when he got there, the dog was gone. Lucas scrambled back to the control room. "What happened?"

"The dog just . . . ," cried Lens. "The camera! It must have glitched. One frame paused, then it jumped forward, and the dog was gone and you were in the room. What did we just see?"

Lucas ripped open his bag and pulled out the journal. He flipped through it until he found what he was looking for. "Look, guys, here! Casper, favorite toy: striped ball."

"What are you saying?" asked Bess.

"I'm saying," Lucas began, holding the ball, "maybe there's more than one beast in Hounds Hollow."

CHAPTER 22

Lucas's words settled in the dim flicker of the control room.

"No way," said Lens. "We've seen the beast. We have pictures of the beast. It's the same creature every time. At no point was it a tiny white mutt."

Lucas shrugged. "You're right, but what if Silas *knew* about the beast? What if he knew that the dogs came back to haunt the town?" He ran over and motioned toward the controls. "What if he rebuilt this house to trap the dogs inside—to contain them so that they couldn't hurt anyone? Think about it! This house is not normal! Doors that open up to brick walls, stairs that lead to nowhere, all in a house that is constantly being built. And the giant box of dog food that Gale gave us—she said that Silas had paid up on the deliveries for a long time. The food is still going to come in. Silas wasn't building the weirdest house in the world, he was building a maze—no, a *prison*—to trap those animals in the house!"

Bess nodded, while Lens let out an audible gulp. Deep in their hearts, no matter how strange Lucas sounded, they knew he was making sense.

"Then, these names on the control panel . . . ," said Bess. "What if each area is where that dog is being held?"

"You mean Silas had workers in the same place as the undead dogs?" asked Lens. "That's cold! You couldn't pay me enough to work in a haunted place like this."

"Well, don't forget, we came inside the house for free," Bess reminded him. Then she turned to Lucas. "There were five dogs, right? But there are only four names here. Which one is missing?"

Lucas traced over each name on yellow tape. "Shadow. Shadow is the only name missing. He was Abel's dog."

"Do you think . . . ?" asked Bess.

Lens looked back and forth as Bess and Lucas shared an unspoken moment. "Okay, for those of us who aren't part of your mind-meld, can someone please tell me what you're thinking?"

"Shadow escaped," said Lucas. "He lost his owner, then lost his pack, then lost his life. And now . . ."

"Now what?!" asked Lens impatiently.

"I think Shadow is the beast that's haunting Hounds Hollow."

Lens let out a whimper. "Okay, maybe I didn't want to know that."

"So what does Shadow want?" asked Bess. "To get the pack back together?"

Lens doubled over and clutched his stomach. "Ugh, a pack of beasts. I can't think about that."

"All right, then, let's not worry about Shadow right now," said Lucas as he pointed to the screens. "Thanks to Silas, we might know where to look for the other dogs. Maybe we can catch them?"

Bess laughed. "Catch them how? We have no idea how we found Casper, or why he's so nice. You go hunting for the other beasts, you're a dead man walking."

She tried to stop herself, but the words stumbled out of her mouth clumsily. Lens shot her a look, but Bess already knew she'd said too much.

"I know." The words barely made it out of Lucas's throat.

Yip. Casper was back, happily wagging his tail. The kids all screamed as the dog stood on his hind legs and pawed at Lucas's knees.

"What do you want?" he asked.

Casper started spinning circles around the red striped ball on the ground. Lucas picked it up and handed it to the dog. The thin pup took it in his mouth and sat obediently, watching the kids.

Lucas leaned down. "So you're Casper, huh? Like the real deal Casper?"

The white dog gave him a nod and a second, smaller bark from around the ball.

"Um, Lucas. Be careful and remember that your little guy is also an undead little beast," whispered Bess.

Lens lifted his camera, but Lucas waved him off. "No pictures."

"No pictures?" asked Lens as he snapped the camera shut. "Come on, who's gonna believe this ever happened without pictures?"

"*We'll* believe it," said Lucas. "Other than the three of us, no one needs to know about this. This beast—I mean, dog— he's here for us. He's here for a reason."

"Great. Do you talk dog, Lucas?" asked Bess. "'Cause unless you do, or unless they talk human, understanding each other is going to be hard."

Casper sat there, not moving. Lucas moved closer, half expecting the pup to disappear at any moment. "Did you and your friends rip into the box of dog food yesterday?"

Yip. Casper's bark made the gaslights fade this time.

"I'll take that as a yes," said Lucas. "You were hungry?"

Yip.

"Holy mongrel, he's having a conversation with that dog," said Bess.

"With a *ghost* dog," corrected Lens.

Lucas ignored both of them and moved closer to Casper. An intense heat emanated from the dog. The edges of his fur flickered slightly, like flames in a burning fire. Lucas was startled but tried to stay calm. "Is this ball your favorite toy?"

Yip. Casper walked forward, and as he did, he shifted back to his normal mutt shape. The flames were gone.

Lucas reached down and petted him. A warmth moved up his hand. The heat wasn't threatening or dangerous; it was relaxing, like a crackling bonfire when Lucas's parents took him camping. He suddenly had the urge to sing songs, make s'mores, and tell, of all things, ghost stories.

"Where are the others?" Lucas asked.

Casper didn't answer this time, but he did become restless. Lucas felt the fur on the back of his neck stand up as the pup shifted away anxiously. The warmth around Casper pulsed hotter as he moved. The little dog stopped and gave Lucas a long, cold stare. The beast's eyes flared red, then cooled to a pitch darker than black.

"Lucas," whispered Lens. "Don't make him angry. It seems like you're making him angry."

Lucas nodded and took a deep breath. "Last question. Can you help us find the beast?"

Again, silence. Suddenly Casper began to growl, and the white hairs on his back stood on end. The tiny pup crouched forward, like a wolf stalking its prey, white teeth glared at Lucas's question.

"Dude, I told you not to make him angry!" said Lens, who backed up.

But Lucas stood his ground and held his hand out. "What? What is it? What did I do?"

"You mentioned the beast," said Bess.

Upon hearing the name a second time, Casper shifted his appearance in the blink of an eye. The dog dropped the ball as his dopey puppy smile and waggy little tail crumbled into tattered skin that hung off the creature's gray, rippling muscles. A wild sneer curled on Casper's lips as if he smelled blood in the air. Lucas grabbed the ball and stumbled back to his friends. They tried to leave the room, but Casper blocked the door. They were trapped.

"Could you both stop using that word?" begged Lens. "He clearly doesn't like it."

Bess smiled. "Beast," she taunted, and the ghoulish dog bristled. A low growl shuddered in the room, like a jagged zipper opening slowly.

"Why did you do that?" Lucas snapped.

He looked for a microphone or some button on the control panel that might call for help, but there was nothing. Casper's mouth snapped, his claws dug into the floor, and his tiny body thrummed with a tense energy that cast heat like the sun. Underneath it all, the dull hiss of gas lighting kept the room aglow.

"'Come on over,' you said," whispered Lens. "'I've got something to show you. It'll be fun!' you said. You never mentioned ghost dogs!"

Balls, thought Lucas. *Dogs love balls. Dogs love to play fetch. Maybe that's true for ghost dogs!*

Lucas held the ball out to show Casper, and then chucked it as far as he could. The ball thunked against the back of the barn doors as the tiny beast skittered after it. Instantly the room plummeted back to a normal temperature. Then, as if nothing strange had happened, the cute white mutt strutted back in with the ball in his mouth and dropped it next to Lucas.

"Lens, can you throw the ball again?" asked Lucas as he grabbed Silas's Hound Pound journal.

"Me, throw a ball to that?" Lens was frozen still.

Bess picked up the ball instead and waved it at Casper. "Here, creepy critter, here you go. You want your ball? Well, go get it."

She rolled the ball into one of the stalls, and as soon as Casper went inside, she slammed the wrought-iron gate closed. Casper sat by the ball; he blinked curiously, but he didn't attempt to escape.

As the boys came rushing in, Bess held her finger to her lips.

"He looks almost . . . happy," said Lens.

"Some dogs see crates like a security blanket," said Bess. "It gives them a sense of safety. This barn is his original home, so it should put Casper at ease. This place survived the fire, after all. Safety."

"Bess, you're a genius!" said Lucas as he gave her a hug, but she pulled away nervously.

"It's one dog, Lucas," said Bess. "We're never going to catch the rest of the pack."

"Actually, I think we can." Lucas flipped open the journal and tapped on a list. "See here, Silas made a list of each dog's favorite toy. Casper loved the red striped ball. I think that's what, I don't know, tamed him, or made him more dog than beast."

"So?" asked Bess.

"So Silas left all the dog toys locked in the desk!" he cheered. "We've already found them! Now all we need to do is find the other dogs!"

"Oh, sure, like that's the easy part," Lens complained. "I mean, are we seriously going to capture wild devil dogs in your house?"

Before Lucas could answer, a buzzer sounded from the control room like an alarm. The kids ran back inside to find a blinking light under a row of controls. All eyes flicked up to the screens as the cameras froze on a four-legged gray smudge dragging itself through the hall. The image moved like ripped-up paper drifting through the air, like it was flipping over in a million pieces instead of walking like a dog. Lucas could almost hear the violins picking their high strings like they did in horror movies when something creepy was happening, but the microphones didn't register any noise.

"What in the world is that?" whimpered Lens.

"That's our next target," said Lucas, glancing at the name written on the yellow tape. "Dakota."

CHAPTER 23

Lucas armed himself with a backpack full of ancient dog toys. He labeled them, matching each toy to each dog according to the journal. His parents used to put similar labels on toys he'd bring to the hospital during overnight tests. The hairs rose on his arms just thinking about the ice-cold air-conditioning in those rooms.

But that was a long time ago in a city far away. Now he was walking into one of the deeper wings of Sweetwater Manor with rubber bones and chew toys to face off against a ghost. Somewhere on the second floor, after eight right-hand turns, probably a few wrong turns, and passing at least five different cuckoo clocks, Lucas, Bess, and Lens finally reached Dakota's room. It was Lens who had pieced together a system of the camera locations like a map based on notes Silas had left behind. Whether Silas left the notes for them or for someone else, Lucas couldn't be sure. But as they walked, Lens spotted each camera and verified the number to lead them through the maze.

As they walked, Lucas noticed several doorknobs that had the same bone mark etched into them like the trapdoors he'd found on his first trip inside the house. Before he could say anything, Bess waved him on impatiently, and Lucas ran to catch up. If he lost track of Lens, he'd never find his way back.

The hallway decor transitioned from fancy white wallpaper with blue peacock patterns to an uneven shiplap of wood that reminded Lucas of log cabins.

"We're close to where the alarm sounded," Lens said in barely more than a whisper. "Bess, why don't you take the lead?"

Bess stepped forward and Lucas followed. He wielded a squeaker clown toy in his hand like a sword. The label wrapped around the clown's neck read *Dakota*.

"Put that stupid thing down." Bess pushed at his arm.

Lucas lifted it back up and gave it a squeak. "Laugh now, but when it works, you'll thank me."

The three friends continued down the hallway until it opened up into a huge room. A cathedral ceiling arched above them as a gray stone fireplace crackled with an unattended fire. The only light in the room came from the fireplace. Flames popped loudly and danced, showing off the comfortable and rustic furniture. Leather chairs with brass-studded accents sat empty next to soft velvet couches that were buried under an avalanche of throw pillows.

"I don't suppose you brought any s'mores in that backpack?" asked Bess.

Lucas stepped into the glow of the strange fire. "Well, I

wasn't expecting to find a working fireplace in the middle of my haunted house, so, no."

He turned to face the open room. It was so massive that the far edges were out of reach from the fire's light, but shadows loomed. "I don't suppose *you* brought a flashlight?"

Lens shook his head. "*That* would have been a good idea. Why isn't the sun shining in here?"

Large windows reached all around the room, but it was pitch-black outside. Lucas went over to one and peered through the dark glass. "There are walls built behind these windows. Why would Silas wall this place in?"

"Why did Silas do anything?" asked Bess. "It's part of his trap. Dakota must be here."

Lens found a lamp and turned the knob. It clicked, but the light stayed out. "No electricity, either."

"This is the rustic cabin room," answered Bess. "Of course there's no power. Silas was a stickler for details like that. Just look above us."

Lucas and Lens peered toward the ceiling. A giant chandelier of antlers and unlit candles hung over them. Or at least Lucas hoped they were antlers; they could just as easily have been bones. The boys quickly stepped aside so they weren't directly underneath it.

Then Lens held up his camera. "I have a flash. Will that work?"

Lucas gulped. The last time Lens used his flash, it had been a horror show in the forest. "Sure . . . ," he said hesitantly. "Let's give it a try."

The flash went off, sending a flare of light into the darkness. Instantly the kids were not alone. As the gloom returned, they could not unsee what was lurking in the corner. A hulking beast stood six feet tall on two legs, reaching out its claws.

Lucas knew that there was only one thing to do: use the squeaker. Turning to Bess, he shouted, "Cover me!"

He jumped and charged the beast, squeezing the clown squeaker furiously. It sounded like a demonic, high-pitched laugh echoing in the tall room. *Squee-Ker, Squee-Ker, Squee-Ker, Squee-Ker.* The toy clown's eyes, ears, and tongue popped out with every frantic clutch of Lucas's fist.

Bess, armed with throw pillows she found on the couch, threw them at her target, but they bounced off harmlessly.

When Lucas crashed into the belly of the strange animal, he realized what they were up against. It was only a stuffed and mounted grizzly bear trophy. It rocked gently on its pedestal as Lucas slumped down against its legs. "You can come out now. We successfully defeated a giant teddy bear."

With one final deflated squeak, Lucas nudged the outstretched arms of the hunter's trophy. The bear's eyes were glassy and cold. Its claws were polished and softened at the tips, erasing any sharp or cutting edges. Lucas wondered why it was in the room.

As his eyes became used to the darkness, he could make out more shapes. A deer head hung on the wall. An antelope posed in another corner as if it were running. Even a green-scaled crocodile was curled in an eternal hiss, baring its teeth.

Lens snapped another picture of a small fox perched on a side table like a cat hopping around furniture in the den. "This place is creepy, no doubt."

"There goes our element of surprise," said Bess. "Did you have to squeak the squeaker so many times?"

Lucas picked up a pillow and threw it at Bess. "Did you have to start a pillow fight?"

"Hey, I use what I have." A smile crept up at the corners of Bess's mouth. It almost looked like she was having a good time. "And I have a lot of pillows here."

The kids listened as silence covered the room like a tarp. Lucas could feel the quiet around his shoulders. He glanced at the fireplace. The flames licked against the logs, turning red and yellow at the tips and blue at the base. As they flickered, Lucas walked closer and put his hand to his ear. "Guys, the fire. It's not making noise anymore."

Bess wiped the back of her neck with her hand. "Well, it's putting out a lot of heat. I'm getting a sunburn over here."

Suddenly a warm breeze blew through the room and slammed every door. The kids jumped as the unlit candles flickered to life and burned brighter and brighter and brighter.

"No, no, no," Lucas said as he squinted his eyes in the harsh new light. "I think we found Dakota."

A low snarl bristled in the space. It seemed to be right beside each of the kids, sending Lens curling into one of the leather chairs, while Bess dove into the pillows. In the glare of the candles, a gray shadow stalked forward.

The shadow was out of focus like a smudge that heaved as it moved closer and closer. Lucas thought he was watching an actual nightmare trying to tear its way out of a dream. He pinched himself to make sure he was awake. And he was.

With every step the shadow took, the light amped up, making it harder for Lucas to keep his eyes open. Heat washed over him in ripples, and Lucas could feel the rubber toy in his hand go softer and softer in the high temperature. He let it drop to the floor.

A bark shattered the silence like broken glass, making Lucas quiver. Dakota was right next to him. Then the hound stood on two legs and placed her paws on Lucas's chest. A burning-hot nose sniffed around him as Lucas became trapped in the dog's gray cloud. He could hear the animal's hot breath, like ashes blowing from a volcano. It smelled of sulfur and rot, like the oxygen in the room had been replaced with death.

Then a pillow whipped past Lucas and smacked the dog in the face.

"Pillow fight!" screamed Bess.

The hound bared her muddy, black teeth at the pillow, seizing it in her jaws and tearing it apart. Bess pulled Lucas out of the way, then rushed straight toward Dakota.

"Bess! No!" he objected, but it was too late.

Squee-Ker, Squee-Ker. The shrill sound of the toy clown burst into the room like a thunderclap. Bess had picked it up and now she squeezed it again and again. *Squee-Ker, Squee-Ker.*

The hound snapped its gnarled mouth, lurching violently outside of the gray cloud for the first time. The movement was quick and Bess almost dropped the toy. Dakota was completely disfigured. Any fur the dog once had was gone, and in its place a black char of muscles and bone pulsed with a new curiosity.

Bess approached the animal and kept squeezing the toy. With each squeal, the lights in the room dimmed and the gray cloud shrunk back from the hound. Dakota was beginning to look more and more like a normal dog. Brown, white, and black hair sprouted from the dark patches of burned flesh. Soon Lucas could tell that the dog had been a shepherd breed before the fire. In her new form, Dakota sat and slowly wagged her tail.

Bess knelt in front of the dog. It cautiously sniffed the clown toy, then sniffed Bess's hand. "Dakota?" she asked.

Woof! the dog answered.

Bess gave a relieved smile to Lucas and Lens, who were both armed with more pillows and ready to battle. The toy had worked. She leaned down, still holding the squeaker between herself and Dakota. "My name is Bess. I'd like you to come with me back to your real home. Okay?"

Dakota tilted her head at the word *home.* Then she let out a happy whine and brushed against the toy in Bess's hand. Bess took it as an invitation and petted the dog's head. Dakota's hair was soft, but still bristled with energy.

Bess wore a doubtful smile. "No way. No way it's this easy, right?"

"Maybe it's like opening a locked door," suggested Lens. "All we needed was the key."

"But what if there's a reason the door was locked in the first place?" said Bess. "I don't like it. A toy can't be a weapon. It feels too simple. Where's the fight? Dakota has been trapped for years and she rolls over at the first sight of a toy?"

"For the record, it didn't seem simple to me," said Lucas.

"All I had to do was stand there," said Bess.

"And not die. Don't forget that part." Lucas's voice remained steady and calm as he watched her pet the dog. The same dog that a few seconds ago was ready to latch her jaws into his throat. "Besides, the toy isn't a weapon. It's a peace offering. I think standing up to your fear is the weapon."

The others were quiet.

Lucas nodded and stood up. "We should go."

Bess went over to the closest door, and Dakota followed with her tail wagging. She reached for the wooden knob, but it wouldn't turn. Quickly, Bess tried the next one, but it was locked, too. Lucas and Lens ran to the other doors. They were all locked.

Then Dakota whimpered and pointed her nose back to the fireplace.

"What's going on, girl?" Bess asked. "Is there something else we need from here? Not that I like taking directions from a monster mutt."

Ignoring Bess, Lens looked at the fire and then to Dakota. The dog had slinked down and made herself smaller, lying with her belly on the floor and her paws tucked under her head. "She's scared," he said. "Believe me, I know a scared animal when I see one."

"There's nothing to be scared of, girl," said Lucas as he walked over to the fireplace. He knocked the stone backing three times lightly. "See? It's harmless."

Then something knocked back and Lucas jumped away. The fire started to crack and pop again, but this time the noise grew louder. Hissing erupted, too, as the fire grew suddenly out of control. Flames spiked into the room and the fire dragged itself out of the fireplace, scorching the wooden floors.

"So not harmless! So not harmless!" screamed Lens as he ran over and grabbed a blanket. He tossed it over the fire to smother it, but the flames were too strong. The fire singed a hole in the blanket and began to vibrate. Four blazing legs slowly unfurled from the fire's belly, lifting the inferno off the ground. A small nose pushed out of the brightness like a knife. It opened up its jaws and clamped them down. A fiery tongue lashed out and licked its flaming lips as if the monster craved the taste of fear in the room.

"What's going on, Dakota?!" snapped Bess.

The fire monster howled at Dakota's name, a woeful bale of burning sadness. The sound nearly melted Lucas's heart. As the beast trudged slowly, the air filled with smoke. Thick clouds billowed around the kids as they dropped to their knees like Dakota had done. The air was cooler down there, but Lucas was still having trouble breathing.

"It's another hound," coughed Bess. "Open your backpack! Get out the dog stuff."

Lucas pulled his arm out of the left strap and flipped the pack around. He unzipped it to dig through everything, but the heat and smoke hit him hard. An attack was coming. Lucas slid the backpack over to Bess, but the toys spilled and scattered across the floor.

Lens acted quickly, gathering the toys and trying each one as the fire beast slumped closer to Lucas. Nothing worked.

The air was gone from Lucas's lungs now. He'd experienced this only once before during a stress test to study his lung strength. But this time it was different. Lucas couldn't simply put on an oxygen mask when he'd reached the breaking point. This time it was real. His hand flapped by his side like a fish out of water, searching for his inhaler. Just as he touched it with his fingers, his body convulsed, and the small, red-and-white canister slid out of his reach.

"Lucas!" screamed Bess as Dakota darted over to him. The dog looked back and forth between Lucas and the inhaler.

Quickly, Bess grabbed an old chew bone and hurled it into the fire, but the monster batted it aside. It kept dragging itself toward Lucas, who was lying on his back. "Lucas! Get up! It's coming for you!" she screamed. "Which dog is it?!"

Woof! Dakota barked.

The flame beast paused for a moment and cocked its head.

Woof! Dakota barked again as she bounded between Lucas and the fire. Dakota barked sharply, as if she were speaking to the fire, warning it to stay away. With each bark, Bess started to truly hear the shepherd.

Woof!

Woof!

Woof!

Doof!

Doofk!

Dook!

"Duke!" yelled Bess. "It's Duke! Find his toy!"

Lens fumbled around on the floor and finally grabbed the pig's ear. The note around it read *Duke*. "Here, boy! I bet you want some flame-grilled barbecue!"

Lens threw the ear into the fire and plugged his ears. The smoke in the air, the flames around Duke's body, and the crushing heat of the room all exploded inward and formed into a squat, brown bulldog.

Lucas gasped as the air rushed back over him in reverse. The doors in the room blew open and the candles all went out. He patted the ground in the suddenly cold darkness looking for his inhaler, but he only found the wood floor.

Then Bess jerked him upright, shoved the inhaler into his mouth, and pressed down. A jet of cool air reached down his throat as Lucas tried calmly to let the medicine work. His pathways opened and he felt his chest loosen its tight grip. Lucas pressed the inhaler for a second dose, taking a deep, deep breath. Then he smiled and whispered, "What did I miss?"

Bess punched Lucas in the arm—hard. "Never do that again! Never!"

"Ouch! Okay, sorry," said Lucas, rubbing the spot where the punch had landed. "Next time we'll split up the toys. It was a bad idea to have one person carry them."

"That's not what I'm talking about and you know it." She hit him again, then gave him a hug.

Lucas's face went red and he tried to change the subject. "Did we get him? Did we get Duke?"

"We got him, buddy," said Lens. He pointed over to the shepherd and the bulldog as the two dogs sniffed each other, rubbing their noses together. Dakota's tail lifted and wagged, and Duke did the same with his tail nub. The two dogs started chasing each other around the room in a game of tag. Watching the dogs play, Lucas sensed a different feeling swell inside Sweetwater Manor. It felt new. It felt fresh. It felt like Lucas and his friends had unlocked Silas's riddle.

It felt like hope.

CHAPTER 24

The room was full of sleeping ghosts curled up in their stalls.

"I cannot believe this." Lens peeked over the gates at Duke. "It's incredible. He looks so calm. He was basically just fire and flames a little while ago, remember?"

"Yeah, we were there, too," Bess reminded him. She didn't give the dogs a second glance and instead headed straight back to the control room. "Now let's get this viewing party started."

Bess was glued to the screens when Lucas and Lens joined her. One camera flickered to a new scene and Bess cheered. "Workers. We've got workers."

She stopped the camera anytime a worker walked into the scene. If Lucas didn't know any better, he'd swear that Bess was more interested in them than in Silas's Hound Pound.

As the evening went on, Lucas kept his eye on the camera feed that lead to his room just in case his parents came knocking. Lens wandered in and out to check on his horse, while Bess kept staring up at the flickering screens. Lucas wondered if this was close to normal, like, *Mom, I'm going over to Lucas's house to watch TV.* But what Bess really meant was *Mom, I'm going over to Lucas's haunted mansion to look for potentially deadly ghosts.* No, this was not normal. Even Lucas could see that.

After another hour, Bess cracked. "Jeez, you'd think this place wasn't haunted at all. Where are those hounds?"

"Maybe they're sleeping?" suggested Lens. "Which sounds like a good idea. Wake me when you find something."

He lay down on the floor and put his backpack under his head. Bess kicked his feet, then returned to her surveillance.

Lucas used the downtime to catch up on some reading. He pulled out the *Haunted History* book. As he flipped through the pages, most of the ghost histories revolved around human travesties. The girl who died on prom night in a car accident and now hitchhikes as a ghost trying to get back to her house. The ancient soldier who died on the battlefield but never realized it, so he kept walking back home, and when he got there, he saw his own funeral. One after another, the stories all centered around people. He turned to the back of the book to check the index. Animal hauntings were on scattered pages—a sure sign that the author either wasn't interested or never studied these types of cases.

Lucas rubbed the back of his neck. He felt like he'd been run over by a bulldozer. Finally he yawned and felt his whole body ache. "Maybe we could pause for tonight? I'm not sure I'm ready for another hunt."

Bess gave him her patented crooked smile. "We pick it up tomorrow, then. Three down, two to go."

Lucas looked at Lens, who only shrugged. They both knew they were powerless against Bess's drive to uncover what was happening in Hounds Hollow. It was magnetic.

"Okay," Lucas relented as Bess and Lens waved goodbye and saw themselves out.

The rest of the night was nowhere near as exciting. After he checked on the sleeping dogs and shut the secret door, Lucas ate dinner with his parents. It was chicken and brussels sprouts with what his mom said was balls-balm-ick glades, or something fancy like that. Whatever it was, it was good. Then Lucas tried to maintain a normal night by playing Wolf Life and reading his *Goosebumps* book before bed. But he didn't make it far into the book before he passed out. It took every ounce of effort he had left just to put his CPAP mask on before he was asleep.

Lucas woke to the sound of sniffing. The small, incessant noise moved all around his room. He groggily lifted off his mask and buried his face in his pillow. It smelled like smoke from Duke's blaze. The sniffing paused at his movement, but started again a second later. It was closer to his bed now.

Next to him, Lucky lifted his head. The cat's eyes glowed in the dark room, tracking something Lucas couldn't see. Suddenly the mysterious thing leapt onto Lucas's blanket and sent Lucky into a fit. The cat hissed, then darted across the bed, onto the floor, and out of the room. Lucas was alone.

Slowly, the strange, new weight walked toward Lucas in the dark. Pressing against his blanket, its sniffing became louder and louder. Lucas was about to kick off the covers when a tiny white dog trotted out of the shadows and licked his face.

"Casper?" Lucas whispered. He rubbed his eyes to make sure he wasn't dreaming. "What are you doing here? How'd you get out of your stall?"

The dog nuzzled his nose against Lucas's cheek and then jumped back playfully.

"You freaked out poor Lucky. What do you want?" Lucas asked quietly. He looked to the window. It was still night.

The dog leapt toward him again, plopping onto its belly with its paws outstretched. Lucas petted him behind the ears. Again, the pup was burning to the touch. Then Casper gnawed the blankets and jumped back, pulling them off.

"You want me to get up?" Lucas asked.

Yip.

"It's late, buddy," said Lucas. "Can't this wait until the morning? And maybe when the house is, like, ninety percent less freaking me out?"

Casper spun in a quick circle and paused again. *Yip.*

"Yeah, you're right. This house isn't ever going to be *less* scary, huh?" Lucas rolled out of bed and grabbed a flashlight from the side table and his backpack from the floor. He turned on the torch, and the sudden light surprised him. It didn't disturb Casper, though. The dog jumped off the bed and went to the door. After a few blinks, Lucas could see again. He ran the flashlight over to the mirror door in the opposite direction. It was open.

"Are the others still in there?" asked Lucas.

Hmm, Casper whimpered again. Then he scratched the bedroom door.

Lucas clutched his shoulder strap as he waved the flashlight back and forth, weighing his options. He had promised Bess and Lens that he wouldn't go hunting without them. But was he going hunting? Maybe Casper just needed to go to the bathroom. *Do ghosts even go to the bathroom?* he wondered. They ate food, apparently. They ate a lot of food. And Lucas did not want to clean up a ghost accident.

He opened the door and Casper skittered out. The speed caught Lucas by surprise and he raced to catch up. The white dog skipped past the front door, past his parents' room, and then darted to the kitchen.

When Lucas finally caught up to Casper, the dog was standing on his hind legs with his front paws leaning on a door that Lucas had never noticed. "What's in there, buddy?"

Casper lightly scratched at the door with both paws like he was digging.

"I guess I'm going to find out." Lucas flashed his light over the doorknob to check for a bone etching, but there wasn't one. He pulled the door open and Casper scrambled inside.

A set of stairs dropped down into a space so dark Lucas's flashlight barely made a dent in the gloom. There were no light switches or pulls to be found. As he stood at the top of the stairs, Lucas could hear Casper sniffing around at the bottom. Then the tiny dog bounded back up and gave a bark that made Lucas flinch. The house had been so quiet that the mutt's yip made Lucas's heart race.

"You're crazy if you think I'm going down there," Lucas told the dog. "Nothing good ever happens in the basement of a haunted house."

Casper kept sniffing. It was a high-pitched, slightly wet sound that echoed back up from below. Then Lucas heard a new sound coming from behind him in the house. More sniffing noises. Different sniffing noises. These sniffs were heavy and long, almost slobbering in their messy way.

Lucas clicked off the flashlight and held his breath. Another noise followed—the sound of the kitchen door creaking open. Lucas wasn't alone anymore.

Carefully he closed the basement door and walked down

the stairs backward, keeping an eye on the entrance. When Lucas reached the bottom, the floor was soft and earthy, like being outside. He wanted so badly to turn on his flashlight, but was afraid of what he might find. Suddenly another beam danced under the door at the top of the stairs. Whoever else was in the house, they were coming this way.

Lucas turned to run, but slipped and fell. Puffs of dirt clouded up into his face. He clicked on his light and found that the entire floor was brown soil, just like in the woods, but Lucas was still inside the house. The ground was misshapen, lumpy, uneven, and untamed. And instead of ancient trees with twisting roots underneath, the walls around him were unfinished, just the bare bones of wood frames stuffed with pink fluff like cotton candy.

The door at the top of the stairs opened and Lucas shut off his light. He scrambled over the ground on all fours until he found a corner and huddled there, waiting. A spotlight shone down the steps and moved slowly across the dirt floor.

"Loo-kasss," a voice whispered lightly. "Are you down there?"

The light switched off and darkness swallowed the room again. More sniffing followed, the long, gulping sniffs Lucas had heard earlier. The sounds were getting closer and closer, until they stopped right in front of him. Lucas couldn't see anything, but he could feel the presence of two huge beasts by his side. With his last bit of courage, Lucas clenched a fistful of dirt in one hand and clicked on the flashlight with the other.

A brown bulldog and a black shepherd stood in front of Lucas. Duke and Dakota didn't flinch at all from his heroic lunge, but instead sat with their tongues hanging to the side. They licked their chops and continued their heavy breathing, peaceful and calm.

"Really? You're cornered and your only solution is to throw dirt?" It was Lens, smiling from the bottom of the stairs.

Bess was right behind him, but she had Lucas locked in a cold grimace.

Lucas relaxed as all the nervous energy rushed out of him. "I had the element of surprise. Maybe the dirt would get in the bad guy's eyes?"

"And maybe these hounds could have torn you apart," snapped Bess. "You promised you wouldn't explore without us."

"No, I promised I wouldn't *hunt*," Lucas corrected her. "And I'm not. Besides, you're the ones breaking and entering. Who let you into the house?"

"Ask the two ghost hounds in front of you," said Lens. "Duke practically pulled me out of bed. That guy's a slobber monster."

Bess leaned down and scooped up a pile of earth, then let it sift back down through her fist. "Now, why did Dakota bring me here, Lucas? What is this place all about?"

"I don't know, maybe a garden?" he suggested.

"A garden? In the basement? Where there's no light?" Bess shook her head. "No way. This place is . . . unique. It's not even built, really. The rest of Sweetwater Manor is pristine. There are workers here every day, building and building and building. Then you have this place. Dirt floor, unfinished walls."

"You're right. Silas must have kept it this way on purpose." Lucas stepped cautiously between Duke and Dakota. The two dogs ignored him and lay on the cool ground. Lucas ran his flashlight around the room until he found Casper nestled between two dirt mounds.

Looking down, Lucas realized there were more mounds in the basement. So many more. They were small, but someone had made these mounds with a great amount of care. On closer inspection, each one had a small, smooth rock placed on top like a marker. A last effort of memory and love. Bess was right. This secret place was unique, and Silas Sweetwater kept it untouched for a very good reason. The basement was a graveyard.

"Nobody move." Lucas stepped between the mounds. "Remember the Hound Pound? Well, I think we found the rest of the gang."

"I'm gonna be sick," whispered Lens.

Casper sat up and almost smiled at the kids. He yipped again, and the sound made Lucas pause. "Yeah, buddy, thanks for sharing, but I think the human kids need to leave now. The sun is probably almost up, and we've got that big end-of-summer barbecue. So hanging around a basement graveyard, while cool, is just not my thing. Okay?"

But Casper didn't answer this time. Instead the small dog trotted up and down the rows of graves. Dim lights began to glow from each mound.

"Time to go," Bess warned.

Lens held his camera like a weapon, like it was the only thing that could stop what was about to happen. At the other end of the room, Duke and Dakota gave a sharp bark and shuffled in to join Casper.

As if they were searching for buried treasure, the dogs began to dig. Lucas, Bess, and Lens backed away toward the stairs, but then the ground beneath them began to lift and fall, like it was breathing. Paws dug out from the mounds, followed by noses pushing through the dirt. The dead dogs pulled themselves out, each one covered in mud and grime. Casper gave another bark and the dogs all shook wildly, shrugging off the remnants of their graves. Once clean, the dogs were bathed in moonlight, even though there were no windows in the basement. Lucas stared as the pack crowded around Casper and sat obediently, watching the kids.

"I am never sleeping again," Lens whispered to himself.

Every instinct in Lucas's body should have told him to run. What do you when zombies rise from the grave? You run, duh! But Lucas, to his own surprise, did the opposite. He walked to the dogs and knelt with one knee on the churned-up ground.

"Lucas, this isn't puppy playtime," said Bess. "Get over here before something bad happens."

"I've got the toys here," said Lucas. He slid his backpack around and unzipped it. "Besides, Bess, look at them. They're like regular dogs."

"They're not dogs," insisted Bess. "Don't call them dogs. It makes them sound normal."

Lucas ignored her as he spread out the toys. One by one the dogs cautiously inched forward and chose a toy, dragging it back. He nodded toward the pups, trying not to make any sudden moves. "See? They're not beasts."

"I don't care. Let's get out of here." Bess grabbed Lucas's shirt and tugged him back. "In my experience, hanging out with the living dead never leads to anything awesome."

But Lucas couldn't pull his eyes away from the pack. Casper stared back at Lucas, then let out a tiny whimper that sounded like nails on a chalkboard.

From out of nowhere, wind howled through the basement as the skeleton walls buckled inward. A loud crack came from above them, followed by a dragging sound across the floor upstairs.

Something new was in the house. A fiery wind picked up, blowing Bess's hair wildly as she grabbed Lucas's hand. The door to the basement crashed open. Lucas, Bess, and Lens aimed their flashlights on the steps as a giant, dark smudge stalked down the stairs. The beast had found them.

CHAPTER 25

There was never a sound in Lucas's life so terrifying as when the pack of ghost dogs around him began to bark. The dogs hissed and screeched, and worse, it actually felt like a thousand animals ramming into a steel door. His chest rattled and his eardrums popped as the dark basement suddenly lit up in a blazing haze, casting everything into a mirage. If it weren't for his friends' hands gripping his own so tightly, Lucas would have sworn he was having a fever dream. Any minute he could wake up.

But this wasn't a dream.

Bess was the first to let go. She reached into her pocket and pulled out a flat rock. Lucas watched as she held the rock up in front of the beast and ran straight at the dark smudge.

"What are you doing?!" Lucas screamed.

Bess pressed the rock against the beast. Its strong neck and jaw arched backward in pain as the stone released sparks that made all of the animals let loose a wretched howl. Lucas covered his ears, but Lens seized the opportunity to shove him forward and up the stairs.

"Go! Go! Go!" Lens screamed, but Lucas couldn't leave Bess.

He swiveled away from Lens and stumbled back down.

The other dogs shifted from their earthly shapes into broken, haunted hounds. Only Casper, Duke, and Dakota remained true to their form. The beast had Bess pinned against the dirt. With a giant paw, it swatted the rock away, leaving her defenseless. A dark sneer spread across the beast's face, bearing burned black fangs. Bess closed her eyes and waited for the inevitable.

Then Dakota leapt onto the beast's back with a snarl that echoed sharply. But the smaller dog was no match for the beast and was quickly thrown aside like a wet towel. Dakota landed in the dirt with a thud as Casper and Duke ran to her side. The other hounds surrounded them with a jagged growl that dared them to try and stop their leader again.

Watching it all, Lucas felt his chest tighten. Then he remembered the dog whistle around his neck. He pulled at it like a rip cord and blew into the metal opening. A high-pitched whine sent all the animals screeching for a moment, then they went silent and cowered back from him.

"Get up, Bess!" Lucas cried.

Stunned, the beast whipped around. Its red eyes pierced through him, sending a ping directly into his heart. Lucas blew the whistle again, and the beast yawned widely to shake the hypnotic sound from its ears. Lucas seized the opportunity to pull Bess away from the beast's claws.

The kids stormed up the stairs and into the hallway. Lens slammed the basement door closed, then jerked his hand back. Smoke rose from the doorknob. "Ouch! It's hot!"

"What are you doing?" Bess snapped at her friends. "I had him!"

"What are *we* doing?" Lucas cried. "What are *you* doing? The beast was going to pluck you like a guitar! And what was with that rock anyway?"

"It's a secret" was all Bess said.

Lucas shook his head with frustration. "That's it. We need to get my parents. This is way more than we can handle."

"Wait, guys." Lens held his finger up to his lips. "Listen."

The house had fallen eerily quiet.

Lens shook his burned hand in the cool air. "I think the dogs left."

Lucas put his ear to the basement door to listen. It was dead silent. "Maybe you're right? I don't hear anything."

As he pulled away, a thunderous *crack* split through the door like an ax, and a charred muzzle snapped inches from Lucas's face.

Lens leapt back and screamed, "I WAS WRONG! I WAS WRONG! THERE'S SOMETHING DOWN THERE!"

"Upstairs!" called Lucas, and the others followed.

Clicking claws on the hardwood floor scratched behind them as Lucas led the way down the second-floor hall.

"Where are your parents, dude?!" screamed Lens.

"Deep sleepers!" Lucas hollered. "We're from the city, remember?!"

As they rounded a corner, Bess stopped. "I think we should stay and fight."

"Are you crazy?" asked Lens as he pushed her forward, moving away from the danger. "How are you going to fight a ghost? The dog whistle wouldn't even work on the beast. And he's leading the rest of the pack."

"They're not ghosts," said Bess.

"I don't care," snapped Lens. "Whatever they are, they want to make us their chew toys. And I am not a squeaker. Neither are you."

Lucas held up his finger and wheeled around. "I know what to do, but you might not like it."

A snarl echoed down the hall.

"I'm in," said Lens. "Let's just get out of here now."

Pacing toward them, the beast's paws singed the hundred-year-old flooring with each step. It paused and sniffed the air, lifting its head high to catch whatever curious scent it had found.

"What's it doing?" asked Bess.

"Don't know, don't care," said Lucas as he ran forward. "There's another hallway on the left back here. You two take it."

Lens bolted, then turned back around. "Wait! What about you?"

"I have a plan!" screamed Lucas as he hustled in the other direction and blew the dog whistle.

The beast roared, then charged after him. The whistle had worked. Now he hoped the rest of the plan wasn't crazy. From behind him, Lucas heard the beast howl, which sparked several other howls in response. The walls shook around him.

They're communicating, thought Lucas. And sure enough, from the shadows ahead of him at the end of the hall, another hound stepped out. Adrenaline pumped through his body as Lucas's heart raced. He was surrounded.

Lucas pulled open the closest door and jumped inside, slamming it shut behind him. The room was long and narrow— another hallway! His sneakers squeaked on the wood floor as he took off into a fast break. Lucas's backpack rubbed against his shoulders as he heard the beast behind him. He didn't have a real plan other than to try and get the dogs to chase him instead of Bess and Lens. They were healthy. They had lives to lead. And luckily, Lucas's plan had worked, though now he wasn't so sure it was the best plan.

He kept running through doors that spiraled into different hallways. The logic of Silas's house was absolutely dizzying. He felt the floor shift upward into an incline as he went, which at least made him comfortable that he wasn't running in a circle back to the waiting jaws of death.

He finally reached a door that opened into a large room. It was the size of a banquet hall and completely dark. Lucas huffed and leaned against the wall, taking a moment to catch his breath. At the other end of the room, he saw the shadow of a staircase. It was the only way out. Lucas blew the dog whistle again to make sure the hounds were still on his trail . . . and his trail alone. Then he pushed forward.

Navigating the shadows, Lucas kept his gaze trained on the stairs. In the darkness, he bumped against large shapes that lumbered beside him. They looked like mannequins. Lucas shook his head. Just when he thought this house couldn't get weirder, it found a new way to be creepy.

Still the hounds were coming. Lucas pushed through the mannequin's floppy arms. They dangled and swung lifelessly as he passed. He looked behind him to the entrance. It was still solid and shut, but the howling was getting closer. He needed to move faster and this room, clogged with display dummies, wasn't helping. Lucas turned back around and smacked face-first into one of the mannequins. "Sorry," he apologized. It was a knee-jerk reaction, and Lucas felt silly saying it to no one. Until the mannequin answered him.

"You should not be here." The voice was low and flat at first. Lucas looked up and the mannequin opened its eyes. No, his eyes. The plaid shirt, the hard hats, the shoes covered in sawdust and mud. These were the workers . . . and this must be where they went at night!

"You should not be here," the man said again, only louder this time. "You should not be here."

With every warning, more voices joined the zombie chorus. The words rattled all around Lucas, and he was happy to take the hint. A hand with an angry-looking bite mark grabbed his arm. It was cold and strong. Lucas jerked back, but the worker quietly held on. Lucas struggled, loosening the worker's grip until he was free. Then he screamed and shoved through the waking workers, who sleepily reached for him. Lucas shrugged off their grips and finally made it up the stairs. He opened the door, casting a light over the sea of workers, all of whom were standing shoulder to shoulder. They looked at him with their dead eyes and reached out, still trying to capture him. Then Lucas slammed the door shut and ran as fast as his legs could carry him away from that awful room.

Having zombie dogs chase him was one thing, being trapped with zombie workers was another. But the workers would have to wait; the beast was getting closer. Lucas stopped at a door when he recognized where he was. He'd definitely been lost down this hallway before. Stumbling forward, Lucas held out his arms and touched the doorknobs as he jogged. Finally, he found the knob he wanted.

As the howling grew louder, Lucas wondered what in the world he was doing. He also wished that maybe he had just stayed in bed and put his CPAP machine back on. But at the time, it didn't seem like Casper would have led him into a dangerous place. Hadn't he sparred with the beast earlier? It didn't seem like they were on the same side anymore.

Sharp cries pierced the house, mournful and angry. They reminded Lucas of the Hounds Hollow foxhunt painting from the study. Some of the men on horseback held trumpets to call the other hunters, telling them which way the fox had escaped. Only in this hallway, he was the fox—and he was going to fight back.

Like a light turning off, the howls ended abruptly, and the silence was even more unsettling. Now the sound of his own breath made Lucas anxious. He was beginning to doubt his plan. Because even if he didn't know what was going to happen next, he knew what was about to walk around the corner.

The shadow was quiet as it stepped forward, like a scene in a horror movie with the volume muted. And Lucas watched. There was no sound except his own quick breaths. Hypnotized by the creature's alien-like skin that moved like black static down the hall, Lucas challenged the beast. "You want me? Come and get me."

The words had seemed brave and bold when he thought of them, but once spoken out loud, Lucas couldn't hide his fear. His voice warbled like an unsteady tightrope walker.

The beast didn't care. It kept moving closer.

Lucas clenched his fist, waiting for the right time to strike. In the darkness of the beast's head, two red eyes began to glow where before there had been nothing. The demon awakened and moved faster now, shifting into a smooth gallop that was no louder than clouds moving through the sky.

Lucas counted the footfalls as the beast ran. One, two, three, and on four, the beast crouched and launched itself, flying with black claws outstretched. Quickly, Lucas reached for the bone-etched knob and pushed.

The door flung open, ripping Lucas out of the house. It was the same third-floor trap he'd almost fallen from on his first day in Sweetwater Manor. The beast followed him, but it wasn't expecting a massive drop.

Lucas clung to the door handle and watched as the beast flew by him. It landed with a crash and released an agonized wail. Blinding pain raced up and down Lucas's arms, but he held tight. Beneath him, the dark shadows around the beast faded as it lay motionless in the bushes. With the mysterious shroud pulled back, the beast was merely a large black dog. It nudged itself out of the bushes with its two rear legs and flipped onto its back. The beast was a Rottweiler.

"Scout?" Lucas called, and the dog looked up at him.

The dog's front legs were twisted from the fall, but Scout still pushed himself along until the other hounds came. Scout's black coat had gone gray at the edges, as had the other dogs'. As the rest of the pack approached, Lucas could see that many were limping, and their fur was matted and shaggy.

The pack surrounded Scout and enveloped him in a warm glow. Just as Lucas had witnessed after the car accident, the dog's legs eerily snapped back into place with a bloodcurdling crunching sound. The Rottweiler slowly turned over and stood up on all four legs, recovered. He looked up at Lucas again, who still hung from the door like a human piñata. Scout motioned with his head and Lucas knew that they would meet again, and that it would be soon. The pack charged into the deep green forest beyond the house and disappeared.

"Lucas! Where are you?!" The calls echoed in the hallway just as the sun broke over the horizon. Bess and Lens had come looking for him.

"Over here," Lucas called back.

They both leaned their heads out the doorway with Dakota and Duke by their sides.

Lucas grimaced. His shoulder was tingling with furious pins and needles as one tiny word fell from his lips. "Help?"

Bess held the back of Lens's shirt as he reached out and took hold of Lucas's hand. Then, as they pulled the door closed,

Lucas found his footing and climbed inside. The three kids slumped against the wall with their eyes closed.

A new shadow emerged in the dull light of the hallway.

"What in the merciful world are y'all doing up here that's making enough commotion to wake the walking dead?" Eartha Dobbs stood over them wielding a frying pan like a battle-ax. "Who are these people, Lucas? They bothering you?"

Lucas jumped up and waved for her to stop. The ache in his shoulders flared. "No," he said through gritted teeth. "These are my friends."

"I don't remember your parents giving you permission to have friends sleep over," said Eartha. "Especially this deep into the house. You know, Silas would have never stood for this."

"Yes, he would have," snapped Bess as she stood up behind Lucas.

"How do you suppose you know what Silas woulda wanted better than me?" asked Eartha. "He told me everything."

"Everything?" asked Lucas.

"Did I stutter?" Eartha shifted the pan to her side, which Lucas assumed was the equivalent of holstering it. "Ev-ur-ee-thing. Do you think I just wandered down this hall in the middle of the night? No, sir. I had this scrappy little terrier mutt whining at my door until I followed him all the way up here."

Casper stepped forward and gave a happy yip before running into Lucas's arms. "Casper, you went for help!"

"Oh mercy, you learned their names." Eartha clicked her tongue. "You shoulda never learned their names."

"Listen, Eartha," Lucas interrupted. "We need your help. Scout's back and so is the Hound Pound."

"And we think they're after something in this house," Bess added.

Lens was still sitting on the ground, far away from the trap-door. Eartha turned to him. "This true what they're saying?"

"Yes, ma'am." Sliding up, he reached into his back pocket and handed her a photo he'd taken of the dogs.

Eartha studied it for a second, then let out a heavy sigh. "I knew them curious critters were going to get into trouble sooner or later. Follow me, y'all. We've got a lotta talking to do before your parents wake up."

CHAPTER 26

Back in Eartha's cottage, Lucas sat on the couch with two ziplock packs of ice on his shoulders this time. The chill made his neck and arms hurt even more, but Eartha insisted that if he didn't try to cool down the pain, it would only get worse. Eartha sat in her favorite chair with her arms crossed.

"Well?" asked Bess abruptly. "You brought us here to tell us something, so tell us."

"Tsk, tsk, tsk." Eartha shook her head at the young girl. "Used to be in my day, we had respect for our elders."

"We do, Eartha," Lucas promised. "But we're also scared to death right now. My parents are asleep in a house full of haunted dogs, and who knows what else, and we have no idea what's going on."

"One of you does, I think." Eartha stared at Bess, who looked around the room to avoid making eye contact. "One of you knows part of the story, but doesn't want to share it. So I'll go first, and then maybe you'll feel like opening up, dear."

Lens flashed his eyes at Bess. "What's she talking about?"

"I . . . I have no idea." Bess's legs were bouncing up and down while the rest of her seemed cool and collected.

Eartha laughed. "Okay. I should start by admitting that I don't understand as much as I know."

"What do you mean?" asked Lucas.

"Honey, I'm a housekeeper," Eartha explained. "It's like being a pilot. I know how to fly the plane. I can take off and land, but that doesn't mean I know how to fix the plane if it breaks."

Lucas felt the cold water drip down his back and shuddered. "At least tell us about the dogs."

Casper, Dakota, and Duke sat at attention before Eartha. They had definitely been in her house before and were comfortable around her.

Eartha smiled at them. "Silas loved those pups. Loved them more than anything else in this world. And they loved him. He was young when the fire struck. Heck, he barely made it out alive. Silas's parents had to hold him down to keep him from running back inside to save his dogs. See, his parents knew that if they let Silas back in the house, they'd lose their only remaining child. There were powerful emotions at work on the night of the fire."

Lucas couldn't imagine what Silas had gone through. Watching a fire tear apart his pets, his house, and everything he loved, without being able to help. It must have been awful. Lucas changed the subject. "Did Silas really lose his brother to tuberculosis?"

Eartha nodded. "Yes, and it was horrible. Townsfolk swore there was something wrong with little Abel, something evil in his disease. Thought it had more to do with demons than doctors. When Abel passed, no one came to the funeral, except Silas and his parents. In fact, Silas told me that according to town rules, Abel couldn't even be buried within the Sweetwater plot for fear that his sickness would spread down the family line."

"Come on, you're just messing with us," said Lens.

"Am I?" answered Eartha. "Remember, hon, we're not talking about the most modern times. When a disease like this struck, everyone feared it. People in town stopped talking to the Sweetwaters after Abel's sickness. And as Abel's health faded, Silas was left all alone to mind the dogs. He spent all his time with them. Even made a home for them in the old barn next to his room."

"His room?" Lucas interrupted. "So I've been sleeping in Silas's room?"

"Mmm-hmm," said Eartha.

Lucas closed his eyes and pictured his bedroom. The blue walls, the missing dog paintings, and the gaslit hallway to the barn. Then he opened his eyes wide. "Wait, the gaslights. The barn didn't burn down in the fire. So if the dogs lived there, they should've been okay, right?"

Eartha took a deep breath, then hung her head. "This is the hard part, kids. Silas had his parents to keep him from running into the fire to save his dogs. Those dogs, though, they loved

Silas every bit as hard as he loved them. And those dogs never had parents. They were strays."

"I don't get it," said Lens. "They were strays, so what?"

Lucas felt a lump in his throat. "The dogs didn't have parents to stop them from running into the fire to save Silas. Only, he wasn't there and the dogs got trapped in the inferno."

Silence struck the room as the true history was revealed. After a moment, Lucas continued. "What happened after the fire?"

"The Sweetwaters rebuilt their home," said Eartha. "And Silas learned how to be alone. He avoided town as much as possible. He rarely interacted with anyone. Then, after his parents passed, he decided to keep building."

"No." Lucas leaned closer. "What *really* happened?"

Eartha shifted nervously in her chair. "Dogs are man's best friends. I can't say how, when, or much else, but those dogs . . . they came back to Silas. Only, when they came back, they brought something else with them. Whether it was anger, rage, or fear, I don't know. But Silas never felt safe around them, so he built extensions on the house. Turned it into a darn maze trying to keep those dogs trapped or wandering curiously. Even after I took over caring for them, Silas would never let me be alone with the dogs. Heck, I reckon they must have nearly killed him several times."

"Didn't they remember him?" asked Lucas. "Like, why would they ever hurt him?"

Eartha shrugged as she looked at the dogs in front of her. "Honey, a scared animal will bite anything to keep itself safe. That's why I live by Silas's strict rules. I leave their food in the manor at night, then I run here, safe in my locked room."

"Why would ghost dogs eat real food?" asked Lens.

Bess huffed. "They're not ghosts. They're real, like other animals, but kinda . . ." She searched for the right word. "Haunted."

Lucas slowly grabbed his backpack and pulled out the *Haunted History* book. He flipped through the pages until he found the term he had earmarked. "My parents gave me this book before one of my hospital visits. I don't know why. Maybe they thought I needed to find something scarier than being sick? But after studying it the past few days, I have a theory about the Hound Pound. Have you ever heard of familiars?"

Lucas held up the book to show them a picture of a black cat silhouetted on a fence with the moon behind it. "The concept is most linked to witchcraft. You've heard of a witch's pet cat? That's a familiar. They aren't ghosts or monsters; they're more like demons. They live because they are linked to something unnatural. So, technically, Bess is right—the dogs aren't ghosts. But that doesn't explain how *you* knew they weren't ghosts, Bess. Or why you keep insisting these rocks will work against the beast."

All eyes were on Bess. She crossed her arms and tucked her legs under herself on the couch. "I'd rather not talk about this in front of any adults."

Eartha leaned forward and pointed at Bess. "And I'd rather you not put your filthy shoes on my couch. Now you best start talking before I call your mother and tell her what you've been up to these past few months."

Bess shifted her legs immediately and sat upright. She stared at the blank wall across the room, and her gaze went glassy. "I was in the forest, months before Silas died, and I saw him. He was with the beast. I couldn't tell what was going on, but he was lying on the ground and the beast had just bitten him or something. I said I'd get help, but he told me to stay put or the beast might chase me down, too.

"The beast paced circles around the two of us. When it got bored, it ran off. I helped Silas get home and he told me the story. After the fire, his family rebuilt the house. The dogs were gone, but Silas started noticing odd things in the home. Dirt in his bedsheets when he woke up, hearing clicks on the hardwood floors, or scratching coming from the other side of the wall. He thought he was going crazy."

Only it wasn't crazy to Lucas. Bess had just described what he'd experienced in Sweetwater Manor. He shuddered thinking about the dirt in his bed or the scratching snarls from the walled-up room—a place where ghostly paw prints had led him.

"Then, one day," continued Bess, "his dog Scout appeared. Silas was visiting his brother's grave, and the dog just trotted out of the woods like he was back from some big adventure. But that wasn't the only thing to come out of the woods."

"The other dogs followed, too, right?" Lens guessed.

"No." Bess paused, but she kept looking straight ahead, as if she were boring a hole into the past and focusing on what Silas told her back then. "No, just two. Scout and Shadow. They were the only dogs at first. Then slowly, more appeared. And each time a dog came back, Silas told me his heart broke a little more."

"Why wasn't he happy?" asked Lucas. "I mean, his dogs came back."

Bess pulled out of her thousand-yard stare and looked at him. "The dogs came back, but they came back different. He couldn't control them. They were wild. He feared for the town and everyone in it. That's why he bought up so much property around here and put up cameras."

"He wasn't scared of what was outside the house getting *in*," said Lucas. "He was scared of what was inside the house getting *out*."

Bess nodded. "There's more. And it's not gonna be easy to hear. In fact, it's the one part of Silas's story that made me think he was a complete lunatic. I pretended to listen then, but now . . . I think he was telling the truth."

Lucas turned and the bags of ice shifted off his shoulders, landing on his knees with a slushy thwack. "What did he tell you, Bess?"

She took a deep breath. "His dogs weren't the only things that came back after the fire. His brother, Abel, did, too."

Lucas felt a chill, and it wasn't from the ice packs this time.

Bess reached into her pocket and pulled out another stone like the one that had short-circuited the beast. She rubbed it in her palm. "Silas found Abel in the house. He was a boy, the same age as when he . . . passed on. This new Abel, he never talked. Never said a word. Silas told me that Abel didn't have to explain why he was there."

"Why?" asked Lens.

"I don't know," said Bess. "He didn't tell me. But Silas did say that Abel was always scared around the dogs. Avoided them to the point that Abel kind of disappeared from Silas's life all over again. You asked me about the rocks earlier. They are from the border around Abel's grave. Silas told me that they would scare the dogs off, but they would also stop them if they ever needed to be . . . stopped." The last word barely made it out of her mouth.

Lucas frowned and clenched his fists. "I also asked you about the boy in the house on my first day here. You lied. You acted like I was crazy."

"Sure, like I was supposed to say, 'Howdy, neighbor, you know that kid you saw? He's a ghost!'" Bess threw her arms up and let them flap back down. "Besides, I needed to get into the house, and you were my way in."

She gasped as soon as she said the last words and went quiet.

Lucas raised his eyebrows. "Why did you need to get in the house?"

"To find my dad, okay?" Bess's voice wavered as she closed her eyes and steadied her breathing. "See, I have my own theory about the dogs. A few years back, I lost my father. You probably all know. The whole town knows, but no one wants to talk about it. He didn't die, he just disappeared. In a normal town, I'd just think what everyone else thinks. Deadbeat dad runs away from his family. But my dad wasn't a deadbeat, and our town isn't normal. There's a lot of folks disappearing in Hounds Hollow."

"So you think the beast ate everyone?" Lens seemed horrified at the thought.

"No. I'm saying that there's something magnetic about those dogs." Bess tapped her chest over her heart. "I feel it here every time I see them. I know you feel it, too, Lucas."

Suddenly the missing persons board crowded with photographs crashed into the mysterious room full of workers. The pieces fell into place for Lucas. The missing people had been in front of him the whole time and he'd never thought twice about it. "The workers," Lucas whispered. "Eartha . . . the workers?"

Eartha shifted uncomfortably in her chair. She stood up and moved into the kitchen. The light from the morning was spreading over the forest, chasing away the dark blue cover of night. Birds were waking up and the cicadas' buzz rose.

"That's the thing about lonely Silas and his giant house," said Bess as she curled back up and put her feet on the sofa. This time Eartha didn't scold her. "It takes a lot of workers to build such a detailed place. I've never seen a single truck parked outside. I've never even seen a single worker leave at night."

"Dude . . . no, dude." Lens tried to express his feelings, but the words escaped him.

Eartha made the sign of the cross as Lucas gently took the rock Bess had given him out of his pocket. Holding it, Lucas felt connected to this strange, new world. It was smooth, edgeless, cold, and hard. Lucas squeezed it tight.

"Eartha, it's all true, isn't it?" he asked.

The old woman gazed out the sink window toward Sweetwater Manor. She stood with her arms braced against the counter and flipped on the faucet. Water rumbled against the empty metallic basin as Eartha grabbed soap and scrubbed her hands. "Silas never wanted to hurt anybody," she mumbled. Her voice was as distant as her stare. "I had my orders. I took care of the house. I took care of the dogs."

Lens shook his head and whispered to Lucas. "I think we broke her."

Ignoring Eartha, Lucas opened the *Haunted History* book again. "There's got to be a way to stop this."

"Maybe we could wake up the workers," suggested Lens.

"No," Lucas said. "They won't listen to us. The spell is too strong."

Lens started pacing. "Then we tell the police. This has gotten too dangerous."

Lucas shook his head. "What happens when the dogs put a curse on the police, too? Or worse? Eartha said it—a scared animal will do anything to protect itself."

"Well, do you have any other bright ideas?" Bess punched the couch cushion, then jumped up and pointed to Eartha. "'Cause we're going to turn into that if we don't do something."

Lucas flipped back to the book. "Maybe. According to this, familiars work for a higher mystical power, but in rare cases, familiars become linked to other spirits. And in those cases, the two powers essentially trap each other."

"Um, in English this time," said Lens.

"Abel Sweetwater and the dogs are connected," Lucas answered. "They are tied together, like familiars. They are *each other's* familiars. Lost souls bonded by horrible events."

"Um, dude, how is that going to help us?" asked Lens.

Lucas's eyes went wide. "Abel's hiding. The dogs are hunting. Maybe the dogs have been looking for him all this time? If we can bring the dogs to him, maybe the curse will end."

"Lucas, you said *maybe* like a million times," said Bess. "Do you really think the familiars will cancel each other out? Is that, like, basic familiar math?"

Thoughts raced through Lucas's mind. "I don't know, but I think it's worth a try. You said Abel disappeared from Silas's life, but I don't think he went far. In fact, I think I know exactly where he might be hiding. Are you guys up for another adventure?"

Lens peeked at the clock. "My parents know I'm up early every morning over at Bolt's stall. I'm good to go until the barbecue, but if I miss that, I'm toast. Who else is going to take pictures for the paper?" He held up his camera.

Bess walked over to the kitchen and turned off the faucet. Then she dried Eartha's hands with a towel and guided her back to the oversized chair. As Eartha sat down, the old woman smiled at Bess for a moment, then closed her eyes and started humming a slow melody.

"My mom gets like this sometimes," Bess said. "Just freezes in the middle of doing dishes and goes all . . . glitchy. If finding Abel can bring back my dad, then I'm in."

Lucas pulled out his inhaler and drew in a deep breath. "Okay. Let's go save this place."

CHAPTER 27

Without the mustard paw prints leading the way, Lucas thought they would have a hard time finding the walled-in room. But with Casper, Dakota, and Duke by their sides, the pack moved swiftly.

As they passed doors with bones etched on the knobs, Lens pointed them out.

"So these are all trapdoors?" asked Lens.

"I think Silas installed them to keep the dogs and Abel confused and lost," said Lucas.

Bess was at the rear of the group, walking backward in case anything followed them. Every step awoke a new creak or moan in the old floorboards of the house.

"Are we close?" she asked.

Dakota barked softly.

"Sounds like it's around here," said Lucas. All at once the long night hit him. His eyes were heavy, his arms throbbed, and his whole body felt like it needed to hibernate for twenty straight hours. Without realizing it, Lucas had stopped dead in the middle of the hallway.

Casper turned and trotted back to Lucas, wagging his tail happily. In a strange way, seeing the white mutt was like wearing the CPAP machine. Breathing became easier. The sleepiness drained away and Lucas ran on.

When the dogs finally stopped, they each put their front paws on a wall with thick, carpet-like wallpaper. It was an ugly shade of green that only succeeded in making the hallway darker than it should be.

"I thought the wall was supposed to be unfinished," said Bess.

Lucas ran his hands over the wallpaper, moving all the way to the corner edge where the next hallway turned. The decorated walls extended down that way, too. Then Lucas found it—the crease in the wallpaper. Slipping his fingers under, he tugged at the strip, and it yanked away from the drywall.

"Looks like someone finished it," said Lucas. "Here, help me. Let's clear this ugly green fuzz off the wall."

Lens and Bess each searched for a seam and tore into the wallpaper. It was so fresh that the strips came down easily. When they were done, the dogs inspected the blank wall. Casper spun in circles and began to bark loudly. Each sharp snap made Lens and Bess nervously search for the other dogs in the pack, but Lucas understood what Casper meant.

"We need to go through this wall."

Bess nodded, but Lens wasn't sure. "Or we could leave the wall just as it was built. What if it's a load-bearing wall? Besides, we don't have sledgehammers. How are we going to knock down a—"

But before he could finish, Lucas kicked the wall. His leg pushed through all the way up to his thigh and got stuck. He stumbled, but then regained his balance. Pulling his leg out, Lucas kicked the wall again. Bess joined him this time, as the drywall turned her black sneakers white.

Once the hole was wide enough, Lucas and Bess cleared the rest with their hands. A black opening sat before them. It looked dangerous and magical at the same time. Lucas stepped inside first.

Bess had one leg in before she stopped. "You coming, Lens? Or are you going to stay outside and wait for the rest of the pack?"

The three dogs gazed quizzically up at Lens. "You know, I used to be a dog person, but cats are starting to look really awesome. I'm coming with you."

The room smelled like rotten eggs and smoke. It made everyone gag at first. Lucas found the light switch on the wall and clicked it on. The small room was filled with framed photos, news clippings, and documents. They covered nearly every square inch of the room like wallpaper. Against the back wall, there was a small brown cot with a blanket draped over it so that the bed almost looked like it was floating.

Next to the cot, a wooden chair and desk sat lonely and curious.

"Someone lived in here," said Lucas.

"Not just someone," said Lens, pointing to a picture on the wall. "I think it was Abel."

While Bess studied the photo, Lucas walked deeper into the room, wondering what it must have been like to live there. He sat down on the cot and felt the mattress sag under his weight. The blanket was stiff and rough to the touch, coarse like old wool. From the bed, Lucas had a good view of the hole in the wall.

"Do you guys notice anything missing from this room?" he asked.

"Like the past eighty years?" said Lens.

"Windows," said Bess. "There aren't any windows in this room. Just walls covered with family pictures."

"That's strange, right?" Lucas moved over to the desk. Pulling the lone top drawer toward him, he found a journal inside that looked a lot like the Hound Pound journal. He opened it. The first few pages were filled with what looked like a first grader's handwriting. All the words were either spelled wrong or spelled phonetically, but as the pages progressed, the style of handwriting matured, too. Papers on US history and book reports gave way to longer passages that read more like a diary:

The sun was hot today, and Mother told me that I needed to stay indoors, lest I burn. But the dogs needed their walk and Silas had to help Father, so when Mother wasn't looking, I snuck out. The dogs are getting strong. I almost dropped the leash many times. I took the dogs through the woods and into town. I like it there. Watching the other people almost makes me feel normal. The people in town are nice to each other, but they are not so nice to me. Silas says I scare them. When I ask him why I scare them, he says it's because people are dumbbells. The dogs are never scared of me. Shadow sleeps with me every night. Mother was mad that I went out today. She's worried about my health. I am tired from all the sun, but it was worth the trip.

The journal ended there. Lucas flipped backward, reading earlier entries. Each one told the same story. Abel was lonely. Outside of his dogs and his family, he felt unwanted by the world.

Lucas closed the book slowly. This journal was from a different world. These were Abel's final, private thoughts, written in a windowless room, hidden away from other people. But Lucas had lived this life, too. Abel's room reminded Lucas of the doctor's offices he visited year after year. He thought of how happy he'd been riding the bike Bess gave him just a few days ago. Lucas suddenly found himself relating to Abel in a way he never expected. One thing that doesn't change from the past to the future: It sucks to be sick.

With a nervous jolt, Lucas stood up and tried to shake off his thoughts. He needed to keep a clear mind. This room must have survived the fire, but it had been hidden for a reason, and they needed to find out why.

Suddenly a low growl curled from under the bed.

"Please tell me that was one of our dogs," said Bess. But the trio of pups stood in the makeshift doorway with their tails low.

The blanket over the cot billowed out as the growling grew louder. A rush of intense heat blasted through the small room with such a force that the picture frames cracked and shattered into tiny bits, covering the kids in flecks of glass. A black paw reached out from under the cot and scraped against the wood floor.

"Run!" screamed Lucas. But it was too late.

A dark, shaggy dog pounced from its hiding place, knocking Lens and Bess aside as it landed on Lucas. Shoving its nose in his face, the animal sniffed him all over. Wet drippings from its snout fell onto Lucas's face. His heart beat uncontrollably, but Lucas kept as still as possible. A sneer lifted on the dog's lips, revealing gleaming white teeth, sharp and ready to tear into something. A pair of black eyes stared curiously at the scar on Lucas's chest, then at the others in the room.

"Shadow," Lucas whispered, and the dog huffed and snorted as if the earthly name no longer applied to the black husky.

Powerful paws dug into Lucas's shoulders and legs as Shadow loomed over him. Lucas had never seen an animal this big, much less been tackled by one. Shadow was twice the size of the beast. The husky leaned closer and licked the dog whistle that still hung around Lucas's neck. Shadow's bright pink tongue glowed against its dark fur as the dog snapped at the whistle.

Lucas winced at first, but then realized his mistake. "It was Silas, wasn't it? Silas put you in here," he whispered to Shadow. "You smell him on this whistle, don't you? I bet he trapped you in this room because he couldn't control you, could he?"

From the other side of the room, Bess held a rock in her hand. "Down, Shadow!" she commanded.

The dog's back bristled at her voice, but he kept staring at the whistle around Lucas's throat.

"What are you doing, Bess?" Lens mumbled. "Leave the monster doggy alone."

Shadow turned to face him, and Lens winced at the dog's soulless stare. "I mean, leave the *good* doggy alone, the good doggy who wants to run out of the room and join all of his awesome zombie doggy buds?"

Shadow licked his chops again and Bess held her rock out like a sword, when a red ball bounced into the room. Everyone looked through the hole in the wall where Casper stood wagging his tail. With a single yip, Casper nodded to the ball, as if suggesting that Shadow play a game of catch. In a flash, Shadow jumped off Lucas, grabbed the ball in its mouth, and ran after the smaller dog.

Lucas grabbed his chest, rolled over, and jumped up. "We need to follow them! Maybe they'll lead us to Abel!"

"And then what?" asked Bess.

Her question grabbed Lucas like a lasso and held him in place. "I don't know. I mean, reading Abel's journal, it sounds like he wanted to be around other people. He hated being alone all the time. He just wanted to feel normal."

"That's crazy," said Bess. "Because the dogs don't want anyone around. I mean, hasn't the beast been keeping everyone away from this house?"

"I love thinking this mystery through," Lens interrupted, "but Shadow didn't look like he wanted to cuddle. That crazy dog is on a mission and we just sprung him out of jail. We've got to keep them from getting outside the house!"

"You're right," said Lucas as he started running down the hall again. "We've got to warn the town. If I'm right, then they're in danger. The dogs are loose and so is Abel."

"Should be easy enough," Lens hollered as they scrambled through the house. "Everyone in Hounds Hollow will be at the barbecue today."

"Oh no." Bess pushed past Lucas and Lens to take the lead. "Everyone in Hounds Hollow . . . the barbecue! That must be where Abel is going!"

Quickly, the kids wound through the maze of the house, following the fresh scratches from the dogs running on wood floors. When they got to the kitchen, the back door was wide open. Lucas was heading outside when he found a note from his mom.

Gone to help set up the barbecue. Excited to mingle with the locals! Breakfast is on the table, but we'll be back soon. Love, Mom

A whimper came from the corner by the fireplace. It was Casper, Dakota, and Duke. They were alone, and Shadow was gone. The dogs trotted to the kids and nuzzled against them.

Casper nodded silently and let out a high-pitched cry.

"It's not your fault," said Lucas. "You were trying to save us from Shadow."

"Where is Shadow?" asked Bess.

"More importantly, where's Abel?" said Lens.

A scream shattered the quiet of the morning. Lucas rushed out the back door to find Eartha lying on the ground. She was clutching her chest and gasping for air.

"Are you okay?!" Lucas sat by her and cradled her head in his lap.

Eartha's eyes bulged out of her head as she strained to breathe. Her lips moved, but no words came out. Lucas leaned closer, but he could barely make out her strained whispers. "Ay-*wheeze*-bull." Then Eartha touched her arm where a black mark was burned into her skin. "Ay-*wheeze*-bull . . . heeze . . . free."

Quickly, Lucas grabbed his inhaler and put it in Eartha's mouth. With two quick clicks, the medicine misted into her lungs and the older woman let out a cough, followed by two deep breaths of air. Then she passed out.

Bess and Lens raced to Lucas's side.

"What in the world?!" said Bess.

"It's Abel. He did this to Eartha. He's outside the house." Lucas felt Eartha's deep breathing push through her unconscious body. The scar on her arm was starting to spread. "What if there's still something wrong with Abel, and Silas knew it? What if Abel wants to wipe out all of Hounds Hollow?"

"Then we need to stop him." Bess was every bit as steely eyed and determined as she was on the first day Lucas had met her.

"Great, so we just go stop Abel and his undead hound dog," said Lens. "It's so obvious, why didn't I think of it.

Oh yeah, that's right, because we have no idea how to stop them!"

Lucas laid Eartha's head lightly on the ground. "*We* don't, but I know who does. Right, Casper?"

The tiny dog gave a sharp bark from behind them.

"See, I think we've had something else wrong about the Hound Pound," said Lucas. "What if . . . what if the dogs weren't hunting people after all? What if they were stationed in the house to protect Hounds Hollow from Abel?"

"Did you forget about those dogs attacking us in the house?" asked Bess. "Silas basically had them all trapped."

"No," said Lucas. "You're wrong. He loved those dogs. I've read his notebooks over and over again. Silas knew that Dakota loved the outdoors, so he built her a cabin. He knew that Duke loved to sit by the fire, so he built a fireplace for him. He also knew that Duke and Dakota never left each other's side, so he kept them together. I think Casper and his friends—even the beast—are the only animals that can save Hounds Hollow. And I think I know how to call them."

Lucas held up his dog whistle and blew with his deepest breath. Even though he couldn't hear the high-pitched sound, he felt the world shutter around him. Just as before in the basement of the house, a warm glow came from the edges of the forest as the rest of the pack entered from the trees. They moved in line next to Casper, Dakota, and Duke.

Bess looked over the army. "Bad news. Scout's not here."

"He won't be," said Lucas. "He's not like the others. Scout was Silas's dog. And if I know Silas, he trained Scout to do one thing: find Abel."

"Well, that's what we're going to do, too," said Bess.

"All right!" cheered Lens. "Let's go kick some beast butt."

CHAPTER 28

"You know, we're basically on a foxhunt," Lens hollered as his horse, Bolt, thundered through the forest.

Lucas and Bess pedaled hard on their bikes, also following the pack's lead. The dogs had caught a scent instantly and taken off as soon as Lucas had gathered them. At first he'd worried they were escaping, but every dog headed in the same direction. Lucas barely made it onto his bike before they disappeared into the woods.

Now Lucas's heart was beating wildly inside his chest. There was no plan; he was acting on complete instinct. He remembered the foxhunt paintings back in the house, how the riders stood victorious on horseback while the hounds surrounded the fox. But Lens was wrong. They weren't hunting a fox. They were out to stop an ancient and deadly wrong that had come back to correct itself.

"Turn!" Bess cried as she swerved left after the pack.

Casper had taken the lead. The other dogs were right behind him, though they spread out into groups. It was a tactic Lucas had seen before in his Wolf Life game. But this wasn't a game— this was real life. In the game, when the wolves reached their prey, they ate it. But what would happen at the end of *this* fox-hunt, Lucas wondered?

"Right!" Bess called, her voice steady as the trees whipped past.

Lucas suddenly realized that he'd been here before, racing through the forest toward the Devil's Drop. He looked to either side of him, and the dogs turned to shadowy blurs.

"I know where we are!" Lucas said, but the others had raced ahead and couldn't hear him.

He pedaled faster. Bess and Lens had become one with the pack. It was as if they were hypnotized by the hunt. Lucas stood up on his bike and pumped the handlebars from left to right as he sped up. With his legs burning, Lucas finally pulled in front of his friends and skidded to a halt. He waved his arms and screamed, "Guys, stop!"

Lens eased up on Bolt while Bess slammed on her brakes, but the dogs disappeared into the woods.

Behind Lucas, the entire town of Hounds Hollow was preparing the park for the barbecue. Grills were blazing, filled with hamburgers, hot dogs, corn, and brisket, while tables were full of chips, potato salad, and other sides. Everyone gazed at the kids.

Gale walked over, angrily shaking a serving spoon with mashed potatoes on it. "I thought I made it one hundred percent clear that there would be no horses allowed at our event, Deshaun!"

Quickly, Lucas threw his bike down, pulled off his helmet, and found his parents packing ice into coolers. "Thank goodness! Are you okay?"

"Lucas, what's going on?" asked Mom.

"I'll tell you what's going on," snapped Gale. "This town, this town has a tradition. Every year, we come together and we celebrate being neighbors. We share stories, we share food, and we share what makes Hounds Hollow so special. And as your neighbor, I asked politely for you to leave your filthy animal at home!"

Lens nodded as he searched the faces in the crowd for Abel. "I know and I'm sorry, but . . ."

"No buts—" Gale's voice turned cold and thin as the air around the campground heated up. The older woman touched her throat gently and tried to speak again, but the words melted in her mouth. Gale's eyes flickered around like birds trapped in a cage as she dropped to her knees and struggled to talk. A black mark bloomed on her neck. *"Can't . . . breathe."*

Behind her, a gray boy had a hand on her back, rubbing it lightly like a mother trying to calm down her child. Gale looked up at the boy with a sense of terror as her throat closed tighter and tighter.

"Hello. My name is Abel," said the boy. "I'm looking for my dog. Have you seen him?"

The old woman fainted backward into the dirt. Lucas, Bess, and Lens were frozen as Abel turned back to them. His face was soft around the corners, like a very old, blurry photograph. Only his white eyes and his twisted smile were visible. The rest of his face looked almost erased.

"Hello. My name is Abel," the boy repeated. "I'm looking for my dog. Have you seen him?"

As soon as Gale hit the ground, the rest of Hounds Hollow jumped up and screamed. People ran in every direction, but the beast was waiting for them. Beyond Abel, Lucas watched as the dark creature that must have been Scout pounced from man to woman to child, picking them all off one by one. With one bite, the townsfolk fell under the beast's spell: As quickly as they had erupted in a frenzy of panic and fear, they suddenly became calm and passive, like zombies.

"Mom! Dad! Run!" screamed Lucas, but of course his parents weren't the kind of people who ran from trouble. As the madness spread, picnic tables were tossed over. Uncooked meat and potato chips were scattered on the ground and trampled underfoot. Paper plates blew in the wind.

And still, Lucas's parents walked over to Abel.

"Hello. My name is Abel," the boy told Lucas's mother. "I'm looking for my dog. Have you seen him?"

"Hello, Abel. My name is Holly Trainer, and this is Kyle. Are you lost? Can we help you find your family?"

Lucas lunged forward, trying to grab his parents, but was blocked by people running everywhere. Screams and snarls filled the morning.

"Hello. My name is Abel," the boy repeated in his little kid voice. "I'm looking for my dog. Have you seen him?"

"Mom! Stay away from Abel!"

His mother turned and gave Lucas a smile as if to say, *Don't worry, we'll be okay; we're just helping this innocent little boy.* But then her face changed. Her smile opened into an agonizing gasp. Lucas's father fell over, too, kicking in the dirt as he reached for his throat. Behind them both stood Abel. Suddenly Lucas wished he'd told his parents about the boy when Abel first appeared in the house, even if it meant going back to the hospital. Anything was better than watching his parents suffer like this.

Other voices swallowed him in a swirl of horrible cries. One second Lucas was staring at Abel, and the next, the gray boy was gone. He ran to his parents and used his inhaler as he'd done with Eartha. His parents went limp as they fell into a deep sleep. "Stay here, Mom and Dad. I'll make this right."

Lucas stood up and surveyed the grounds. The entire population of Hounds Hollow was coming unhinged. Half were drowning on the ground while the other half were mindlessly walking back toward Sweetwater Manor. He watched as the beast rushed into the woods and did not return. Screams echoed from far away, and Lucas knew that the beast was continuing its job: making more workers.

Quickly, he grabbed the dog whistle and blew the silent alarm. The ghost dogs faded back into view, sitting at attention.

The gray boy stepped out from behind a tree. His white hair and pale skin floated against the dark backdrop of the forest. He grinned and gave Lucas a small wave. "Hello. My name is Abel. I'm looking for my dog. Have you seen him?"

"We already know your name is Abel!" It was Bess. She and Dakota were protecting a group of other kids hiding under a picnic table. "These dogs belong to your brother, Silas. They're here to stop you!"

"Have we met?" the gray boy asked. He shuffled closer, and Bess held up her stone.

"Stay back!" she warned.

But Abel didn't listen. With a swift movement, the gray boy slid across the ground and snatched the rock from Bess. He turned it over in his gray hand. "Oh my. Where did you find this? I used to collect rocks. Did you know that? Yes, skipping stones! They float over the water if you know how to throw them just right. Do you know how to float?"

Abel waved the rock in front of Bess and she lifted up from the ground. The tips of her shoes pointed down as she struggled to touch the forest floor. Instead she hung in midair, like a swimmer treading water.

"What are you doing to her?!" shouted Lens, who ran forward with Duke.

"Playing," said Abel. Then he changed the subject. "I like your dogs. Are they nice? Do they hunt?"

Lucas heard something in Abel's voice.

"They do," Lucas confirmed.

Abel put the rock in his pocket and clapped his hands at the dogs. None of them moved to him. "They don't seem to obey."

"They obey their master," challenged Bess.

"And who might that be?" asked Abel. "Is it you, Bess Armstrong?"

Lucas flinched hearing Abel use his friend's name.

The gray boy smiled. "No, it's not you. Do any of you know what they call the leader of a foxhunt? The master of hounds. Are you the master of hounds, Lucas Trainer?"

The pack dogs surrounded Lucas and growled like chain saws. "It's over, Abel."

"Is it time to go home?" The gray boy turned in a circle, holding a hand to his ear and looking deep into the woods. "I didn't hear your parents call you back. I didn't hear my parents call me back, either."

While it was hard to make out his face, Lucas could swear that Abel was oblivious to the horror he had created around him. The remaining people of Hounds Hollow stayed hidden in the distance, too scared to run and too scared to stay.

Abel disappeared, then reappeared next to a bearded man hiding behind a tree. "Peekaboo, I found you."

The man scurried backward, trying to get away from the gray boy.

Abel's smile turned down. "What's wrong? Aren't we playing a game? Why does everyone look so frightened?"

He flash-walked again, appearing in one place and then another. Each time the crowd whimpered and squealed. Abel finally stopped and flashed back in front of Lucas. "I understand now. It's a scare game! Oh, can I be the monster? I make a very good monster."

"You're not a monster, Abel," said Lucas.

"Tell *them* that." Abel motioned to the people shivering around him.

Lucas nodded and thought back to Abel's journal. "Yes, well, they can be *dumbbells* sometimes. Especially with a, um, surprise like you."

There was a glint in Abel's white eyes. "*Dumbbells*. My brother used to say that all the time. Where is Silas? I miss him."

"Abel, what do you remember?" asked Lucas.

"Oh, I remember everything," the gray boy replied. His voice was unsettlingly calm and casual. "I was sick and I died. I remember my parents and Silas crying over me while I was in my casket. They dressed me in these clothes. Then I remember people from town interrupting my funeral. Men and women said I couldn't be buried with my family. They said I was evil and that my sickness was going to spread if they didn't burn it away."

With Abel focused on Lucas, Lens slipped behind Bess and pulled her back to the ground. As she landed, Bess repeated the phrase, "Burn it away."

"The town," Lucas said. "The town set fire to your house."

"They came at night," said Abel as he kicked at the ground with his shoe. He was acting like a little boy getting restless. "They had torches. They burned it down. Ashes to ashes, dust to dust. Oh, but what they made was so . . . much . . . worse."

"Silas knew," said Bess. "He survived and he knew when you came back that he had to keep you inside the house."

"Not just me, the doggies, too," said Abel. "Except for Scout, his favorite pup. He could never control Scout. Anyway, I'm bored. Can we play another game?"

"Inside the house, you led me to a trapdoor," Lucas said as Lens and Bess carefully stepped beside him into the circle of dogs. "Was that a game?"

"Of course," said Abel with a smile. "Did you like it? I had no idea that your little mutt was playing, too. He caught you by the hair of your chinny-chin-chin."

Lucas looked at Casper. "You saved me that day?"

The dog answered with a sharp bark.

Abel rolled his washed-out eyes. "See, *you* have a dog. Silas has a dog. Where's my dog?"

"You mean Shadow?" asked Bess. "We found him, but he's long gone by now. He ran away from the house faster than any dog I've ever seen, and you'll never ever find him."

The pack of dogs around the kids hung their heads and let out low whines.

"What's going on?" asked Lens. "Why are they acting like this?"

"Oh man," Lucas said under his breath. "I don't think we were supposed to tell Abel about Shadow."

The gray boy clapped his hands and spun happily in a circle. "Is this true? It is, isn't it! Bess Armstrong is not a liar. Oh, thank you, thank you."

Then with another flash-walk, the gray boy disappeared.

"Where'd he go?" Bess stepped out from the circle.

"He went to find his dog," said Lucas. "You shouldn't have said anything, Bess. I—"

Bess whipped around. "You what? Had things under control? Look at all these people, Lucas. Look at Gale! Sure she's not the best person in Hounds Hollow, but she didn't deserve that. Look at your parents! I mean, he *levitated* me into the air. Abel's not a good kid."

Lucas ignored her and waved to anyone who was still

hiding. "Sorry! The barbecue's canceled. Go home and lock your doors."

The crowd didn't have to be told twice. They scattered and the sound of cars starting rumbled through the forest.

"We need to stop this before it happens again." Lucas looked down at his parents, peacefully lying in the dirt. He didn't want to think about whether or not they would ever wake up. "We need to find Abel. To do that, we need to find Shadow."

"I have an idea where he might be." Lens knelt down by the dogs and held out his hand. The animals sniffed at it, warming to him. "It's like in every Disney movie. Dogs always head home."

Bess shook her head. "There's no way that Shadow would go back to Sweetwater Manor. It was a prison, not a home."

"I wasn't talking about the house," said Lens. "Like I said, dogs always head home."

CHAPTER 29

The hedge maze rose tall above Lucas, Bess, and Lens as they marched with the dogs toward the darkening center. A sunny morning had shifted into an overcast afternoon, and the heat became stronger, almost boiling, with every step the kids took.

"I've never seen weather like this in Hounds Hollow," said Bess. "It's been hot, but this is like . . ."

Lucas caught her eye and nodded. "Like a fire? It means we're on the right track."

The thin rows of the maze opened up into the same small field they'd seen before. The shack was still dark and leaning to the side as if it were made of the same thin skin and brittle bones as Abel.

All was quiet, except for the warm breeze that swirled around the clearing.

"So how does this work?" asked Bess.

Lucas shrugged. The windows in the old shack were open as the faded curtains waved lazily in and out. "Abel?" he called out.

The front door creaked as the gray boy shuffled outside. "You are good at hide-and-seek. Are you sure you had your eyes closed when I left?"

As the door slapped shut behind him, Abel pointed to the

Hound Pound. "Hi, fellas, have you seen Shadow? I thought he would be here."

The dogs stood still as Abel approached, but Lucas stepped in front of them. Abel flash-walked right up to Lucas. The gray boy's face was different this close. There were pocketed ridges around his cheeks where his skull pressed against the deteriorating flesh, and his eyes sunk deep into his head. "There are other games we can play," he told Lucas.

Suddenly a black shadow crashed through the hedges, its dark smudge glittering from the quick movement. Abel fell down at the sight and cowered. It wasn't his dog, Shadow. It was Silas's pet, Scout. The beast stalked slowly. His large paws dug into the unkempt field as bristling heat sparked over the beast's fur.

The gray boy looked from Scout back to Lucas. "Please don't hurt me. I'm scared. Lucas, Bess, Deshaun, please."

"I think you deserve what you get," Bess snapped.

Scout licked his chops and snarled at her. Then, with a twist of his powerful neck, the beast set his eyes on Abel again. As he sniffed the air, his black tail went straight up and his snout pointed directly at the gray boy. The beast had found his prey.

Before the beast could attack, another giant animal burst into the maze. Shadow and Scout collided, rolling into a ball of snapping and biting. The other dogs howled with rage at the dogfight and paced toward the battle, but Lucas held out his hand and commanded, "Stay!"

The animals stopped, but they did not back down.

From his crouched position, Abel covered his ears and rocked back and forth, crying, "Stop them, please! My Shadow's getting hurt!"

The beasts swatted with their hind legs and crashed into each other's chests as their sharp teeth snapped. Watching it, Lucas felt sick to his stomach.

Bess ran over to Lens. "The cameras! Can you trigger off all of the cameras we set around the shack?"

"You want pictures of this?" Lens asked. "I'm trying to *forget* what I'm seeing!"

"For the flashes, Lens!" hollered Bess.

"Light doesn't affect the beast, remember?" Lens pointed out. "It won't stop him."

"Just do it!" cried Bess.

Lens nodded, then fumbled through his pockets to pull out a device that looked like a walkie-talkie. He pulled up an antenna and clicked a button. Instantly, green lights on each camera glowed to life.

"Don't do anything until I say so, okay?" Bess asked.

"What are you planning, Bess?" Lucas grabbed her arm, but Bess shook his hand away.

"Just give me your whistle," she said. "Trust me."

He slid the necklace off and handed it to her without another word.

Everyone watched as Shadow and Scout charged through one of the walls of the old shack. The wooden boards snapped like twigs. When the animals tumbled back out, Scout threw Shadow aside. The husky slammed against the ground, then popped back up. Lucas could see both dogs clearly for the first time. Their dark fur was covered in dirt and dust from the fight. Their skinny ribs rattled as each breathed hard. They were both wearing down.

As the two dogs paced, waiting for the next strike, Bess jumped between them.

"What are you doing?!" Lucas blurted out, but Bess ignored him.

The beasts ignored her, too. Their eyes were locked only on each other. Paw over paw, Shadow and Scout stepped carefully, like warriors sizing each other up, looking for a weakness, or a point of attack.

"Now!" screamed Bess, and Lens flipped a second button.

Flashes from the cameras popped, creating a chaos of bright lights from all angles. Shadow bucked like a startled horse and cowered backward. His tail shifted between his legs and his back curled up as the dog snapped at each flash.

Scout sensed Shadow's fear and was about to pounce when Bess blew the dog whistle. She was so close to Scout that the loud noise made the beast instinctually sit at attention. Bess stood above the beast and held her hand out. "Stay," she commanded.

Behind her, Lens turned off the cameras, but the effect of the lights still had a hold on Shadow. The black husky crouched onto his belly and whimpered. He laid his head on the ground and slid back, trying to hide underneath the bushes at the edge of the maze.

"You saved my dog!" cheered Abel. He flash-walked to Bess and threw his arms around her in a hug. "Thank you! Thank you!"

Dakota howled as the air squeezed out of Bess immediately. Her knees buckled and her body went limp. She dropped the dog whistle. Abel let go of Bess and she fell, lifeless. Then the gray boy picked up the whistle and looked at it curiously.

"No!" screamed Lens. "You are a monster!"

He marched over to Abel and raised his fist, but Lucas caught his arm from behind.

"What are you doing?" cried Lens. "This kid is a curse! Let Scout tear him apart and Hounds Hollow will be done with him."

Abel cringed at Lens's words and tripped onto the ground. "He is angry. Why is he angry?"

"Seriously?!" roared Lens. "Don't you see what you've done? That's my best friend lying on the ground turning blue. She was fine before you touched her!"

"Lens, stop," Lucas said calmly. "He doesn't understand."

"What?" Lens's shoulders tensed. "How can you say that? He tried to kill you in the house. Those dogs, they have all been after him. He's the reason for all of this. Silas knew what he was up to. That's why he went to the trouble of locking his brother up in that fancy prison. If we let him go, he's going to hurt more people. We can't let that happen."

Lucas looked back at Bess. Dakota was sitting beside her. The dog licked her upturned hand and whimpered.

"We were wrong," said Lucas. "Silas was wrong, too. Abel didn't want to hurt anyone. He only wanted to be normal."

"Normal isn't going around and killing people," snapped Lens.

"He's sick," Lucas explained. "He's sick and he's scared and all he wants is to be normal. Believe me, I know what that's like. I know what it's like for people to be scared of you because you're different. For people to think that you have some disease that will spread to them or to their kids. Hounds Hollow was so frightened of Abel Sweetwater that they burned down his house with his family inside. Look at him, Lens. He's our age. He was our age and he died alone. Then he came back alone and the only thing he wanted was his dog. So what did Silas do? He hid Shadow in a windowless, doorless room and trapped Abel separately in the house so they could never escape or be together. Why? Because Silas was scared. Well, I'm through being scared."

Lucas walked over and held out his hand to Abel. "Hello. My name is Lucas Trainer. I know where your dog is."

The gray boy took his hand and stood up. His skin was freezing compared to the intense heat of the dogs. Lucas felt a coldness bloom from the inside of his body and stumbled for a moment, but fought hard to keep standing. The dead feeling, that was the curse. That was what Bess, his parents, Eartha, Gale, and the others had felt when Abel touched them. But the secret was, it was the same feeling Lucas had lived with for his entire life. Only he never thought about it as death. To him, it was life.

"You are not scared?" asked Abel.

"No," Lucas answered. "Now let me take you to Shadow."

As they came closer to where Shadow was hiding, the ground began to shake. Lens cradled Bess as the remaining dogs linked into a circle of fire around them. The dogs started to burn bright and harsh, casting a warmth over Lens and Bess that they'd never felt before.

Slowly, Bess began to blink. Her fingers squeezed around Lens's hand. She whispered, "Close your eyes. Don't look."

Lens closed his eyes and hugged his friend tight.

Lucas and Abel were across the field, calling for Shadow to come out. The husky nervously peeked its snout through the hedge and sniffed the air. Catching Abel's scent, Shadow crawled forward on his belly with his tail wagging wildly.

"Hi, Shadow. It's me, boy." Abel fell to his knees and threw his arms around the beast. "It's me. It's me," he repeated over and over again as he nuzzled his face into the husky's deep, black fur.

Lucas smiled. "You're home now, Abel. It's time to rest."

Tendrils of fog laced through the forest as a new kind of heat emanated from Abel and Shadow. A crackling sound like fire rose around Lucas, and the rest of the pack behind him began to howl. The sound wasn't horrible or sad. It was euphoric.

The fog swarmed around Abel, Shadow, and Lucas, moving faster and faster. Lucas had the sense that he wasn't even on Earth anymore. He tried to find Lens and Bess, but they were gone. He only saw the pack circle. Each of the dogs had their heads tipped up to the sky, singing out in a language that Lucas couldn't understand.

Abel stroked Shadow calmly in the eye of the storm. "Thank you, Lucas Trainer. I can rest now."

Then, as soon as it began, it was over, and the silence reached deep inside Lucas, casting him into the darkest night he'd ever known.

CHAPTER 30

A steady beeping woke Lucas up. He was lying in a field of brightly colored flowers. The beeping kept on, like the alarm on his CPAP machine. Groggily, Lucas reached over to try and shut it off, when he felt a tug on his inner arm. There was a tube coming out of his skin. He grabbed it and pulled.

"He's awake!" His mother sat next to him and gently moved his hand away from the IV in his arm. "No, no, Lucas, you need that, honey. It's me, Mom. You're in the hospital. Lucas, you're safe."

Lucas let out a strong cough and felt his body shake. He sniffled and studied the room. Blinking machines were all around him, hidden behind a strange garden of plants and flowers. He touched the petals on one particularly large orchid.

"Oh, these?" It was his father, sitting on his other side. "Well, looks like you're a popular guy with Hounds Hollow. I think everyone in town sent you flowers. We had to take some home; they wouldn't allow any more in your room here."

Lucas licked his lips. They were chapped and dry. "Bess? Lens?"

"Right here." They both stumbled over each other trying to get to Lucas, then hugged him hard. Lucas could hear his parents shift uncomfortably, but they didn't stop his friends.

Lucas took their hands and held them weakly. "Is it . . . ?" he started.

"It's over." Bess smiled and nodded behind her. A man he'd never seen before was sitting next to Bess's mother. "Lucas, this is my dad."

Lucas coughed again. "It's nice to meet you finally, sir."

Bess's father reached down and patted her mother's knee. "Lucas, you have no idea how nice it is to meet you."

Lucas leaned back, resting his head against the pillow on the bed. "Mom, Dad, could we have the room for a minute?"

His parents shared a look, then his mother said, "Of course. We'll be just outside."

After the adults left, Lucas shifted himself up and took a deep breath. "Are the dogs . . . ?"

Bess nodded. "Gone."

"And . . . Abel?" Lucas struggled to get the name out.

"He's gone, too," said Lens. "And you, I mean, when we found you lying in the dirt. We thought you were . . ."

Bess interrupted him and held up a copy of the *Hounds Hollow Gazette*. "You were right, Lucas. All the missing people, they're back. You did that."

Lucas coughed again, and this time an ugly wad of phlegm caught in his throat. He spit it into a tissue. "Oh, that can't be good."

There was a knock at the door as a doctor walked in.

"Actually, that means the body is working properly. Hi, Lucas, I'm Dr. Ward."

She checked the chart at the end of his bed, then gave him a smile. He'd seen that same smile a hundred times before. It said, *You, son, are still very sick.*

Lucas nodded. "Hi, Dr. Ward. Am I okay?"

"Let's call your parents in for this." As they joined Lucas, Dr. Ward held an X-ray sheet in her hand. She slid the X-ray into a light box. It was strange to Lucas, having his friends peer into his insides. In the image, a gray haze hung over his bones like clouds above the earth. "This X-ray was taken by your last doctor."

Then, Dr. Ward slid a second X-ray in. "*This* is the X-ray we just took."

As the doctor moved her finger back and forth between the X-rays, what she said might as well have been in another language. Still, his parents nodded as if they understood, and tears welled in their eyes. Lucas didn't need to know what the doctor was saying exactly because he could see the difference in the X-rays immediately. The black cloud was smaller. It wasn't gone, but it didn't cover as much of his lungs now.

"What does this mean?" he asked.

"It means that whatever you've been doing, keep it up," said Dr. Ward.

Lucas let out another booming cough. It was louder than he'd coughed in a long time. His parents threw their arms around him.

Then Dr. Ward cleared her throat. "It also means that I'd like to perform a few more tests before you leave. If you don't mind."

"What's one more test?" Lucas asked with a smile.

The ride back from the hospital was fast but crowded. Lucas had to share the back seat with so many get-well gifts, he felt like he was delivering for a floral shop. He stared out the window as the trees stood in the forest, watching over him as he returned to Sweetwater Manor. He strained to see beyond the trees, searching for a black movement, and felt his heart jump at the thought of spotting the beast again. But the woods were still and quiet.

His father turned the car onto the loose gravel driveway, and Lucas could hear the pebbles crunch underneath the tires just like the first time he rode up to the house. The full beauty of Sweetwater Manor presented itself to him.

Eartha Dobbs stood by the front porch, waving at his return. As soon as they parked, Eartha opened his door and gave Lucas a squeeze that would have cleared an entire bottle of toothpaste. "Boy, I cannot believe you messed with those dogs! I told you they were dangerous! I have half a mind to punish you if you ever, ever, *ever* do something like that again."

"I missed you, too, Eartha," Lucas mumbled into her shoulder.

She pulled him back and gave Lucas a wink. "I'm glad you did, though—but don't never tell no one I said that."

"Your secret's safe with me." He gave her arm another squeeze.

The cicadas were back, buzzing wildly in the late afternoon. They were so loud that he could practically feel their noise in the air. "I . . . uh, Mom, Dad. Do you mind if I visit the maze?"

"Sure, honey, we can go down there," she said.

"Thanks, Mom, but can you maybe give me a minute there . . . alone?" asked Lucas.

His mom looked to Eartha and his father, then nodded. "Five minutes, then it's time for dinner. I can't believe it's gotten so dark out already. It'll be night before we know it. Anyway, we'll be right here if you need us."

"I know. Thanks, Mom." He put his arms around her and his mother bent down to kiss his head.

"You're getting so tall, Lucas," she said. "I hadn't noticed until just now."

"That's how life works, Mom," he said.

When Lucas rounded the corner of the house, he was surprised to find that the maze was gone. The hedges and grass path that had been so easy to become lost in were no more than black shrubs and dried brown patches. He stepped down the slope carefully and surveyed the damage. At the center of nothing, the shack still stood unscathed except for the hole in the wall where Scout and Shadow had fought.

Lucas stood in front of the shack and opened the door. It was empty inside. Even Lens's photo collection of the beast was gone. "Hello?" he said to nobody. And nobody answered. The space was as quiet as a tomb.

When he headed back outside, Lucky the cat was there. He stretched under the bright moon that hung low in the sky, then sauntered over to Lucas and nuzzled between his legs, letting out a deep, rhythmic purr. "I missed you, too, Lucky."

In moonlight, a dark circle appeared in the field. Lucas knelt and put his hand on the ground. It pulsed with a warmth that sent a shiver up his arm. He remembered the dog pack as they surrounded Bess and Lens. It had been only a week since everything had happened, but it felt like years.

With a deep breath, Lucas took in the calming smell of freshly cut grass. He felt silly all of a sudden, being outside by himself when his parents were inside waiting for him, but there was something he had to do. Lucas cleared his throat.

"Casper, Dakota, Duke, Shadow, Scout, and all the others . . . thank you. Thank you for never giving up. I'm sorry we were wrong in the beginning and I'm sorry we didn't listen. That we saw you as monsters and ran from you. And I'm sorry that I couldn't save you. I hope you can finally rest now."

Then he added, "I hope you can finally rest, too, Abel Sweetwater."

Lucas closed his eyes, clasped his hands in his lap, and said a prayer for the Hound Pound. As he did, he felt a small, rough tongue licking his wrist.

When he opened his eyes, all of the dogs stood at attention in front of Lucas. This time they were blue and glimmering. He looked down to Casper, who climbed in his lap and curled up. Lucas hugged the small dog tightly. So many feelings welled up inside him that his chest and throat were suddenly crowded, like water rushing into an open crack.

Standing behind the pack were Silas and Abel Sweetwater, with Scout and Shadow by their sides. The older Silas and younger Abel both waved to Lucas, and he waved silently back. Then the tips of their fingers faded and blew away like a drift of sparkles. First their arms, then their bodies and smiling faces were carried off like embers spreading out in the night.

The same thing happened to the dogs, each of them wagging their tails happily as they faded from this world and entered another. Casper licked Lucas's face, pulling his attention downward.

Lucas sucked in a ragged breath. "I know, I know. You have to go, too, don't you?"

Casper rolled over on his back and kicked his paws playfully in the air. Lucas smiled an ugly, heartbroken smile, and rubbed Casper's belly one last time. Then the small white dog disappeared into the wind, carried up into the night sky to join the stars above.

Lucas breathed in, and he knew he was not alone.

ACKNOWLEDGMENTS

When anyone writes a book, whether they know it or not, there are ghosts alive inside the story. But these ghosts are not to be feared . . . usually. Instead, think of these spirits as the people, the animals, or the quirky experiences in one's life that helped lead to the final product you are holding in your hands. *Hounds Hollow* is no different.

Thank you first to my wife, Adrienne, who didn't flinch when we found ourselves on a dirt road in the middle of nowhere without directions and stumbled upon that broken-down barn with faded, cartoon puppy faces painted on its walls. And thank you for not punching me when I called dibs on whatever story might live in that haunted shack. Turns out it was this one.

Thank you to my daughter, Wren, who took long walks with me, dreaming up different horrifying scenarios that could happen in a haunted house with ghost dogs.

Thank you to my son, Desmond, who constantly proves how powerful and magical it is to be a good person.

Thank you to my agent, Josh Adams, for telling me to write this book when I called him with a single-sentence idea.

Thank you to Nicholas Eliopulos, David Levithan, and

Nancy Mercado, for seeing the possibility in a pack of dogs, a haunted house, and a kid named Lucas.

A big thank-you to Orlando Dos Reis, for taking over as the editor for this book in the final stages and helping make it way better than I thought it could be. Thank you to Nina Goffi for the great cover design. Thank you to the copy editors who make this book look like I knew how to spell.

Thank you to my parents, Thom and Linda, as well as my in-laws, Greg and Janet, for listening to me talk about this book for a long time and never asking me why it wasn't finished yet.

Thank you to my brother, Matt, for always putting up with my overactive imagination.

And finally, thanks to the family dogs I have had the honor to know and love over the years: Bo-Peep, Panda Bear, Molly, Bear, Max, Scooter, and Ellie. You are loved.

ABOUT THE AUTHOR

Jeffrey Salane grew up in Columbia, South Carolina, but moved north to study in Massachusetts and New York City. After spending many years playing in several bands, he now works as an editor and writer, and he is the author of the Lawless series. He lives with his wife and kids in Brooklyn, New York. Follow him online at jeffreysalane.com.